DELILAH

RHODRI WYN OWEN

Gomer

First published in 2019 by Gomer Press,
Llandysul, Ceredigion SA44 4JL

ISBN 978 1 78562 313 4

A CIP record for this title is available from the British Library.

This book is published with the financial support of
the Books Council of Wales.

Printed and bound in Wales at
Gomer Press, Llandysul, Ceredigion
www.gomer.co.uk

For Lizzie, Siôn and Wil,
who were there for me.
Thank you.

Acknowledgements

This book wouldn't have been published without the endeavours of Rebecca F. John and Sue Roberts of Gomer Press, to whom I offer my admiration and thanks.

I missed out on the days of hot metal printing, but I was lucky enough to work in newspapers before the last few characters belonging to that era of the job had moved on. These old-school newspapermen fired my imagination and, among them, I'll always be grateful to Wilf Orchard, Peter Hollinson, Denis Gane and John Ritson. None of them are in this book, but I hope some of their spirit is.

Prologue

I was fine until I saw the body fall. A dead weight, it dropped like a stone. For a second or two I forgot how to breathe until a man's voice dragged me back to reality.

'You look like you've seen a ghost.'

As my eyes refocused I saw a line of Royal Marine commandos in combat fatigues snap off their abseiling hooks and stand to attention. I'd only caught a sideways glimpse of one of them plummeting through the air but it had been enough to trigger a terrifying flashback to the last time I had been here.

I turned to see a smile on the face of a young man in the seat next to mine. 'Yeah, the commandos,' I replied in a thin voice which needed a cough to thicken it. 'They took me a little by surprise.'

'You wouldn't get me jumping off the top of that stand on a length of rope,' he continued. 'That roof's over a hundred feet high.'

'I can believe it,' I said, though I knew full well.

'Some stadium this, though, isn't it?' he said, gesturing to our surroundings.

From our position in the lower tier of this brand new cathedral of rugby the view was not unlimited but was still remarkable. Below us an enormous groundsheet bearing the logo of the tournament organisers had been draped like an altar cloth across the playing area. At each end thin white posts stretched like giant candlesticks halfway up towards the arched steel ribbing of the underside of the roof. In the stands around us a simmering mass of humanity in black and red was waiting impatiently for the sermonising of the opening ceremony to end, and for the opening game of the world's biggest rugby tournament to begin. A world in communion.

A day that had been circled on calendars around the world, mine included, had at last arrived. Though the progress of the new national stadium's construction had been the subject of heated debate, the deadlines had to all intents and purposes been met. Unlikely as it had seemed, and I had read the facts and figures enough times in the newspapers, a structure which should have taken four years to build had been completed in just two-and-a-half. And now, in front of a global television audience of billions, a small nation would bask in the greatest exposure it had ever been afforded.

'Your first visit?'

'I was here for the inaugural match a few months ago,' I replied.

'Some game that, wasn't it?'

'Apparently so ... I didn't get to see it all.'

There was a sudden swell of excitement in the stands as down behind the posts at one end of the pitch a regimental band struck up the first staccato stabs of an instantly recognisable tune. The hymns had begun.

'Hang on a minute,' said the young man next to me. 'You're the one who ...'

I could see him moving his lips but his words were submerged beneath a wave of sound. Led by the massed choirs whose harmonies were being piped through the stadium's PA system, the crowd around us had burst into song:

'I saw the light on the night that I passed by her window.
(Da da da daaa, da da da)
I saw the flickering shadows of love on her blind.
Sheeeeeee was my woman,
As she deceived me I watched and went out of my mind.'

With something approaching religious fervour the crowd around us launched into the traditional pre-match rendition of the old Tom Jones hit 'Delilah'. As usual it was more of a performance than a song, with the lyrics joyfully embellished and melodramatically acted out. But as the verses unfolded my thoughts turned inward, and I came to understand that the tale told in this familiar old standard had taken on a whole new meaning. And I realised I would never again be able to enjoy this ritual in the same carefree way as the thousands gathered around me.

My thoughts had drifted to another woman who had found herself the victim of man's desire. A woman described by the one man who had truly loved her as 'young and innocent and wild'. A woman whose life had also been brutally taken from her, and whose remains, it now hit home to me, lay buried somewhere beneath our feet. A woman whose murder sparked a chain of events that for thirty years blighted the lives of the men who had desired her.

PART ONE

CHAPTER 1

It arrived on a Tuesday, in a box on a sack trolley wheeled into the newsroom by two press-room workers in ink-smudged overalls.

'Where do you want it, Humph?' said George Mellor, the older of the two men, and the one slightly out of breath.

'Where do I want what, George?' came a rich, deep and uninterested voice from behind a fully-extended copy of *Sporting Life*, above which a trail of cigarette smoke spiralled through a dust-laden ray of morning sunlight.

'It's the new computer,' replied George, his abundant belly testing the patience of the long zip on the front of his murky boiler suit. 'Came over on the circulation van this morning.'

The *Sporting Life*, soon to become a collector's item when its print edition would make way after 140 years for sportinglife.com, shuddered as Humph Blake began to fold it back on itself. He stubbed out the last half inch of his Benson & Hedges cigarette in his blue White Horse whisky ashtray and took a long pull from his mug of tea. 'Just leave the box by the fax machine, George. There's a bloke coming over from head office sometime to put it all together.'

'Okay, Humph.'

Humph Blake rose up and walked across to where George had left his delivery. Tall and reedy, with light blue eyes and a thin, greying Clark Gable moustache the standout features of his tired but kindly-looking face, Humph was the editor of the *Gazette*, the weekly newspaper for the town of Porthcoed, fifteen miles from the nation's capital.

Humph was the paper's father figure, its longest-serving son and, due to his well-known fondness for a tipple, its often unholy spirit. Old school from his soft-soled shoes to the betting-shop pencil he sported behind his ear on production day, Humph loved few things better than the *Gazette*, and his heart and soul came off each page with the ink on your hand.

'It's Tuesday the fifth of May, 1998, ladies and gentlemen of the newspaper industry, and the future of our profession has just arrived,' he said. He paused to fish a fresh cigarette from the waist pocket of his light brown cardigan and then looked over in my direction. 'We're all fucked.'

Chapter 2

It was Wednesday the following week before the 'bloke from head office' arrived and the contents of the box emerged. With its inbuilt fan whirring self-importantly, the newly-installed Internet Terminal – its capped-up initials were implicit – sat in sleek glory on a desk in the centre of the newsroom, upstaging a dusty fax machine, a careworn printer and a battered photocopier.

When I showed up for work that morning it was surrounded by a cluster of curious *Gazette* staff. As computer equipment went it was a cut above the jaundiced plastic word processors that sat on each desk in the room and its looks did not deceive. Whereas the stories we reporters knocked up each week blinked fitfully on our screens in light green characters set against a green-black background, the Internet Terminal's screen glowed in Windows 95 white. And while our finished articles were printed off noisily on a continuous roll of green-striped and perforated tear sheet – ideal for the dreaded story spike on Humph's desk – the Internet Terminal's dedicated printer purred, effortlessly yielding a faithful screen shot on individual sheets of crisp A4. It's fair to say the *Gazette* lagged a little behind the times when it came to the revolution in office technology.

'The Internet Terminal is to be used as an instrument of reference,' announced Teg Rowlands with pomp and ceremony underpinned by a thinly-concealed layer of threat. 'And the word from head office is that nobody is allowed on the Internet Terminal for more than ten minutes at a time.'

If Humph was the father of the newspaper, then Teg was its mother figure, nurturing but no-nonsense. Fragrant, brassy and thirty-nine for a few decades now, Teg, whose heavily-permed hair was best described this month as sangria red, ran the *Gazette*'s front desk. The widow of the Reverend Goronwy Rowlands, late of Moriah Chapel in Baker Street, Teg was the public face of the paper to anyone who called in to place a small ad, engagement notice or lost dog appeal. The story went that Teg had met Goronwy in London in the fifties while working as a secretary for Churchill at Downing Street. By equal parts glamorous, foul-mouthed and church-going, she gave a feminine form and a local twist to Winston's riddle wrapped in a mystery inside an enigma.

'The Internet Terminal is *not* here for shirking, for checking the form on the horses, or for printing out colour pictures of women's tits, okay?'

Teg liked to finish with a flourish. Amid the ripple of laughter from those gathered around her, I noticed Humph stub out another cigarette and rise from the desk at which he practically lived in the opposite corner of the newsroom. There was a suitably impressive office in another part of the *Gazette* building with his name on the door, but Humph preferred to spend his long days alongside his reporters, and the editor's office was used instead as an over-sized stationery cupboard.

Shoving an early, pencil-scratched layout of next week's *Gazette* under his arm, Humph walked through the dispersing huddle to my desk, set beside a window at the front of the newsroom, where he stood above me, scratching his moustache with his forefinger. 'Got a minute, Twm?' he asked, turning to walk in the direction of the office door. 'Quick eye-opener?'

While his offer suggested a morning coffee, in Humph's case this was occasionally interchangeable with an early pint. I checked the office clock, decided on the former and grabbed my jacket.

The ageing lift clunked clumsily down two floors towards ground level. In the silence between us I sensed that Humph had something on his mind, though he wasn't in a hurry to reveal it. We crossed the street to Grumpy's, shutting its glass-panelled door on the roar of a BT works crew tearing up the tarmac on Station Road. May or December, Grumpy's café, a regular haunt for *Gazette* staff, was engulfed in a sweet-smelling damp fug that steamed up its windows.

'Two brews, is it, Humph?'

'If you mean two mugs of your finest tea, Grumpy, each infused for a respectable amount of time by a brand new teabag and not just parked briefly in the same postcode as one of yesterday's leftovers, then yes, please. Mr Bradley and I will be in the corner.'

'All right,' replied Grumpy, adding, in a voice just loud enough to be heard above the eggs he was deep-frying, 'Though I think we can live without the wisecracks, thank you …'

In or out of the newsroom Humph was a corner-dweller. He liked to have his back against two walls and a clear view of the room in front of him, as if he expected trouble was on its way and he wanted to see it coming.

'Twm,' said Humph after a moment of silence. 'There's a strong scent of change in the air, have you noticed it?'

'I think that's probably one of Grumpy's breakfasts,' I replied, but Humph wasn't biting.

'First they got rid of manual typewriters. Did you ever hear a newsroom full of typewriters half an hour before deadline?'

'Only in the movies. *All The President's Men*. You know that bit at the end when Redford and Hoffman are just clacking away with two fingers in front of Nixon on the telly?'

'When I first started in this game I never thought I'd be able to hear myself think in the middle of that racket, let alone write a story,' continued Humph. 'But after a while it got to the point where I couldn't concentrate without that wall of sound around me.'

Grumpy arrived and placed two mugs of dark brown tea on

the table between us. Humph waited for him to turn his back before reaching for his hip flask and tilting it in my direction. 'Probably a little early for me,' I protested, but Humph went ahead anyway, drizzling two fingers of whisky into my tea before adding a glug or two more to his own.

'These new bloody keyboards,' continued Humph, now stirring in the Scotch with a teaspoon. 'They're too quiet. The newsroom is too quiet. Journalism isn't meant to happen in silence, Twm. A newsroom should sound like a betting ring at a racecourse or the taproom of a pub. There should be people talking over each other, energy, blood pumping... And now we get "the Internet Terminal". It's the beginning of the end if you ask me.'

'What's on your mind, Humph?'

'You've been with us for what, two years now? You're just about the sharpest tool in the *Gazette*'s box. You're a natural. You've got a good nose for a story and you know how to write one up too.'

The six years, not two, that I'd spent under Humph on the *Gazette* had taught me that I wasn't going to like what was coming. If you counted the paper's veteran council reporter, Coma Jenkins, and two recent acquisitions, the Germolene Twins – as Humph had christened them – who were due to resit their GCSEs in the summer, the paper boasted just four reporters. And none of us were in danger of being snapped up by the *Washington Post* any time soon. So, rather than respond to Humph's unreliable flattery, I simply met his gaze through a cloud of his freshly exhaled cigarette smoke. As the smoke dissipated, the expression on Humph's face changed, and I felt I was looking at the unfamiliar features of a stranger.

'I'm in a spot of trouble,' he said. 'Unless I can lay my hands on five grand in the next three weeks it's curtains for me, and quite possibly for the *Gazette* too.'

Chapter 3

It had cost me a small fortune in gin to discover what little I knew about Humph Blake's life story. Although he was widely recognised and liked in and around Porthcoed, where it was generally appreciated that no smarter newsman had seen his name printed under the masthead, few people really knew him. He rarely spoke about himself and when he did he liked to keep you off balance, sometimes with humour, sometimes with anger. I'd already learned that a relationship with Humph was like a game of chess. If you showed him a few moves early on and stayed in the game you could win his respect. If you succeeded in gaining his esteem his loyalty could be fierce. But if you showed him any sign of weakness he would ruthlessly unpick you, lose interest and move on to the next person.

It was during my first taste of the *Gazette*'s infamous annual Christmas party at the Railway, the *Gazette*'s local, that I'd managed to tease some detail out of Teg with a few glasses of Bombay Sapphire. Humph himself had already told me that he'd started out many years before as a cub reporter on the *Gazette* and I'd always supposed he'd been one of those one-paper men, the journalistic equivalent of the rare and cherished rugby or football star who played for one club throughout their long and illustrious careers. Many sons and daughters of Porthcoed had sought and found a way out of this small, sometimes suffocating community, but it had never occurred to me that Humph might have wanted to do the same. And yet through juniper-flavoured stage whispers in the Railway snug I learned from Teg that back in the sixties Humph had been 'seduced by the bright lights' of the capital.

'At the time it seemed like the next stop along the main

line to Fleet Street,' said Teg. 'Young Humph was a bit of a star, lovely. But to everyone's surprise, after a couple of years on the *Western Morning Record* he ran back home to Porthcoed, arriving with what we all noticed was one helluva thirst.'

Taking the hint, I accepted Teg's lipstick-smudged tumbler from her and squeezed my way through the revellers to the bar where Humph was holding court with the press-room boys. Based in the capital city just down the road, the *Western Morning Record* was the nation's pre-eminent newspaper and it was odd that a natural-born newsman like Humph had apparently not made the grade there. Watching him stop mid-anecdote to scream at George Mellor for drinking from a pint glass he thought was his, incorrectly as it turned out, I reflected on his 'thirst', as Teg had put it. Along with a minor weakness for racehorses, a little too much drink had been part of Humph's make-up since the first day I'd met him. Many times, long after the last edition of the *Gazette* had been run off the presses, I'd seen beer or whisky send him to sleep in his chair. But though his overworked mind occasionally surrendered consciousness, I had never once heard it surrender common sense. Alcohol and journalism still mixed in those days and, drunk or sober, in the newsroom or in the pub, Humph was the controlling force of the *Gazette*. He had a ready cynicism and a combustible temper, but if you had enough of a heart beating in your own chest then, as I saw in the attentive faces around him that night at the bar of the Railway, he was a man who inspired loyalty and love.

'Humph's taken a real shine to you, Twm Bradley,' breathed Teg, lifting her refilled highball. 'For some reason you've been a bit of a project for him since the moment you arrived. And he's not the only one at the *Gazette* to have spotted your potential, if you follow my meaning.' The look on Teg's gin-flushed face, as she licked her tongue across the gap between her two front teeth and then winked, left little room for misunderstanding.

'Don't even think about it, Teg,' came a shout from Humph across the smoke-filled Railway snug. 'Woman like you would snap a young shaver like him clean in two.' As if Humph's remark had been an injury-time penalty kick slotted home from the touchline, the room erupted in cheers. Cheers, I noticed, led by Teg herself.

Teg had been right, though. Gradually, as the years passed, and not always in the most sympathetic manner, Humph had been my mentor, lifting the veil from 'the game' of journalism, as he called it, to reveal what lay underneath. 'It's not complicated, Twm,' he would tell me. 'The truth behind every story is found out there in the real world, not in the newsroom or on the end of a fax machine. Stories are based on facts, not hearsay. And chasing one down is a physical thing. The phone is your friend but you need to use your feet. To hell with press releases, get out of the office. Meet people and ask them questions. Look into their eyes when they talk to you and remember that nothing they say can ever be taken for granted.'

'Humph and Bren never had kids,' said Teg. 'Don't know why, exactly. But I think maybe you remind him of a part of himself that needs putting right.'

I didn't buy Teg's cod psychology. In a headline or in real life Humph Blake hated a cliché. And he had never once shown me an ounce of regret or self-doubt; almost no sign of a weakness at all if you considered his uncanny ability to function on alcohol. For so long I had been the pupil to Humph's teacher, but suddenly and without warning the tectonic plates beneath us had shifted and left me decidedly off balance. Sitting across the table from him in Grumpy's, after he had dropped his guard so unexpectedly, I tried to find the right words to offer him, but he cut straight across me.

'It's not what you're thinking, Twm. Everyone who knows me knows I like the horses and I'm partial to a drop of Scotch in my tea. But it's not what you're thinking.'

'What am I thinking?' I stuttered.

Humph looked around the café until eventually his gaze fell down to the mug in his hands, which he tilted slightly to examine the dregs at the bottom. Then he lifted his head and looked straight at me. 'There's a bit of a hole in *Gazette* accounts that I can't answer for,' he said almost apologetically.

'You mean a five grand "bit of a hole"?' I asked him.

'The money's gone and I just don't know how.'

'Five thousand quid?' I hissed, now leaning conspiratorially across the table towards him. 'How do you mean "gone"?'

'Just gone. As in not there any more.'

'It's got to be an accounting error. I mean ... someone's got their sums wrong. Have you asked Teg to take a look at the books, double-check?'

'Teg knows nothing about this and that's how it's going to stay, okay?' Humph hissed quickly back at me. 'Nor Coma. No one knows about this except you and me. The money has gone. You'll just have to believe me.'

A rare moment of silence in the café was filled by the sound of Grumpy cursing to himself behind his counter.

'The trouble is that any time now the *Gazette*'s accounts are all going to go online,' Humph continued. 'And when the robots in the accounts department at Bentall Newspaper Group get a live look at the sums for the *Porthcoed Gazette* they are going to notice that we don't add up.'

He shot a look across at Grumpy before taking a pull straight from his flask. 'Why do things always have to change?' he continued. 'When the accounts were all kept on paper it was so much more straightforward. You had something tangible in your hand ...'

'More wriggle room to bullshit head office, you mean?'

Humph's eyebrows rose in acknowledgement of my point and he turned his mug in his hands. 'There's no way I'm bullshitting my way out of this one, believe me, or I'd have tried.'

'Surely you can think of a way to buy yourself a little time, until you can sort out your maths and figure out where the money's gone?'

'Oh I know where the money went. I just don't know how it got there,' he said, lifting his forefinger to scratch his moustache.

'Where did it go?'

'Into Bren's bank account.'

'Your Bren?'

'Yeah. It's the one she uses for the housekeeping.'

I looked into Humph's eyes, wanting to laugh but finding myself dumbstruck for a second time that day. 'Well, for God's sake, Humph, move it back quickly before some bugger finds out about it.'

'I can't, because it's gone again. And so has Bren.'

Chapter 4

It had all the makings of just the sort of small-town scandal that Humph himself loved to publish. But, before I had a chance to cross-examine him any further, he promptly announced that he had that week's edition of the *Gazette* to put to bed and disappeared back over the road to the office.

I was so stunned at what I'd heard that I was halfway to my next job, a press conference at the Recreation Ground, before I realised I hadn't even asked him about Bren, his wife of almost thirty years.

Bren Blake had been my favourite teacher at school. After moving to Porthcoed in my early teens, everyone had been a stranger to me when I'd started out at the Comp and Bren had recognised this quickly and had done her best to help settle me in. 'You must be Twm Bradley,' she'd said to me that first morning as I'd taken my seat in her English class. 'You look like a bit of a writer to me, Twm. How about you and I start a school newsletter?' She'd smiled at me with warm, intelligent eyes and winked. After school that night I'd learned from my mother that Bren had been on the phone to her the previous evening to find out what interested me, and any remaining anxiety about a new school had evaporated.

I'd never forgotten the care Bren had taken and I'd loved her for that kindness and the many more she'd shown me since. But what Humph had told me about her had me confused. Where had she gone? Was he worried? He couldn't honestly think she had anything to do with the *Gazette*'s missing five grand?

That morning's presser at the Rec represented the last remaining story for that week's paper, so following Humph back to the office to ask him was not an option. The story was in the running for either the front-page splash or the page-five lead, depending on what Ivan Harris had to say.

To concentrate my mind on the task at hand I started to run over what I knew about Ivan Harris. Harris was a local-born entrepreneur who had left Porthcoed in his twenties to make a fortune in the construction industry. He'd begun his working life as a labourer and risen up through the ranks, eventually making his first million building cheap timeshare apartments on the Costa Blanca. I'd covered his ostentatious homecoming just over a year earlier, when out of nowhere he'd unveiled himself as the new owner and chairman of Porthcoed Rugby Football Club.

The Buzzards had been struggling badly on and off the pitch at the time and were expecting the administrators to blow the final whistle at any moment. Harris had told me back then that his intention was to return the club to the glory days it had enjoyed in the seventies.

I knew from my research that Harris had himself turned out once or twice for Porthcoed as a tight-head prop of no great ability and no little aggression. As chairman he had appointed one of the club's only two living ex-internationals, hooker Gwyn Shell, as coach. Then he'd covered the Rec with adverts for the club's new sponsor, Harris Construction, and recruited players from Romania, Tonga and Italy. The club's freefall was brought to a halt.

A year on, both the town and the rugby world were waiting to hear how this son of Porthcoed was intending to take the club to the next level. There had been worried whispers from the *Gazette*'s contacts at the club that he intended to demolish the Rec and cover it with cheap houses. And, after all, wasn't building stuff exactly what multi-millionaire construction firm bosses did? The big question was what might happen to a club with no home ground to play at?

These were turbulent times in domestic rugby. As a reporter covering this story I'd made it my business to keep up with the sport's difficult transition from amateur to professional status. Across the country I knew a small collection of rugby-loving businessmen, 'benefactors' as they were known, were busy working out how to drag the game out of the club bar and into the twenty-first century and safeguard their investment in the process. But there were whispers of disharmony in the game at local level with talk that some clubs might rebel against the governing body, and seek fixtures with bigger clubs across the border.

Ivan Harris, however, had a reputation as a resourceful man. He'd worked his way out of his parents' end-of-terrace home and into a sprawling terracotta villa up on Deri mountain, from where he and the second Mrs Harris, a 29-year-old nail salon owner from Abergerran by the name of Jacqui, could gaze down over the entire town.

Arriving at the tall, wrought-iron gates of the Rec car park, freshly painted in the club's colours of red and black, my thoughts were interrupted by the familiar sound of cameras firing off. I looked up to see the man himself – stocky of build, with short grey-blond hair and a pasty complexion running slightly to pink – emerge from the back of a large saloon car. Checking the button on his suit jacket, perhaps aware of the paunch underneath, Harris paused, smiling for the half-dozen photographers whose vigil next to the 'Reserved for Club Chairman' sign had paid off.

'Thanks for coming, boys,' he said, and turned towards the clubhouse entrance.

A sharp and also occasionally blunt negotiator, Harris had used his purchase of the Buzzards to worm his way into the game's corridors of power just after the governing body had announced it was to build a new national stadium in the heart of the capital. Suddenly the construction firm originally commissioned to do the job had lost its contract, along with all its suppliers and subcontractors, and Harris Construction had stepped into the breach.

Businessmen with Harris's skill set and bank balance were few and far between in domestic rugby and very few doors were closed to him. All the same, with the national stadium now his number one priority, no one knew what he would do next with Porthcoed RFC, and it was my job to find out.

'Morning Twm,' said club president Ken Thomas, handing me a glossy-fronted press pack and a complimentary blue-glass bottle of mineral water as I filed into the bustling clubhouse.

'This lot must have cost you a small fortune,' I laughed, opening the folder to find a six-page press release and glossy photos of Ivan Harris within. 'Whatever happened to half a side of badly-typed A4 and Mrs T's bakestones?'

'Ivan got a couple of his marketing girls to pull this together. It's the way it's all going these days. All very professional.'

'It's a brave new world, Ken. So what's the form today, then?'

'You'll have to wait and see. The presentation should start in a few minutes.'

I took my seat near the front of the clubhouse, wondering where an old-school rugby man like Ken had picked up a word like 'presentation'. As I waited for the event to begin I ran my eye over the small gathering. The usual suspects from the local rugby and news media merry-go-round were present and correct, but one unfamiliar face stood out amid the crowd.

On the other side of the room sat a young woman whose striking look spoke more of London than any provincial media organisation. Porthcoed simply didn't do that kind of chic. Dressed in fashionable black, her complexion was milk white and fresh; her lips cherry red. Her fair hair, cropped closely to the back of her long neck, tumbled across her forehead from the dark roots of her side-parting. She effortlessly radiated confidence and cool. Instinctively aware of someone looking at her she turned her eyes to meet mine. I thought I saw the first glint of a smile before I was distracted by a voice from over my shoulder.

Turning round I was presented with the thin smile of a small balding man in a sky blue Berghaus hiking jacket. Gesturing with his thumb to the camera crew in tow behind him, he smiled politely and asked, 'Would you mind awfully moving to another seat?'

'Yes, I would,' I replied, and returned my focus to the woman in the crowd whose gaze had now fallen onto her press pack.

'Twm?' came another voice a minute or two later. Ken Thomas's voice. 'Do us a favour and budge over a bit, will you? It's the TV boys over from the city, see. They say they need a better angle onto the podium, and your head's getting in the way.'

With the Hairdo, his camera operator and sound man in the process of setting up right behind me, I reluctantly obliged, sliding two seats across to the side. 'Hairdo' was the recognised vernacular at the *Gazette* for a regional television journalist. While their counterparts in radio were regarded with professional respect – many a *Gazette* trainee had moved on to the radio – Hairdos were not. They habitually arrived late at press conferences, rearranged everything to their own satisfaction at the expense of all other journalists in the room, and then later on the telly draped themselves all over their story. It wasn't a job for a proper reporter.

The clubhouse lights dimmed, and the conversational hum around me began to die down. On a large screen behind the podium a video sprang into life. In a dizzying procession of rapidly-cut sequences, set against what I recognised as The Chemical Brothers' track 'Dig Your Own Hole', we were presented with Ivan Harris's vision for Porthcoed RFC. A vision, I couldn't help but notice, that had slick production values but lacked anything specific in the way of actual newsworthy or reportable detail. The professional game had become all smoke and mirrors. Club rugby was belatedly auditioning for the MTV era.

The screen dimmed and a single spotlight picked out the figure of Ivan Harris, open-collared and tieless in his well-cut, shiny dark blue suit, smiling confidently from the podium in front of us. Next to him stood Ken, a microphone in his hand.

'Mr Harris will now take your questions,' announced Ken.

Getting to my feet I caught Ken's eye and was about to speak when he cut me off.

'Er, yes, you have a question, Mike? Sorry, Twm, do you mind – Mike behind you has a question for Ivan.'

I had no choice but to give way to the Hairdo and sit back down.

'Ah yeah, thanks Ken. Mike James-Jenkins, WTV. Mr Harris … a very *confident* promotional video I think we can say. This seems to mark, almost, a quantum leap in the development of Porthcoed RFC, once great but now a sleeping giant. Is this the message you are sending out to the rest of the rugby world? That the Buzzards are on their way back?'

Chapter 5

'Shut the door behind you, Smudge, will you? Humph's not here so I'll be in the chair this afternoon, okay?'

On the Wednesday afternoon I'd headed into the *Gazette*'s conference room just before 3 p.m., taken my usual spot at the round table circled by an assortment of old chairs apparently plucked from a school or church hall, and waited for Humph and the others to arrive.

The Germolene Twins had been the next to show, followed by the *Gazette*'s veteran production manager Albie Evans, photographer-cum-picture editor Smudge Tucker and eventually the senior, rotund and unkempt figure of the *Gazette* legend that was Coma Jenkins.

Coma had taken Humph's usual place at the table, tilting his head down and delivering his bombshell over the besmirched half-rim spectacles he always wore midway down his nose. Like all bombshells it was followed by a moment of stunned silence, which Albie was the first to break, his trademark stammer doing nothing to lessen the disbelief in the room.

'You mean Humph's n-not ... c-coming?'

'No.'

'Well, a'll be ... b-buggered.'

'It is a matter of common knowledge that Humph Blake has missed only two editorial conferences at the *Gazette* in the past thirty-odd years,' added Smudge, a swarthy south Londoner in his late thirties with an abundance of thick, oily black hair, a winning smile and a small silver stud in his left ear. 'First time was when Porthcoed drew with the All Blacks ...'

'... and the second was the time he had Norton's Coin at 100-1 for the Cheltenham Gold Cup,' Coma confirmed. 'Yes, we all know that old chestnut, Smudge, but he's not here and Teg hasn't been able to get him on the phone. So, let's just push on, shall we? What's the story up at the Rec, then, Twm? Have we got our Ivan Harris splash?'

If there had been a front-page lead to be found in Ivan Harris's video clip or the question-and-answer session that followed it, then I hadn't spotted it. I'd gone to the Rec presser expecting some concrete detail on Ivan Harris's plans for the club, or at least for the club ground, but I had walked straight into a set-up job.

Harris's slick video duly earned him a three-minute slot on that evening's local television news. In a triumph of style over content, WTV began its bulletin with clips from the promo. Two slick sound bites from the anchor foreshadowed a special report: 'Provincial rugby's marketing makeover ... Construction millionaire drags Porthcoed into the professional era.' Job done.

The uncomfortable truth was that I hadn't been able to put a question to Ivan Harris during the entire presser. I had not been alone in my fate. No other print journalist had been allowed to get a word in either. The whole event had been stage-managed for the cameras. We print hacks had been merely extras draped across the set. I'd put this to Ken Thomas as the presser was winding up, and Mike the Hairdo was leading Harris away for 'a quick one-on-one', as he described it, on the club pitch. Ken had merely shrugged apologetically at me and walked off.

That week's *Gazette* led with a Coma Jenkins-penned splash on a plan to demolish public toilets in Porthcoed town centre to make room for more parking spaces.

Chapter 6

The newsroom was empty when I arrived at half eight the next day. I sat at my desk and rearranged a mess of accumulated paperwork to locate my desk phone. I dialled nine for an outside line and called Humph at home. After three rings the line clicked and fell silent.

'Humph?'

I rang back but once more the line was disconnected. Was that Humph, I wondered, or something to do with the groundworks on Station Road?

Thursday, the day when the *Gazette* hit the news-stands, was also the first day of the paper's weekly publishing cycle, and usually started slowly. I knew the newsroom wouldn't fill up until around ten, so I walked out of the building and, leaping to avoid an oncoming BT van, landed in the doorway of Grumpy's.

After swapping pleasantries with Grumpy I took a copy of the *Daily Mirror* from the café's newspaper rack and headed for my usual window table. I needed to sit quietly and work through the events of the past twenty-four hours to try to make some sense of Humph's behaviour. Five grand missing from the *Gazette* accounts and the suggestion that Bren had somehow done a bunk with it? That was so far off the chart that I was still having trouble accepting it.

'Don't tell me you had a tenner on that bloody nag, too?' said Grumpy, delivering a mug of tea to my table then wiping the sweaty dome of his receding pink forehead with a murky Charles and Diana tea towel that he pulled from the waist of his apron.

'Which nag?' I replied.

'It was daylight bloody robbery, never mind delight,' said Grumpy, gesturing to the back page of the *Mirror* on the table in front of me. 'Bloody horse ran in two lengths clear. Sixty-five-to-bloody-one. The donkey I had my tenner on is probably parked round the back of the glue factory by now.'

I looked down and scanned the story. A horse named Daylight Delight, a rank outsider, had won yesterday's big race at Chester. Somewhere in a corner of my brain a small light started to flash, but by the time I noticed it Grumpy had retreated to the other side of his counter.

'You said "too", Grumpy,' I called to him across the mostly empty café. 'You said: "Don't tell me you had a tenner on that nag, too." Did Humph have money on that horse?'

'Jammy sod,' came the mumbled reply. 'I never win anything.'

'He told you that himself? When did you see him?'

'He was in first thing this morning. Him and a young lady. Posh sort.'

'What did she look like?'

'Oh, I don't know,' said Grumpy, starting to turn a giant can of baked beans under a large can-opener fixed to a white-tiled wall. 'Nice-looking girl. Blonde. Bit pale. Practically anaemic, now I think about it. Never seen the inside of a black pudding, that's for sure. Ow, shit!'

'You say they came in together?'

'I've cut my bloody thumb now,' said Grumpy. He inspected the damage to his swollen digit, shoving it briefly into his mouth before wiping off the top of the can of beans with the smiling face of the heir to the throne.

'They sat together, Grumpy?' I repeated.

There was a brief interlude while my question caught up with him. 'Er, yeah. Same table you're at now. Don't you worry about me, Twm, I'm all right. I'm just bleeding over the baked beans.'

'How long were they here?'

'Mmm? Oh, not long. They had a bit of a falling out, they did. Humph stood up, shouted something at the girl and then he stormed off. I felt a bit sorry for her to be honest. Very pale, she was. I found one of her business cards on the table after she'd left. I pinned it up there on the noticeboard.'

I crossed the café to the wall by the door. It wasn't hard to spot. Pinned between a fluorescent pink postcard offering 'Dirty Chat' on an 0800 phone line, and an irony-free letter from the British Heart Foundation thanking Grumpy's of Porthcoed for a donation of £16.71, was a much smaller, clean-looking business card.

I drew out the drawing pin and examined the card. Beneath the familiar-looking masthead of a national broadsheet newspaper I read: 'Mara McKenzie, News Reporter'. Humph losing his rag with a Fleet Street reporter? That wasn't necessarily something that should worry me but, given the way things were going, it did.

Chapter 7

I left Grumpy's and went back over the road to the *Gazette*. There was still no sign of Humph and no one in the newsroom had heard from him. Coma took the morning conference, after which I put in a few preliminary phone calls on the stories I was working up for that week's paper. After a lunch consisting of a sandwich from Grumpy's and a plastic cup of thin metallic-tasting coffee from the newsroom's vending machine I went down to reception to find Teg.

'Nothing at all from the mysterious Humph,' she breathed. 'Not a clue as to what the bugger's up to.'

Out on Station Road I was glad of the warm sunshine, though with the roadworks there was little more than dust to see or breathe until I had turned the corner onto Bridge Street. As I walked I ran over what I had learned from Grumpy. It seemed likely that Mara McKenzie was the woman I had seen at the Rec presser, but what had she been doing there? Ivan Harris's marketing team may well have tried to rouse interest among the nationals for the Harris revolution at Porthcoed but this was at best still a sports story, and a fairly parochial one at that. What drew a broadsheet news reporter 150 miles down the motorway to a town like Porthcoed? Something to do with Harris's national stadium contract, perhaps? There was nothing quite like the first stirrings of professional jealousy to get my mind ticking over, and the prospect of being scooped in my own back yard added a few inches to each stride.

I needed to know what had passed between Mara McKenzie and Humph Blake at Grumpy's earlier that morning. I had often seen Humph outsmart regional and national newspapers over the occasional big story that broke on his home patch, so it was a possibility that he was just running a little interference with the girl from Fleet Street. But Humph wasn't a man to lose his rag in quite that way. Okay, he might unleash one of his infamous rants at one of the Germolene Twins for an aberrant apostrophe, or at Ted Buckett at the Capital News Agency for selling a *Gazette* copyrighted picture without permission, but it was unlike him to unload on someone he'd just met, especially a young woman.

The air inside Dai Whitehouse's bookie shop was no fresher than the dusty air out on Station Road had been but the atmosphere was electric. In the glare of two long neon strip lights, a combination of pipe, cigarette and roll-up smoke hung like a layer of cirrus cloud over the shop floor, which was occupied by a familiar and solitary figure. All bar one of Dai's customers were ringed around the edges of the room, their attention focused inwards on George Mellor. Seeing no sign of Humph among the crowd I made my way to the counter past George, who was deep in concentration, his eyes fixed on a screen on the opposite wall.

'What's going on?' I asked Dai, who had been a year above me at school and had inherited the bookie's six months earlier when his father had passed on.

'Oh, hi Twm. It's George. He's on the last leg of an accumulator,' said Dai, nodding towards the screen. 'If his horse comes in now I'm seven hundred and fifty quid down.' He took a deep pull of his cigarette. 'And all off a 50p stake.'

'Dai, I'm looking for Humph. Has he been in today?'

At this point the shop's noise level, which had been steadily on the rise, burst into a loud crescendo as on the racecourse in Chester a bay colt answering to the name of Stretarez romped home at 25-1. The shop floor filled and George, tears welling in his eyes, was mobbed.

'Ahh bugger it,' I heard Dai mutter through the maelstrom, before he recovered sufficiently to shout, 'Nice one, George!'

'Dai,' I shouted back. 'Have you seen Humph?'

'No, but he phoned in yesterday to place a bet. Another rank outsider which came in at 65-1. Dodgy as hell if you ask me. I've had a terrible week.'

'Has he come in to collect his winnings?'

'I haven't seen him.' Dai waited a moment and then jerked his head backwards twice, inviting me to lean over the counter towards him.

'I shouldn't really be telling you this, but Humph isn't going to be seeing any of his winnings. He's got what you might call a bit of a tab going.'

'Bad?'

Dai nodded.

'How bad?'

'Just north of five grand. And I've told him I'm going to have to call it in.'

CHAPTER 8

The first couple of rings went unnoticed so I decided to lean on the doorbell. Still no sign of life. I took three steps back and glanced up at a first-floor window. The curtains were open and the window was shut. I stepped back onto the block-paving path and then crossed the small front lawn to peer in through the sitting room window. Everything looked immaculate, as usual, and all in its allotted place.

After leaving Dai Whitehouse's bookie shop I'd driven over to Humph's house in the *Gazette*'s pool car. What I'd learned from Dai had muddied the water still further and now the alarm bell that Humph had set off in my head at Grumpy's was ringing even louder. Money missing from the *Gazette*. The mysterious disappearance of Bren. And now a five grand bookie's bill.

On the left-hand side of the house I reached over the top of a shoulder-high wooden gate and loosened the metal bolt on the other side, sliding it open. 'Anyone in?' I asked as I turned the back corner of the house and walked into the back garden, but with no reply. I wasn't much of a gardener but the back lawn didn't look like it was overdue a trim. On either side of it tall, orderly borders were beginning to come into flower. 'Humph?' I inquired. 'Bren?' There was nothing in response.

I followed the mosaic of garden paving around the back of one border towards the wooden shed where I knew Humph kept a spare back door key, but was stopped in my tracks by a muffled scratching sound. Was someone inside the shed?

'Humph, is that you?'

There was still no reply so I approached the shed door cautiously, half-expecting it to open in my face. I was reaching for its twisted metalwork handle when another sound, this time a metallic double-tap, spun me around until I was facing the rear of the house. By the kitchen door I saw the vicious and loathsome Modlen, Humph and Bren's brown and white long-haired cat, who had just appeared through the cat flap. Modlen flashed her fangs at me and hissed, then there was a loud crack of thunder and I hit the crazy paving. Before I lost consciousness I thought I felt warm fluid trickle down my neck.

Chapter 9

The top of my skull was on fire and throbbing. The skin around my eyes was taut with dried tears and, as I sat in my chair at the kitchen table, my neck was already stiffening to the point where I had to turn my entire upper torso just to accept a mug of tea from Humph.

'Sorry, Twm.'

I felt my head gingerly and then sniffed my hand. 'Did Modlen piss on my head?'

'I beg your pardon?'

'Did the cat piss on my head when I fell to the ground? I can smell something in my hair. Smells like cat's piss.'

'Your head was bleeding. I cleaned the wound with something of Bren's from the bathroom. I think it was Germolene.'

I tried to smile but it hurt too much.

'You took a bit of a knock. I think maybe you're still a bit dazed. Drink your tea.'

'"A bit of a knock"? You smashed a pot of bloody tulips over my head.'

'They were pansies, actually,' Humph replied. 'Bren's going to be mad when she finds out.'

'But why would you do that? In broad daylight?'

'I thought you were someone else.'

'Who?'

Humph slotted a bottle of milk back into the fridge door, closed it and looked back at me. He shrugged.

'And where *is* Bren?'

'You know, I think you're going to need to get off to the Prince Harry for a stitch or two. Maybe more.'

'Humph, I'm not budging until you –'

'Okay … okay.'

There was a pause as Humph sat down at the table and scratched his moustache with his forefinger, seeming to decide where to start.

'As I told you in Grumpy's, Bren's gone,' he said, lighting a cigarette.

'Gone where?'

'I don't know. When I got home on Tuesday night the shed door was open, there was potting compost everywhere and I found her gardening gloves on the paving. It looked to me like there'd been a struggle and I thought Bren must … must have been taken. I was in there tidying up and I thought you were them coming back for me.'

'Hang on a minute, Humph. Back up a little bit. Who's "them"? And what makes you think Bren has been "taken"? She might have gone to stay with her sister or something. Have you checked?' Silence. 'Humph, just what the hell is going on?'

Humph stood up and walked into the sitting room. He returned with a bottle of Scotch. He sat down, unscrewed the bottle top and slugged some whisky into his mug. He offered none to me.

'It's all happened so quickly,' he said after a moment. 'I just haven't had time to think it all through and work out what's going on. And I'm worried sick about Bren.'

'But not so worried sick that you couldn't get on the phone to Dai and back a 65-1 shot at Chester yesterday?'

'Who told you that?'

'Grumpy. And Dai. Grumpy also told me you had an argument with a Fleet Street reporter.'

'She called me,' he said. 'After you and I spoke at Grumpy's. Mara Mc … something. She explained who she was and asked me about the money missing from the *Gazette*. How the hell did she know about that?'

'Don't look at me,' I replied, indignant at the implied accusation. 'I haven't told anyone.'

'I told her to get lost but she rang straight back and said we needed to meet. She said she'd dug up something about me. Something from my past.'

'What did she mean by that?' I asked.

Humph reached forward and rolled the lit end of his cigarette gently round the rim of his ashtray, cleaning off the ash. It was another of his nervous ticks. Then he spoke. 'I could only think it was something that happened years ago, when I was working at the *Record* ...'

CHAPTER 10

In December 1965 life in the city was quite an eye-opener for a young lad from Porthcoed. The sixties were beginning to swing – both the Beatles and the Stones played the Capitol cinema in 'sixty-five. I landed my first real story for the Western Morning Record *with an interview with a guy who'd rushed the Beatles onstage and made a lunge at Paul and George. I missed most of the gig for that little 'scoop', as the guy got thrown out by the bouncers and I had to go out after him.*

Back in those days the Record *was a big newspaper, Twm. Over 100,000 copies sold each day. It wasn't easy for me starting out. Back home in Porthcoed I knew my patch backwards and was trusted with any story. At the* Record *I was just another hick from the sticks. Wet behind the ears. The editor may have seen something in me but it became clear the news desk didn't rate me. I spent the first few months writing nibs. That story from the Beatles gig was the first I'd written that was more than two pars long and not printed under the fold. They still threw it away inside the paper. A picture from the gig made the front page but my story was buried alongside a display ad on page seven. Anyway, it started a slight thaw with the news desk.*

From nibs I graduated to council meetings. Month after month in wood-panelled committee rooms listening to grown men arguing about bin collection. But I stuck at it and one day I got a tip-off from a member of the planning committee that the organisation that owned the land around the old rugby club ground in the city centre was going to sell part of its hallowed real estate to the governing body. The governing body was looking for somewhere to build a national stadium and had already briefly considered using land outside the city. But this was final proof that its preferred choice was to stay in the heart of the capital. The first proper national stadium was going to be built on land right next door to the existing club ground.

I broke the story and knew I had at last won the confidence of the news desk. From then on I was entrusted with bigger stories. And then I found myself on the biggest story I would ever work on for the Record. *And the last.*

It all sprang from a nib. The paper's late-duty reporter had turned up a line from the regular evening calls to the emergency services. Police were concerned about the whereabouts of Angharad Sullivan, a 25-year-old hairdresser who worked at a salon in the city. She had been reported missing by her employer, a French woman.

I turned up for my shift the next morning and immediately picked up on the nib. The news desk agreed to let me work on the story and so I put in a few calls to the police and was told that Angharad hadn't showed up for work on the Saturday morning. I spoke to her boss and went round to her digs and spoke to her landlady who said she hadn't seen Angharad since she'd left work the previous day, excited about a night out with her boyfriend.

I kept digging, toured a few well-known nightclubs around the city asking questions and discovered that Angharad had gone out that Friday night with Eddie Lennox. You may remember him. Lennox was a footballer who had recently signed for City from a big Scottish club. Good looking young feller. Angharad had styled his hair, been out on a date with him and they'd started going steady. Well, as steady as you could with a footballer even back in those days.

The police took in Lennox for questioning and, although Angharad's body was never found, they eventually charged him with her murder. His trial was a big national story back then, and I was the Record's *man in court.*

Lennox always denied killing Angharad but was convicted of her murder, apparently on the strength of two bits of evidence. The first was the discovery of one of Angharad's shoes on the groundworks at the building site for the new stadium. The shoe was spattered with blood from her blood group and had Lennox's fingerprints on it. The second piece of evidence came in the form of a key prosecution witness who claimed to have seen Lennox dispose of her body there. The witness was a foreman working at the stadium site. The big … coincidence … was that he turned out to be Angharad's husband.

This man had met and married Angharad in a whirlwind romance around a year earlier. But the relationship hadn't lasted, and after six increasingly bitter months she'd walked out, taking digs under her maiden name.

At first the coincidence seemed almost too great to be believed, and the feeling was that at any time the entire trial would come crashing to a dramatic halt. But somehow it never did. With her body by this stage deemed irretrievable within the footings of the stadium's North Stand, in the end it came down to the shoe and a beauty competition between Lennox and the prosecution witness. Of course there was talk of a fix but nothing that anyone, including yours truly, could make stick.

Lennox wasn't a likeable character. He was flashy and arrogant. He was widely known for his volcanic on-field temper. And after Angharad's heartbroken husband was cruelly harangued in the witness box by the defence counsel, the jury was coaxed and won over by the prosecution. Lennox was sent down.

You might be interested to know the name of this foreman who claimed he had witnessed his wife's body being dumped in a foundation shaft, and whose testimony in court won over the jury.

It was Harris. Ivan Harris.

Chapter 11

Humph rose from his chair and walked across the kitchen to the sink where he stood and stared silently out of the back window.

The shock of hearing Ivan Harris's name in this context compounded the tension in my neck and the throb of my head from the physical blow Humph had landed on me. Eventually, however, the penny dropped.

'You haven't finished the story, Humph,' I said looking across the kitchen towards the side of his face. 'You haven't said why that was your last story for the *Record*, or what exactly it was that you think Mara McKenzie has dug up from your past.'

Humph stood there unmoved.

'What did she find out?'

Eventually Humph spoke. 'I was getting there. It's just that hearing myself tell that story out loud is like picking over an old wound. A deep wound.'

He took his seat at the table again, lit another cigarette and poured another slug of Scotch into his mug.

Chapter 12

About a week after the end of the trial I was called into the editor's office. The editor of the Record *back in those days was an Englishman named Malcolm Ridley. Bit of a gruff northerner. Not a man to mince his words. Editors were mostly feared in those days, and Ridley was no exception.*

He started by congratulating me on the way I had handled the story, from the moment I had picked it up from a two-par nib to the post-trial backgrounder I'd written on the 'fiery Scots winger-turned-killer'. He said it had been the biggest story the Record *had covered under his lead, that we'd managed to keep one step ahead of the nationals all the way and that the* Record's *proprietor, board of directors and shareholders were all delighted with the resulting upturn in sales and ad revenue.*

He said the story had helped to place him in the strongest position he'd been in during his tenure, and this would allow him to drive through the changes he had always wanted to make at the paper.

But then he gave me this really … cold … look. And he told me: 'I say all this to you, Blake, by way of explanation of why I have decided to accept your resignation with immediate effect. When you leave this office you will kindly clear your desk and leave the building. Your career at the Record *is over …'*

Of course I'd known all along that it could end like this; that the truth would find its way out as it always does. But I was a little surprised that it had happened so soon.

'… That is, Blake,' Ridley told me, 'unless you can look me in the face right here and now and, with your hand on your heart, deny the veracity of the information I have received about your connection with the Lennox murder case – and your failure to

bring this to the attention of your superiors at the Record, not to mention the relevant legal authorities?'

Ridley told me he'd received a tip-off from a source, who would remain nameless, that not only had I known Angharad Sullivan prior to her murder, but that I had enjoyed a lengthy and close personal relationship with her. The source was not unimpeachable, Ridley said, but he added that just the threat of this being true, and of this unfortunate truth coming to light, was too much of a risk for the good name of the newspaper. By which I took it that he meant his good name and all the changes he wanted to make to the paper.

I was young, Twm, and Angharad Sullivan was the love of my life. I didn't know her as Angharad, though. To me she was and always will be Delilah. It was a private joke, a nickname she gave herself, a Biblical reference. She used to laugh and say she took power from the men whose hair she cut. The Beatles gig at the Capitol had been our first date. I thought I'd blown it by leaving her to chase down my story, but afterwards, when I finally convinced her to speak to me again she admitted she'd secretly admired my single-mindedness. We were lovers long before she'd even met or married Ivan Harris, or ever heard of Eddie Lennox. But then suddenly, and for no reason that she would give me, she told me it was over between us. It broke me in two. I had trouble accepting it and hit the booze a little too much for my own good.

Then one morning I came to work and saw her name in that nib, and I had to find her. I knew I should have revealed my conflict of interest right from the start but I also knew that, if I had told the news desk, I wouldn't have been allowed to work on the story. And I wanted to work on that story more than any other story I'd ever worked on.

By the time Lennox was arrested and charged I was in too deep. I made a big mistake. I decided not to step forward and tell the police that I had known Delilah.

It wasn't easy. I was in daily contact with the story for months. My greatest fear was that at some stage during the police and then the prosecution's investigations, someone would mention me in connection with her and the walls would come tumbling down on my head. But somehow that didn't happen ... until my meeting with Ridley after the trial.

I left Ridley in his office, walked straight out of the building and got on a train back to Porthcoed. I told the editor of the Gazette *that I'd grown homesick in the city and wanted my old job back, and I started back the following week on the news desk.*

Ridley made his changes to the Record *and later made the step-up to an editor's job in Fleet Street. He had too much to lose, career-wise, to ever reveal his involvement in a conspiracy to withhold evidence concerning a murder. He died in a drink-drive wreck on the motorway a few years later.*

I never knew who Ridley's unnamed source had been, but I had my ideas and it worried me sick at times, I can tell you. For years I knew that at any time the story could pop back up and wreck my life. But then I met Bren and settled down and became a Gazette *lifer. Eventually I worked out that the walls weren't going to crash down on top of me and I forgot about it. Just about. I managed to put the biggest mistake of my life behind me and got on with the business of being the best, the straightest journalist I could be.*

And then thirty years later, out of the blue, five grand goes missing on my watch, and then Bren disappears ... and along comes Mara Mc ... whatever ... talking about a secret from my past.

CHAPTER 13

'So you knew this girl Delilah and didn't mention it,' I said. 'Was that such a crime?'

There was no reply.

'I don't get it. I mean you were a young reporter,' I continued. 'You went out with her for a while well before she was murdered. Then you made a mistake. Big deal. It's not as if what you did or didn't do had any direct impact on what happened to her or on the verdict of the case. Is it?'

Humph looked down at his drink and scratched his moustache with his forefinger.

'Is it, Humph?'

I never got an answer to that question because at that moment the doorbell rang. Humph looked at me silently, then straightened up and walked stiffly into the sitting room. I was a couple of steps behind him when he unlocked the front door and pulled it towards him on the chain.

'Humphrey Blake?' said the shorter of the two tall men standing on the doorstep.

'Cut the crap, Bryn, you know who I am. We were in school together.'

'So you don't mind if we come in, then.' Humph pushed the door to, unhooked the chain, and opened it to let the two men enter. 'Oh, hello, Twm. What brings you here?'

As a *Gazette* reporter I'd had many dealings over the years with Detective Inspector Bryn Thomas. A heavily-built man with a ruddy complexion and an unruly mop of hair, Bryn Thomas had a reputation as a hard-nosed copper which was in no way contradicted by the way his own zigzagged down his face towards his mouth. An old rugby injury, he'd once told me during a long day at Porthcoed Crown Court. Thomas didn't wait for my answer but walked into the lounge, peered through the door into the kitchen and turned back to face us.

'Humph? Twm? This is my new assistant, DS Templeton, freshly arrived from Bristol. Josh, meet Humph Blake of the *Porthcoed Gazette* and,' sarcastically, 'his "ace reporter" Twm Bradley.'

DS Templeton, standing by the fireplace, nodded down to us from a height of at least six-foot-six.

'Bren not at home?' asked Thomas.

'No, she's out actually, Bryn.'

'Due back soon, is she?'

'She's staying with her sister, I think. In Abergerran.'

I shot a look at Humph.

'You *think*?' queried Thomas.

'We had a bit of a row.'

'Oh. Money, was it?'

Humph was about to respond when Thomas turned to me. 'Is that blood?'

'Uh, yeah. Bit of an accident,' I heard myself reply, touching my head. 'Helping Humph with the gardening.'

'A gardening injury,' grinned Thomas.

At this stage Templeton offered a flat smile of his own and disappeared into the kitchen. We heard the back door open and close.

'Oh for God's sake, get to the point, Bryn,' pleaded Humph. 'What are you doing here?'

'I was wondering the same about the two of you.' Thomas turned once more in my direction. 'Okay, Twm, on your way. I'm just going to have a nice little chat with Humph here.'

CHAPTER 14

I shut the front door behind me and walked to the gate. As I turned to drop the latch I saw Templeton standing beside the house. He nodded again and returned to his inspection of the bolt on the side gate.

I hadn't wanted to leave but I wasn't going to argue with Bryn Thomas. I'd gone to get answers from Humph but I'd left with more questions. Now I was keen to know what had prompted Thomas's sudden interest in Humph and wondered how far he might get with his own line of inquiry, and so I decided to stay close by. As soon as I saw Thomas and Templeton leave the house and drive away, I would go back in and mop up with Humph.

For at least six months now the driver's door of the *Gazette* pool car had opened from the inside only so I unlocked the passenger door and manoeuvred myself awkwardly over the gearstick and handbrake to the driver's side. A twelve-year-old Ford Fiesta with its own eco-system, it bore the odour of a car driven by many and loved by none. The smell had not been improved by the heat of the early-evening sun, so I wound down a window a few inches to let in some air. After trying, and failing, to check my head wound in the vanity mirror on the driver's sunshade I decided against a trip to A&E. The car had no radio so I passed half an hour reading back copies of the *Gazette* which I found strewn amid the empty Coke cans and torn crisp packets in the passenger footwell.

The unmistakable clunk of a house door closing drew me from a two-week-old leader column in which Humph was insisting: 'Mr Harris owes the people of Porthcoed full disclosure of his plans for the Recreation Ground and soon.'

Before I could turn to check if it was Humph's front door that I'd heard, there were footsteps on the road beside me and I looked up to see Bryn Thomas raise his right hand in my direction. I smiled stupidly back and watched as he unlocked the driver's-side door of his dark blue Vauxhall Omega. Templeton opened the Vauxhall's offside rear door and offered Humph the back seat. As soon as the lanky Templeton had folded himself in beside him, the car pulled off. I managed to start the pool car at the third attempt and headed back across town to drop it off at the *Gazette* before walking back to my flat.

Set above a doctor's surgery on Terrace Road, my one-bedroomed apartment could, with a little imagination, have been described as homely. It was reached, via a rickety old iron staircase loosely fixed to the back of the surgery building, from a rear car park where the two GPs and their receptionists parked during the day. The flat was located within easy walking distance of the centre of town; Aarav's corner shop was just a hundred yards away and the Royal Crown pub was right across Terrace Road, so I had all I needed to get by quite happily.

I closed the door behind me, walked through the kitchen and crossed the living room to open a front window, letting in the noise of traffic and a distant ambulance siren. The flat was almost as stuffy as the pool car had been, though thankfully the aroma was a modest improvement.

I slid off my tie – my top button was never done up in those days – and returned to the kitchen to pull a beer from the fridge. I chucked a half-eaten plastic container of curry in the microwave and then collapsed into the living room sofa. I'd just opened the can of beer when I heard the tell-tale rusty creak of my stairway, a useful if unintended domestic security device. I rarely had company these days – invited or otherwise – and so out of curiosity I was on my feet in time to see a small dark silhouette appear on the other side of my frosted glass door. I opened it just as my visitor was reaching for the doorbell. Before either of us could speak we were both stilled by a loud ping from the microwave. I managed to recover first.

'So, you'd be Mara McKenzie,' I said, confronted with the striking face I'd seen at the Rec presser. 'You'd better come in.'

Chapter 15

It may have been the stuffiness of the flat, the steamy odour of curry or the dried blood in my hair that caused Mara McKenzie to stand her ground on the stairway.

'Perhaps we could go somewhere and get a drink?' she asked in a soft, anglicised Scottish accent which took me by surprise. 'I think we need to talk.'

'Okay. You're going to have to give me five minutes, though,' I said. 'I'm, er, still in my work clothes and I'd really like to change.'

'Shall I wait in the pub over the road, then? Come over when you've had a chance to … freshen yourself up.' She smiled, sweetly, and turned to go. I watched her descend for a few moments, then closed the door and headed for the shower.

Entering the bar of the Crown twenty minutes later I saw Mara McKenzie seated at a window table. In the seconds before she noticed me I had another chance to take her in. She was a few years older than me, slim, attractive and poised enough to look perfectly at home sipping a pint of Guinness. When she looked up I gestured towards the bar and performed the universal mime for 'Another pint?' She smiled politely and shook her head.

'I was actually going to ring you but then you showed up,' I said, placing my pint of bitter on the table between us. My hair was still wet after my hurried shower and as I reached into my back trouser pocket a few drops of water landed on the table top. From my wallet I plucked her business card. I wiped the table with the cuff of my jacket and placed it in front of her. 'How did you find *me*?'

'I followed you from Humphrey Blake's house,' she replied.

The slim fingers of her left hand brushed her long fringe away from her forehead, though I noticed it flopped back over again. 'Sorry.'

'How did you know who I was?'

'Well, I didn't at first,' she admitted and her red lips smiled. She had a ready smile, I noticed, and I liked it. 'I saw you come out of Mr Blake's house and watched you … get into your car.' She smiled again, and this time her eyes, deep blue circling black, joined in.

'Oh, you enjoyed that, did you?' I replied. 'Been a while since you drove a local newspaper pool car, I expect.'

'But if you really want to know, it was the name printed on a piece of card above your doorbell that gave away your identity.'

'Well, there are no mugs at your newspaper, clearly,' I said, toasting her with a pull from my pint. 'So what do you want with me?'

As she drank from her Guinness, I spotted a thin pale scar beneath the rim of her right eye socket, a small accident from her youth, perhaps. This scarcely-detectable flaw offered some context, some unknown history which I found curiously appealing. I wanted to know more.

'Now, you've just told me you were going to ring me,' she said, 'so I suppose I could ask you the same question.'

'Well, don't let me stop you,' I told her. 'You want another one of those first?'

'Maybe in a moment,' she countered, and then picked up her business card from the table. 'Where did you find this?'

'There are no mugs at the *Porthcoed Gazette*, either, Miss McKenzie. And, as we can stretch to a small but quite workable weekly expenses claim, are you sure I can't tempt you to join me in another drink?'

'Well, all right then,' she said. As she spoke I glimpsed faint shadows beneath her eyes, just a hint of fatigue hidden beneath the surface of her fresh complexion.

At the bar I drained the last of my bitter, ordered two pints of Guinness, two packets of cheese and onion crisps, and returned to the window table.

'Thanks,' she said, and with a finger drew a line across the milky white head of the stout. 'So, you were about to tell me why you were going to ring me.'

'You know at some stage soon we're going to need to turn this into a proper conversation,' I ventured. 'Unless you'd rather we just carried on avoiding each other's questions?'

'Well, I'll risk it if you will,' she replied, conspiratorially.

'Okay, okay,' I said. 'You can call it professional curiosity, if you like. I was going to call you because I wanted to find out what a reporter from a national newspaper was doing at a small-town rugby club press conference.'

'Oh, I remember you now,' she said, with another smile. 'You were in the front row. Got caught up in a public slanging match with a TV crew. Which you lost, as I seem to recall.'

I decided to just come right out and say it.

'So, is it Ivan Harris you're investigating?' I asked her. 'Or is it Humph Blake?'

CHAPTER 16

Mara McKenzie let my question hang in the air as if she was calculating a precise answer. 'Neither,' she said eventually. 'Or perhaps both.'

I was on the point of remonstrating when she added, 'I'm working on a story about an ex-footballer by the name of Eddie Lennox.'

This time it was my turn to let the silence hang.

'Lennox was jailed for life for murder,' she continued. 'Back in the sixties. He was released from prison within the last year and just now he's looking at working up a miscarriage of justice case. You know, wrongful conviction. Low behaviour in high places. That sort of thing.'

I took an inch from the top of my pint, licked the inevitable Guinness moustache from my upper lip and maintained radio silence.

'I take it from your reaction that you're familiar with the Angharad Sullivan murder?' she asked. 'Even though it was well before our time.'

'I've heard Humph mention it,' I replied.

'Well, it would help our investigation if I could get Mr Blake to answer a few questions about that case. His byline is all over the *Record*'s coverage of the case back then and so I'm across all of that. It's just that I've uncovered … certain information … about the lead-up to the trial, and the trial itself, that I need to clarify.'

'Well, Humph's your man. You'd best speak to him,' I suggested.

'I think you already know that I've tried doing that and got nowhere.'

'Well, Miss McKenzie, if you're going to get caught up in a

slanging match in Porthcoed then Grumpy's café is probably as public a place as any.'

She smiled briefly down at the table to concede the point, then lifted her head and then her glass to mock my earlier toast.

'The trouble is that having just seen your boss being escorted into an unmarked police car, I'm not exactly sure now when I'm going to get another chance to speak with him,' she said.

'But you've talked to Ivan Harris?'

'Well, that didn't quite work out either.'

'Yeah, I know the feeling,' I confessed. 'That entire press conference was a travesty, wasn't it? Ivan Harris doesn't appear to want anyone to know what his plans are for Porthcoed. He only seems interested in the platform that owning the club has given him – getting his feet under the table with the governing body. There, you can have that little titbit for free. Does he know you're on the Lennox trail?'

'I faxed his office a while back asking for an interview,' she explained. 'I may have neglected to mention exactly why. And when I heard nothing back I thought I'd come down here and approach him in person. But I couldn't get anywhere near him.'

'So your Eddie Lennox investigation is not going so smoothly, then?' I observed a little more smugly than I'd intended.

'Oh I wouldn't say that,' she replied, confidently and conceding nothing. 'Listen, how about we get something to eat? My paper's expenses have been known to stretch beyond two bags of Golden Wonder.'

'Just for that remark you're going to buy me the most sought-after dinner in town.'

'Okay.' She delved into an inside jacket pocket and produced a mobile phone. 'Do we need to ring ahead and book?'

'No need,' I assured her, and lifted my Guinness. 'I'm not without a certain pull in this town.'

Chapter 17

Ernie's Fish and Chip Shop on Riverside was not exactly what Mara McKenzie had been expecting, judging by the look on her face as we joined a lengthy queue on the street outside. But twenty minutes later, after her first mouthful of battered cod, even she had to concede that it was fresh, plump and crispy and Ernie's twice-fried chips were pretty much to die for.

'No one's died yet,' I assured her as we ate straight from the chip paper, on a bench just down from the bridge, while the river glistened in the reddening light of the sun.

'You just don't get this in London,' she said.

'A good old-fashioned chippy, you mean, or a sweet-smelling river?'

'Both, now you mention it. We've a wonderful chippy back home in Kelso. Gordon's. It wouldn't be an exaggeration to say this is the best fish supper I've had since I was last at Gordon's.'

'And when was that?' I asked.

'Mmm, let me see now. It must be going on four years ago. Yeah, all of that. I started out on the local paper in Kelso and then moved to *The Scotsman* in Edinburgh. After three years there I made the move down south to the *Daily Mail*.'

'Ouch.'

'It didn't really work out …' she laughed, '… but I had a friend who helped me get a few shifts at the broadsheet he worked at and I was taken on as staff there earlier this year. It's a great newspaper and I love my job.'

'I'm loving your expense account,' I said, slipping another chip into my mouth.

'So has Porthcoed always been home for you?'

'No. I was born in one of those northern seaside villages

that can be hard to pronounce. We moved down to Porthcoed when I was thirteen.'

'We?'

'Mam and I. It didn't work out with my dad. This was where Mam grew up so we came back down south to what she knew.'

'And what's it been like growing up here?'

'Not so different, I'd imagine, from growing up in Kelso.'

'And you started out on the *Gazette*?'

'Yes, after university. Postgraduate diploma in journalism.'

'Ah, an educated man. Your mother must be very proud of you.'

'She was.'

'Was?'

'She died. Cancer. Three years ago now.'

'I'm so sorry ... I didn't ...'

'No, of course. Don't worry about it.'

We both picked at our chips for a while until she spoke again. 'So are you planning on a future in the big city, or are you happy here in Porthcoed?'

'Oh, I'm just taking it as it comes,' I replied. 'No plans. I like it well enough here. I have a comfortable life. And they're a good bunch to work with at the *Gazette*. Real people, you know?'

'So what's your editor like to work for?'

'Humph? Oh, he's a piece of work. He once suspended the entire *Gazette* newsroom for a day because, at my suggestion, we'd opened a few bottles from a crate that the local brewery had sent round as a gift. He made me replace the opened bottles and deliver the full crate back to the brewery. No one buys Humph Blake.'

'So how come he never made it to the nationals? I'd have thought that would have been a natural step up from the *Western Morning Record* ... but he comes back here instead, after the biggest story of his career?'

I'd noticed a gear shift in our conversation. 'Are we on the record, all of a sudden, Miss McKenzie?'

'Just a little deep background, Mr Bradley. I'm going to need to justify that receipt for the fish and chips.'

I folded up the remainder of my meal inside its wrapping and dropped it into a bin next to the bench. 'I think I'd better get going,' I said. 'Thanks for the meal.'

'Was it something I said?' she asked, crumpling her own leftovers into a ball of chip paper.

'No. I've got a splitting headache and an early start tomorrow,' I told her, as we started back towards the bridge. 'I've enjoyed this evening, though. Maybe we can do this again before you head back home. When are you leaving?'

'Well, I'm going to be here for a few days yet,' she replied. 'I'm staying at the Railway. Give me a ring, you've got my card.'

'Good night, Miss McKenzie.'

'Back home in Kelso they call me Mara.'

'Okay. Good night, Mara.'

At the bridge we turned in opposite directions, and fifteen minutes later I found myself back outside Humph's house. The lights were off and there was no obvious sign that he'd returned from the police station. It was a still, warm evening but the windows were shut and the curtains open. I walked slowly back to the flat where I lay on the sofa and drained the now warm can of beer I'd opened earlier that evening. My eyes turned towards a framed photograph of my mother on one of the crowded bookshelves that filled one wall of my sitting room. It was hard to reconcile the warm, full, smiling face I saw there with the pale, hollowed-out shell that it became. Gradually, lulled perhaps by the soothing sound of John Martyn, I fell into a deep sleep.

CHAPTER 18

'My god, Twm, you look rough as shit, my lovely,' said Teg as I walked into reception early the next morning.

'You're all heart, Teg,' I replied, crossing the foyer to the lift. 'Anything from Humph?'

'Not a sign of Humphrey Blake since you two went over to Grumpy's on Wednesday morning,' she declared.

'Okay.'

I got into the lift and pressed the button for the second floor. Just as the doors were closing an out-of-breath Smudge Tucker squeezed himself into the lift. As we started to rattle upwards he attempted to still his breathing enough to speak. In the cramped space I caught the unmistakable odour of nicotine, tea and the oily scent of Smudge's greasy black hair, which fell in curls over the collar of the black leather biker's jacket that he wore all year round.

'Gotta give up the fags,' he panted, flashing a glimpse of a gold filling. 'I've only run across the road from Grumpy's. Had to jump out of the way of one of those little JCBs.'

'Didn't see Humph over there, I suppose?'

'No,' replied Smudge, blowing his nose into a red handkerchief and then briefly inspecting the result before folding it over and tucking it into his jeans pocket. 'What's going on with him, then? He had a face on him like thunder on Wednesday and no one's seen hide nor hair of him since.'

'I wish I knew,' I said. A mildly awkward silence ensued before the lift finally stopped with a shudder and a ring and the doors opened agonisingly slowly.

'Probably in trouble with Bren again,' said Smudge, lifting

his eyebrows as a parting shot. 'See you at the morning conference.'

I headed straight for the vending machine, where I saw the grandfatherly figure of Coma, specs perched mid-nose, pulling a face at a small plastic cup of coffee.

'This stuff tastes like it's dripped out of a rusty radiator,' he said and thrust the cup in my direction. I accepted it and gestured him quietly to one side. In hushed tones I explained how I'd seen Humph being carted off by Bryn Thomas. I was beginning to feel a little uneasy about my promise to Humph not to mention the missing money, or the missing Bren, but I decided that as far as Coma was concerned I'd better not mention either just yet.

'Carted off by Bryn Thomas?' asked Coma, unable to hide his annoyance at the prospect of having to continue running the paper in Humph's absence. 'What the hell does Bryn want with Humph?'

'I've no idea,' I lied, 'but I think it would be wise if we kept this between the two of us, for the time being?'

Coma nodded and shuffled off towards his desk deep in thought.

An hour or so later I was sitting at the Internet Terminal with the thin, greasy taste of a second vending-machine coffee in my mouth, when Coma appeared behind my shoulder.

'That takes me back,' said Coma, tilting his head back to focus on a thirty-year-old picture of Eddie Lennox on the screen. 'Big story back in the day, that was. Especially for Humph. Ivan Harris, too.'

'There might be more to come,' I replied. 'Listen, how are we fixed for this week's paper? Can you manage without me if I come off diary to work on something a little bit more long term?'

Coma looked aghast. 'Twm, we're already one man down with me filling in for Humph on the desk.'

'Come on, Humph's bound to have a few stories squirrelled away for a rainy day. Besides, it's high time the Germolene Twins were given a little more responsibility around here, don't you think? I just need a week. Two at the most.'

'Two?'

'Maybe three, then. Look, I really think there's something brewing here. There's a reporter from London in town nosing around Ivan Harris and she's talking about Lennox and a miscarriage of justice. Now Humph wouldn't want us to get scooped on our own patch, would he? And certainly not on your watch.'

Coma rubbed the underside of his chin with the inside of his thumb and said, 'I'd need you on the Wednesday, to help me with the subbing?'

'I can do that.'

'Okay. All right then. But two weeks is all there is, even if Humph walks back in tomorrow morning. And I'm going to want regular updates on what's going on, okay?'

'Okay. Thanks, Coma.'

'And for God's sake watch how you go with Ivan Harris. He's a nasty bit of work, that one, and if you so much as put a foot wrong with him he's got a string of lawyers who would break a paper like the *Gazette* just for fun.'

CHAPTER 19

Where to start? There was still much I wanted to find out from Humph, but didn't want to ask: the coincidence of his gambling debts; the missing *Gazette* funds. I needed answers. I also needed to know more about what had happened with Bren and why Humph was so jumpy. But as things stood I was clearly second in line behind Porthcoed CID for Humph's attention, and I knew I would have to bide my time.

As for Ivan Harris, I was happy to heed Coma's appeal for caution. There was no way I was going to go asking questions of Harris until I had a much better handle on the Lennox case. So, in direct contravention of head office's recent working-time directive – as outlined in no uncertain terms by Teg – I settled down for a lengthy stint at the Internet Terminal, researching and printing out anything I could find on Eddie Lennox. Mara McKenzie was way ahead of me on this story and I needed to play catch-up.

There wasn't much to show for an hour's trawl – Lennox was old news, and mostly pre-internet – so I flicked through my contacts book and rang up Karl Sillitoe. Karl had begun his career at the *Gazette* as a young lad during World War Two and had gone on to work on the sports desk of the *Record* for many years afterwards. He'd been retired for some time now but kept his eye in with an occasional exclusive, or weekly match report for the *Gazette* from around the local area. I managed to get hold of Karl easily enough and he said he remembered Lennox well.

'Eddie Lennox grew up in Paisley. Some player, he was. One of the best City ever had.'

Karl went on to tell me that Lennox had begun his footballing career as a schoolboy with Hibernian FC in Edinburgh. That was odd for a lad from a town so close to Glasgow. In 1966, at the age of 26, he'd been brought south by City's manager, also a Scot, to inject some fire into a City team struggling to avoid relegation from the old Division Two. A tough guy on the field, Lennox soon made his mark and despite a couple of sendings-off – one for fighting and another for booting the ball into a linesman's face – the Lennox effect seemed to work. City finished third bottom that season, escaping the drop by just three points.

It had taken Lennox very little time to familiarise himself with the capital's nightspots, Karl explained, and the long-haired Scot's lop-sided grin was soon being used in the local press and on billboard posters to advertise the Morocco Club in the docklands.

'It wasn't a surprise, as such, what happened to him, but in many ways it was a tragedy,' said Karl. 'He was no angel, for sure, but that young lad had magic in his boots. He could have been one of the very best Scottish players of all time. But off the field it all seemed to go wrong for him. He wasn't the brightest spark and he just didn't seem to have the judgement for life in the real world, or what passed for the real world back in the Swinging Sixties.'

'Was there something dodgy, do you think, about the trial?' I asked Karl. 'I've heard rumours.'

'It's hard to say,' he replied. 'The city police force didn't have, let's say, the best reputation in those days. But Lennox wasn't helped by his own reputation, that's for sure.'

I thanked Karl for his time and hung up the phone.

I recalled Humph telling me that Lennox had met Delilah Sullivan at a hair salon used by some of the more fashion-conscious City players. The salon had been run by a French woman, he'd said, but he hadn't mentioned her name. I left the *Gazette* and walked across town to the library where I scanned through some microfiche back issues of the *Record*.

It wasn't long before I found what I was looking for. According to the reports, Annie Léchet, Delilah's employer, had been the first to report her missing. I did my sums: if Annie had been in her thirties, or even forties, back in the 1960s there was every chance she would still be alive. But would she still live under her own name in the city? I crossed the library floor to a large set of shelves, from which I took down the city phone book. Flicking it open around halfway through, I turned back a couple of pages and traced my forefinger up the page ... Lecksham ... Leckie ... Léchet, A-M. There was an address near the park. I jotted this down in my notebook, along with her telephone number, and then returned to the microfiche to read up some more on Lennox and his trial. An hour or two later I walked back to the *Gazette* in search of the keys for the pool car.

'Sorry, lovely,' shrugged Teg, from behind the front desk. 'I just gave them to Nigel. Out on a job over Abergerran way, he said. Looked pleased as Punch, he did.'

'Who's Nigel?' I asked.

'Nigel. One of the Germolene Twins,' came the reply. 'Humph and his stupid bloody nicknames ...'

'They don't look old enough to drive,' I countered.

'Nigel passed his test just last week, bless him.'

'What's the other one called, then?'

'That's Aled. Nigel Parry and Aled Edwards. That's what they're called.'

'Oh, okay. It's not a problem,' I said, and glanced up at the clock on the wall behind Teg's reception desk. 'I can take the train.'

CHAPTER 20

Walking out of Central Station I heard the metallic clank of heavy machinery and could see the blue, white or yellow cranes that had risen at mad angles behind the long office block opposite the bus station. There was dust in the air above the world-famous stretch of real estate that ran alongside the river where, thirty years after work had begun on one national stadium, work was now underway on another to replace it. As my bus pulled away from the station with a sudden jerk, a slim supplement slipped out of a copy of the *Western Morning Record* that I'd bought at the station. After retrieving it with some difficulty from the floor under my seat I saw that it was the latest in a series of advertising-led features reporting on the progress of the stadium, one of a number of huge infrastructure developments under way across the capital. I scanned through the copy beneath artist's impressions of both the stadium and the city's dockland regeneration.

With a new millennium approaching this is a city in a hurry. For years now a development corporation has been lining up the public and private investment needed to repurpose our historic docklands for the next era. A great barrage is being stretched across the open end of the Bay and, when the estuary is finally locked out, a permanent inland lagoon will be created. Soon the sight of wading birds wallowing in the ugly mud of low tide will be replaced by a permanent vista of bobbing yachts.

The word 'lagoon' seemed out of place in the city I had come to know, but it was just part of the new lexicon attached to the development. Around the Bay, old docks were suddenly being referred to as new marinas. Warehouses were being reborn as quayside apartment blocks. Alongside historic dockers' pubs, new hotels, restaurants, café bars and nightspots were appearing as a leisure quarter was busily taking shape. The city was a product undergoing a major rebrand.

> *The jewels in the Bay's crown are yet to appear, but space has already been allotted along the waterside for an opera house and a debating chamber for the new devolved government. Just four decades since it became the nation's capital, the city's fathers are working hard to complete its transformation from a thriving, coal-dusted seaport to a cultured European waterfront destination. And the cherry on the top of their cake will be the state-of-the-art new stadium upon which, with the help of the TV cameras attracted to the city by rugby's biggest tournament, the eyes of the world will fall.*

The city fathers weren't saying anything about a body buried beneath their precious 'cherry', I noticed, which seen through the layer of dried dust on the window of my double-decker still looked far from ripe. A steady flow of lorries ferrying building materials onto the massive construction site was causing havoc for the rest of the everyday traffic trying to navigate its way through the city centre and my bus was going nowhere fast. In the heat of the day its lower deck was breathless and some of my fellow travellers were beginning to lose their cool. It was another ten minutes before we left the stadium site behind us and fifteen more before I'd reached my destination.

If the city's twenty-first-century future lay to its south, then my trip to its northern suburbs was like a journey back in time to the city's nineteenth and twentieth-century past. I stepped down from the bus and checked the numbers on a row of grand Edwardian dwellings before setting off on foot along a leafy avenue. I decided that if Annie Léchet owned one of these impressive houses that overlooked the 130 acres of parkland, with its 30-acre lake, then she must have done very well out of the hairdressing business. As it turned out, the address listed next to her name in the phonebook was a lesser, more recently-built glass-fronted property further along the park's west side. I knocked on the front door and waited.

Annie Léchet was a spry-looking woman of around seventy-five. She was small, bird-like, and as immaculately plumed as one might have expected. Her face was sympathetic and her grey eyes, though watery, twinkled from within. I decided to come straight out with the reason for my unannounced visit at the doorstep, and my punt on honesty paid off to the extent that I quickly found myself seated on her plush two-seater sofa, cradling a cup and saucer of fragrant Earl Grey.

'What happened to Delilah was such a tragedy,' said Mme Léchet in good English with just a slight Gallic inflection. 'It was a long time ago now but I still think about her.'

'You knew her as Delilah?'

'Yes, it was a silly name she gave herself. She said it was a secret name, only to be used by those she loved best. Somehow … it suited her better than Angharad.'

'What was she like as a person?'

'Delilah? She was very beautiful and very natural. Kind, caring and honest. But she had a … a wild side to her nature. Impetuous, I think, is the word. Her mother was an Irish barmaid from the docks; her father a Somali merchant seaman who she never knew. She was brought up a strict Catholic by her grandparents. They tried to make her religious, but Delilah liked to rebel. From time to time she was quite unpredictable.'

Once again I sensed that getting straight to the point was my best way forward. 'Madame Léchet, did Eddie Lennox kill her, do you think?'

The question seemed to knock her back, and I cursed myself silently for going too far too soon. But then Mme Léchet began to frame her response.

'I did not know Eddie very well,' she said, 'but I certainly met him a few times. He was an important customer for the salon. A big football star, you know – that was almost like a pop star for us here in the sixties. Good for business! He was a good-looking young man and full of confidence. Cocky, I think, would be your word for it.'

She paused and I gave her time to follow her train of thought.

'He had a violent temper, I knew that. And perhaps not as much respect for women as one would have expected even then. Yes, it is quite possible that he killed her. I have considered that many times and that is what I have found myself thinking.'

'You must have also met Ivan Harris?'

'Ivan married her, of course,' she replied.

'Yes. I was aware of that. What was your impression of him?'

'Eddie, Ivan … in looks and in intellect they were opposites, but unlike opposites they did not … attract. This is not easy, for a man like Ivan, when his wife cheats on him.'

'So Delilah was still married to Ivan when she met Eddie?'

'Yes, married but separated. To begin with it was a big secret, their relationship, of course, but Delilah told me. She confided in me like a mother.'

'But Ivan knew that Delilah was having a relationship with Eddie?'

'Well, yes, he found out. Eddie was so well known, and he was not a discreet man. Vulgar, boastful. Ivan found out about him and Delilah and he beat her. She arrived at my door one night with her face bruised and covered with blood.'

'Mme Léchet, you must have attended the trial. Why do you think the jury believed the testimony of Ivan Harris, and not Eddie Lennox? It must surely have been suspicious that of all people it was Ivan who said he had seen Eddie dumping her body at the stadium?'

'Well, yes, but then that is where Ivan was working, on the building site. And there was some other evidence … the shoe? I can remember Humphrey telling me that strange things can happen with juries. They can form their own prejudices, he told me.'

'Humphrey? Do you mean Humph Blake?'

'Yes, you know Humphrey? Such a lovely man, I was so sad when he and Delilah split up. I told her that Humphrey was the man for her. A good man. But it seems she preferred the more dangerous type.'

'Did you not think it odd that Humph … that Humphrey was reporting on the trial but had not revealed to the police that he had been in a relationship with Delilah?'

'Well, perhaps he did not think that it mattered,' Mme Léchet replied. 'It was over a long time before she married Ivan or met Eddie, was it not? What difference would it have made?'

'Well, it cost him his job at the *Record* for one thing.'

'Is that what Humphrey told you?' Mme Léchet paused suddenly, as if she realised she had told me something she wished she hadn't.

'What other reason could there be?'

Mme Léchet stood up and walked across to the glass-fronted wall where she stood momentarily lost in thought, looking towards the park. Then she turned back towards me.

'You know of the man, Bryn Thomas?'

'Bryn, yes, I do,' I replied. 'He's a senior police officer at Porthcoed CID. He was at school with Humph. I've known him for years.'

'Well, in those days Bryn also worked here in the city, a young police constable. He was not a very nice man. The city back then was a place of shadows. There were men who would come to my salon and demand money from me in case my shop front was broken or the salon burned down.'

'A protection racket?'

'Do not sound so surprised, young man. This is not just something that happens in the movies. Well, Bryn Thomas was, how should I say, in a business relationship with some of these men.'

'Bryn was bent? Corrupt, I mean?'

'There was an element among the police in those days that was, as you say ... bent.'

'And this had something to do with Humph losing his job at the *Record*?'

'Humphrey came to see me before he left. He was a mess. Drunk. He told me there was no future for him here, that he'd never be able to work on another story here that involved the police. He said that if he stayed he would be, how did he say it, putty in Bryn's hands.'

Chapter 21

I left Annie Léchet standing at her front door and crossed the road into the park, where I found an empty bench under a tree overlooking the lake. I pulled out my notebook and jotted down the substance of our conversation while it was still fresh in my mind. Contemporaneous was the journalistic expression. Then I shut my notebook and gazed out across the water. To the sound of fussy ducks being fed bread by a mother and her wheelchair-borne son I ran over in my mind what I'd managed to glean about the Delilah Sullivan case.

The hot take from my conversation with Annie Léchet was Bryn Thomas. I'd known Thomas as a hard-nosed DI for six years but it had never occurred to me that he might be corrupt. And yet the more I thought about it now, the more obvious it seemed. Sometimes it takes a complete stranger to point out something that's right in front of your nose.

The news that Thomas had also been working in the city at the time of Delilah's murder was another revelation to me. First Humph, then Harris and now Thomas. I'd had no idea that these three men, all from Porthcoed, shared such a long and tangled history. Two of them – Humph and Harris – had been in a relationship with the same woman and had played a part in the trial of the man accused of murdering her. I flicked open my notebook and scribbled a reminder to check whether Bryn Thomas had been involved with either Lennox's arrest or trial. As a copper known to Annie Léchet at the time, it seemed perfectly feasible.

There were too many coincidences here. And no journalist likes a coincidence. Was Mara McKenzie on to something with the Eddie Lennox story? What exactly had she found out,

I wondered, about these three men who I thought I had known, but who had apparently been strangers to me?

I tucked my notebook back into my shoulder bag and fished out a small envelope. Just before I'd left her, Annie Léchet had delved into an antique bureau in the corner of her sitting room and brought out a letter. 'You asked me what sort of girl Delilah was,' she'd said. 'This might help you. Take it, read it, but do please keep it safe. I'd very much like to have it back. It's all I have of her.'

The pale pink envelope was old and creased and the Queen looked young and glamorous in profile on a brown stamp marked '4D' in the top corner. Mme Léchet's name and former address was handwritten in blue biro, in forward-leaning letters that were neat and artistic, with the occasional flourish of a loop to start an F or finish a G.

I carefully removed the letter, written on one side of matching pale pink writing paper, and began to read. The letter was dated February 1968, not long before Delilah died:

My Darling Annie,

Thank you so for your luvly note – which I only got this morning. You worry too much about me!! (Always my mum). I know I didnt ring to say I wouldnt be in – I'm sorry. I know I should have and that was wrong. Forgive me?

Life, as ever, went mad. You know how it is, Annie. You have some fun with a guy and before you know it he thinks he owns you. I thought Ivan was all behind me – but somehow he found me again. So I had to dissappear for a day or two. Find a new flat. Try again. But I'm safe now. Safe and sound.

I'll be back at work next week. I promise!! (I know you cant cope without me!!). Try not to worry about me. I'm a big girl – I'll get by.

Luv you always,
Delilah XX

PS – Hey, have you heard that new Tom Jones record? ❤
Delilahs gonna be number one!! ❤

I was about to feed the letter back into the envelope when I noticed something else inside. With care I unfolded a strip of black and white passport-style photographs.

I immediately understood. At the age of eighteen I'd been dragged into a photo booth in Woolies by a girl called Alys Roberts. We'd laughed and kissed and pulled faces at the camera. Alys was long gone now – she took off five years afterwards with a friend of mine and a large chunk of my heart – but I still kept that strip of photos folded flat in a *Jagged Little Pill* CD hat she left at my flat. Here now in front of me, young, vibrant and also very much in love, were Delilah and a young Humph doing just the same. It was definitely Humph. There was no trademark thin grey moustache of course, and the mop of dark hair that fell over his eyes and covered his ears was unfamiliar, but it was him all right. It was a shock to see him looking so animated and happy, and suddenly I felt I was prying into something I recognised from my own past as private and sacrosanct.

Delilah was indeed beautiful. A combination of woman and child, it seemed to me. Sophisticated and yet somehow still raw. Her face was thin, almost gaunt, with high cheekbones and a tight jawline that swept back and up towards the large disc-like earrings that hung from each petite ear. Her abundant dark hair had been pulled away from her face and piled up on top of her head, held there by a pale headband tied playfully at the front with a bow. The depth of her forehead and the arch of her eyebrows seemed to accentuate the defiance in her eyes.

I studied Delilah's string of poses. In the top picture she was pouting, in the next sultry. In the third she had crossed her eyes and was sticking out her tongue. In the last photo she was side-on, kissing young Humph on the cheek. In each of them she radiated life, and I was overcome by the bitter irony.

I refolded the photo-strip and returned it to the envelope, wondering whether Delilah had enclosed it with her letter. I doubted it. It didn't seem to fit somehow. I decided that Annie Léchet had simply gathered all she had left of the girl she'd loved into one place for safe keeping. Just like I had done with Alys Roberts.

My thoughts were interrupted by the thin squeaking of a wheelchair. Having apparently run out of bread, the mother was now pushing her son away from the lake. Behind them, I noticed, the ducks had already turned their attention to an old man with a brown paper bag a little further along the lake edge.

At that moment a middle-aged woman sat down on the other end of my bench. Smartly dressed, she had the look of an office worker stealing a few minutes of much-needed fresh air.

My new bench companion placed a large plastic shopping bag between us, from which she pulled a newspaper, a can of Diet Lilt and a packet of sandwiches. She eyed me up and down for a moment and then unfolded her paper and started to read.

As she took a bite of her sandwich I found myself leaning towards her. By the time she had begun to object to me encroaching on her private space I was all but deaf to her protestations. All my attention was focused on the front-page headline on that afternoon's *City Evening News* which, in 24-point bold capitals, read: 'BODY FOUND AT STADIUM SITE'.

PART TWO

CHAPTER 22

My bench mate baulked at my offer of a fiver for her newspaper so I left the park in search of a newsagent's, which I eventually found half a mile down the road. I paid for a copy of the *Evening News*, flicked it open and started reading in the light of the shop window.

The story looked as if it had been written right on deadline and it wasn't clear until the third or fourth paragraph that the newly discovered body was not the thirty-year-old remains of Delilah Sullivan. This was the body of another woman. Police had been called to the site and had sealed it off for forensics. Suddenly I was aware of the assistant behind the counter calling me back to ask me if I wanted the change from my fiver. I took it from her and left the shop.

I hailed a passing cab back to Central Station and boarded the first train back to Porthcoed. It was late afternoon by the time I arrived at the *Gazette* to find two police cars – one marked, the other a familiar dark blue Vauxhall Omega – parked up on the pavement, out of the way of the roadworks.

Teg was at the front desk, looking quite unruffled. 'What's going on?' I asked her.

'We're being raided, lovely,' she said, as calmly as you like.

'Raided?'

'Bryn Thomas and half a dozen of his boys. One of them even said, "This is a raid."' She shook her head slowly, unimpressed.

I ignored the lift and ran up four flights of stairs. On the second floor the newsroom was in a commotion, with uniformed police officers searching desks and cupboards. As I walked into the room I saw Bryn Thomas standing over Humph's desk, raking through the contents of its drawers.

Coma was hovering next to him, remonstrating. I didn't have to wait long to find out what had brought this on.

'The books, Coma,' said Thomas. 'You said Humph doesn't keep the *Gazette* accounts on a computer, so I need the books.'

'Well, Humph usually has them.'

'I know that, Coma, but where does he keep them? Does he have an office?'

'Well ... there's ... the editor's office down the corridor, but ...'

'Show me. Now.'

Either Humph had told Bryn Thomas about the missing five grand or someone else had tipped off Thomas. My money was on the latter. As Coma and Thomas headed out of the newsroom I turned to see the tall frame of DS Templeton sifting methodically through the contents of a square of filing cabinets in the centre of the newsroom. I passed him and the Germolene Twins, sitting at their desks, stunned and immobile. They looked up at me, hoping for some answer in my expression. I shrugged and sat at my desk. It looked just as it always did, a mess, so it was hard to tell if Thomas's goons had already been through it.

Maybe one thing was different. The bottom left-hand drawer of my desk was shut tight. It never shut tight. I'd been trying to make that drawer shut tight for the best part of six years with no success. I leaned down and tugged at it gently. Nothing. It was either jammed shut or locked. Moving gently so as not to attract attention I quietly slid open the drawers above it in turn. In the top drawer, on top of some folded back copies of the *Gazette*, I saw an unfamiliar small key. It looked like it would fit the lock on the bottom drawer. After a surreptitious glance around the room I took the key, inserted it into the lock on the bottom drawer, turned and pulled the handle. To my amazement the drawer slid smoothly open. Inside lay a folded copy of the *Sporting Life*. I lifted it and it felt bulky. There was clearly something wrapped inside. I pulled back one corner of the paper and exposed the top corner of a familiar, well-worn accounts book. Instinctively I slid the drawer shut again, turned the key and dropped it into my left jacket pocket.

At that moment Bryn Thomas and Coma Jenkins walked back into the newsroom.

'You might have mentioned that it's a stationery cupboard now,' said Thomas testily. 'There is such a thing as wasting police time, you know.'

'I'm just trying to help, Bryn,' came Coma's reply, admirably poker-faced.

'What's over there?' asked Thomas, pointing to the door at the other side of the newsroom.

'Oh, you know,' answered Coma. 'The coffee machine. And then the passage to the kitchen.'

'The kitchen,' Thomas repeated. Instead of checking it himself, he delegated the job to one of his uniforms and crossed the room to speak to Templeton. That was when he noticed me.

'Ah, I see we've finally been joined by our "ace reporter". Been out on assignment have you, Twm?'

'That's right.'

'Where to, might I ask?'

'Just over to see Dai Whitehouse,' I replied. 'Punter of his landed a big accumulator. Might do for an inside lead, you know.' Well, they said the best lies had a flavour of the truth in them.

Thomas turned to Templeton. 'Josh, have we had a little look at Mr Bradley's desk yet?'

'Not yet, boss. Shall I?' asked Templeton.

'I've got it,' replied Thomas.

I stood up and moved aside, allowing Thomas to sift through the papers on the top of my desk. 'No such thing as a clean-desk policy at the *Gazette*, I see,' he quipped.

'It's organised chaos, Bryn. I know where everything is.'

'And would "everything" include any documents concerning the financial records of this newspaper? You know, bank records, petty cash, that sort of thing?'

'That's way above my pay grade.'

Thomas finished his search of the top of my desk and began to check the drawers. He slid open the top drawer, rummaged inside and then slid it shut. He opened the second drawer, pushed aside its contents and found a small ring-bound notebook. He flicked it open and saw page after page of shorthand. He looked at me then dropped the notebook into the drawer and slid it shut. Finally he tugged at the handle of the third drawer. Nothing. He lifted his head back towards me, inquisitively.

'That drawer's jammed,' I explained. 'I've been onto Humph for months now to get it fixed.'

'This drawer isn't jammed, Twm. It's locked. Where's the key?'

'I don't have a key. Like I told you, it's jammed.'

Thomas caught Templeton's eye momentarily and turned back to me. 'My detective sergeant would seem to disagree. Wouldn't you, Josh?'

'Left-hand jacket pocket, boss,' said Templeton.

'Okay, okay,' I said and fished out the key from my pocket.

Thomas scowled at me with genuine menace and hissed, 'Don't you dare fuck with me, Bradley.' He took the key from my hand, unlocked the bottom drawer and delved inside. 'And what have we here?'

The room fell silent as Thomas unfolded the *Sporting Life* and produced the ledger. He set the book down on the rubbish strewn across my desk and opened it, eager with anticipation. As he turned over the first few pages his face suddenly fell.

'What the fuck is this?' asked Thomas.

At this point Coma stepped forward and looked over Thomas's shoulder. 'Oh, that's Humph's form book,' he said.

'He's fond of the horses, is Humph. Likes to keep a tally of how his favourite trainers, jockeys and horses get on, you know.' Coma craned over even further. 'His handwriting's something shocking, though, isn't it?'

Thomas slammed the book shut and dropped it onto the top of my desk. He stared in frustration at Coma and then at me.

'Okay boys,' said Templeton. 'Keep looking.'

CHAPTER 23

I shut the door of the flat behind me and the phone rang off. I'd heard it ringing from halfway up the rickety staircase but in my haste to get inside and pick up I had fumbled my door key. Dropping my shoulder bag in the kitchen I walked into the front room and opened the window, so I was right next to the phone when it went off again. I picked up before the second ring.

'Twm?'

'Humph. You're out?'

'Yeah.' His voice sounded weak and tired. 'They couldn't keep me any longer.'

So much had happened that I had to remind myself that only twenty-four hours had passed since I'd seen Thomas and Templeton taking in Humph for questioning.

'We had a visit from Bryn and his boys this evening,' I told him. 'I've only just got in. They seem to know about the missing five grand. Didn't find anything though.'

'They didn't get it from me,' said Humph. 'I've just spoken with Coma, by the way. I told him all about the cash.'

'What's happening, Humph? Have you heard anything from Bren?' I had more questions than these to ask him.

'Why don't you pop round the house? We'll talk. I need to get in the shower and change my clothes, so give me an hour first, okay?'

I agreed, replaced the handset and headed for the fridge for a cold beer and something to eat. No sooner had I cracked open my beer than the old metal stairs began to creak. I put down the can, walked to the door and swung it open to find Mara's arm reaching towards the door frame. It was the second time we'd played out this routine. And this time she recovered first.

'I don't know why you need a doorbell,' she said. Another smile.

'Yeah, the GPs downstairs want me to replace the staircase, but I keep telling them as long as it doesn't actually collapse I'm fine with it as it is.'

'Do you mind if I come in?'

I turned my head back towards the inside of the flat, ostensibly to examine the wreckage, though in truth I was stalling while I wondered if I'd be able to shake off Mara before I headed round to Humph's. But my hesitation had already become embarrassing so I stood back and ushered her in.

'Nice place,' she offered, looking at the chaos of the kitchen.

I gave Mara a wry smile and walked around her to the kitchen table to pick up my beer. 'I'm a little … disorganised at the moment,' I said. 'You want one of these? Seems every time I open one you arrive on my doorstep.'

I'd decided to hear what she had to say before I made a polite excuse and left; something about having to keep a *Gazette* diary appointment, maybe. I handed her a fresh can and she took it, refusing my offer of a glass.

'Probably a wise choice,' I said. 'I'm a little behind on the washing-up. Go on through. Take a seat.'

As she sat on the sofa, I dragged the chair from my desk, turned it around and sat astride it, facing her with my arms over the back of the chair. 'What can I do for you?'

'The police have released Humph Blake,' she began. Her eyes really were deep blue and black. I hadn't imagined that.

'You don't miss a thing, do you?' I replied.

There was an awkward pause.

'I need to come with you to see Humph,' said Mara.

'I'm sorry?'

'Don't tell me that's not where you're headed as soon as I leave here,' she said.

'Have you been listening in on my phone calls?' I asked her, only half-joking.

'Oh come on, it doesn't take any great imagination to work that out. I want to come with you. Twm, let me come.'

'Why do you need to come with me to see Humph?' I asked. 'You know where he lives.'

'He's not going to let me in. You know that. Our last conversation ended quite abruptly.'

'Mara, no offence, but Humph and I, we're family. He wouldn't appreciate me showing up with you in tow. It would be like, I don't know, some kind of a betrayal or something.'

'What exactly do you think it is that I want from Humph?'

'Well, you tell me,' I challenged her.

'Humph's an old pro,' she replied. 'He's been in newspapers forever. You don't think he can handle a few direct questions from someone like me?'

'Look, Mara, you're a Fleet Street reporter asking Humph about missing *Gazette* funds and you expect me to lead you straight to him?'

'He told you I asked about the money? Oh, that's not … Do you honestly think a paper like mine gives a shit about a few grand going missing at a newspaper like the *Gazette*? No offence but I couldn't care less about that, other than any bearing it may have on the real story we're both working on here … which is who really killed Angharad Sullivan.'

I didn't deny that I too was working on that story now and considered her words for a moment.

'I've been working on the Eddie Lennox story for longer than you have,' she continued. 'The chances are I know things that you haven't been able to find out yet. Things that maybe Humph doesn't even know. But you're the local. You can open doors around here that I cannot. Such as Humph's to begin with.'

'Are you seriously proposing that we join forces and work together on this story?' I asked her. 'That's not how you lot work.'

'Why not? There are no rules here. You open the door to Humph for me and I open the door to Lennox for you.' She paused. 'You want to get to the bottom of what's going on with Humph, am I right? Maybe you're starting to have one or two doubts about a man you thought you knew, and you don't like it.'

I didn't disagree. He hadn't seemed worried enough about Bren the last time I'd seen him.

'Look, if Humph's conscience is clean, and he's in trouble, then maybe we can both help him out.'

'And if Humph's conscience isn't clean?' I asked.

'If that's the case then, family or not, it's a story for both of us.'

Chapter 24

It was twilight when Mara and I turned the corner onto Humph's road. The evening was warm and still, and the air in this leafier part of town was filled with the sweet but pungent aroma of summer. On the walk across town I had been trying to figure out how to explain to Humph why I'd brought her along. The best reason I had come up with so far was Mara's. If he was in trouble then maybe we could both help him out.

We were a hundred yards from Humph's gate when a large, dark saloon car with tinted windows swept past us from behind. There were only two black Bentleys in Porthcoed, and from the number plate – HAR R1S – it was clear that this one didn't belong to Andrew Thomas's funeral parlour.

Mara and I stopped in our tracks as the car slowed up, indicated left and pulled in outside Humph's house. The driver's door opened and out stepped a heavyset, broad-shouldered man, his shaven head shining in the orange sodium street lights. He walked around the front of the car.

'Do you know him?' whispered Mara.

'That's Gwyn Shell. He's the coach of Harris's rugby team. Used to play for our national team. Tough nut.'

Before Shell could catch sight of us, I pulled Mara into the shadows of the nearest gateway and started to peer at the car through the branches of a tall bush. Shell reappeared on the pavement and the near-side rear window of the Bentley slid smoothly open. The conversation was just too far away to make out. I took a step nearer and heard a furious flapping as a bird fought its way out of the bush above us. I swore and was rewarded with an expression of contempt from Mara.

Before we could do anything Gwyn Shell was standing in front of us. He didn't speak, merely smiled in recognition of me and nodded his head to shepherd us in the direction of the Bentley. As Mara and I approached the car, he hovered behind us.

'A familiar face,' said Ivan Harris, eyeing me up from within. 'Lurking in the bushes outside your boss's house? Journalism, Gwyn, it's a shady business.'

'Ivan Harris?' Mara left me standing and walked confidently up to the car window, where she declared her name and the name of her paper. 'I've been trying to get hold of you for a story I'm working on involving Eddie Lennox,' she said. 'Can we speak?'

Without warning she had changed gear from first to third. This was a different persona from the one she had shown me so far. This was Mara in business mode: direct, fearless and quite cold. I had little choice other than to stand back and watch, and I was curious to see how Harris would react.

'From ... London, you say?'

'That's right and my name is Mara McKenzie. You see I tried to get hold of you through your office but without any success, so then I came down to your press conference earlier in the week but I still didn't get to talk with you. So I wonder whether now might be a good time?'

If I hadn't expected the initiative to be turned so quickly on Harris then, judging by the look on his face, neither had he. But he recovered swiftly, reaching inside his coat to produce a business card and then writing on the back of it with a silver pen.

'I'm afraid now wouldn't be convenient, Miss McKenzie. But do give me a ring at another time and I'm sure we can work something out. By the way this is my private mobile number, which I try not to publicise so I'd be grateful for your discretion.' He handed it to Mara and turned to me. 'If it's

Humph Blake you're after, Mr Bradley, then it seems as though we're both out of luck,' Harris said. 'Looks like there's no one home.'

I turned to see Gwyn Shell shutting Humph's front gate with a shake of his head. For a big man he moved lightly on his feet. I hadn't even noticed that he'd left us. Shell walked back around the car to the driver's door and I heard an elegant clunk as it shut. Harris's window rose as smoothly as it had fallen and the car pulled away.

'You go straight at it, don't you?' I said.

'While you just beat around the bush,' Mara replied with a smile. 'So are we going to take Harris at his word, or are we going to have a quick look round ourselves?'

'Humph was at home when he rang me just before you showed up at the flat,' I said, lifting the latch on his front gate. 'He said he was going to have a quick shower and change and that I should call round soon after.' I tilted my wristwatch in the street light. 'He's probably just lying low, keeping out of Harris's way.'

We walked to the front door and I tried the bell. Nothing. As before, the lights were off and the windows closed.

'Let's try round the back,' said Mara, heading for the wooden gate at the side of the house.

'Yeah, okay, but keep your wits about you. Humph has a wicked way with pansies.'

Mara turned to demand an explanation, but I chivvied her along.

Chapter 25

We'd reached the back of the house when we first heard the sirens. It was just another Friday night in Porthcoed as far as I was concerned, so I continued towards the kitchen window. I leaned my head with cupped hands on the window glass, and immediately recoiled in horror. On the sink drainer inside, just an inch or two in front of my face, the demonic Modlen arched her back, her fur raised.

'Are those sirens getting closer?' asked Mara. I had to agree.

We returned to the pavement in front of the house in time to see the flashing lights swing into Humph's road. There was a commotion and curtains started to twitch as two police cars, the same two I'd seen that afternoon on the pavement outside the *Gazette* building, screeched to a halt in front of us. Doors opened and three uniforms pushed past us towards Humph's gate before DI Thomas and DS Templeton appeared.

'He's not in,' I offered.

'Where is he?' Thomas replied.

'Search me.'

'Don't give me your lip,' countered Thomas. 'This is a murder inquiry now.'

'Murder?' asked Mara.

'Who's this?' Thomas asked me. Before I could speak Mara identified herself.

'Who's been murdered?' I asked, but even as the question left my lips I realised I knew its answer.

'A body has been recovered on a construction site in the city,' said Bryn Thomas. 'It looks very much like it's Brenda Blake.'

One of the uniformed officers who'd brushed past us towards the house reappeared on the street. 'Nothing doing, sir. House looks empty bar the cat.'

Thomas turned back to me. 'What are you two doing here anyway?' he asked. 'Never mind. Josh, bring them both in.'

Chapter 26

Alone at a table in the interview room on the basement floor of Porthcoed's Victorian police station, the reality behind Bryn Thomas's words, the finality of them, hit me like a fist in the gut.

I'd known Bren Blake even longer than I'd known Humph. She'd taken early retirement from her teaching career a few years ago, but was still helping young misfits like me, earning a few quid by giving after-school tuition in her and Humph's front room. A kind-hearted and intelligent woman. Dead.

My brain was flooding with questions and doubts. Delilah Sullivan and Bren Blake, both murdered, apparently on the same stadium building site, but thirty years apart. Another questionable coincidence. Humph's mysterious behaviour and sudden disappearance. Why? Ivan Harris and now Bryn Thomas both eager to find him. Thomas, the bent copper, about to question me. The pieces of a jigsaw were floating around my head but I couldn't fit them together in any way that would allow me to see the bigger picture. I took a deep breath and tried to regulate my breathing, trying to calm down and think clearly, but still the ability to concentrate proved beyond me.

I glanced at my watch. Around an hour had passed since a uniformed officer had left me in the interview room. From my wooden chair at the table in the middle of the room I could hear the distant buzz of indistinct conversation and sporadic laughter which, along with the sound of spring-loaded doors squeaking open and slamming shut, echoed through the station. The acoustics of a police station might have been designed to play on your nerves. These were ordinary everyday sounds of a routine working day, but they served to remind the unfortunate soul sitting in my chair that for him or her it was anything but.

The chair creaked as I shifted my weight to get comfortable. How many people, Humph included, had been left waiting here over the years, I wondered? Thomas was giving me time to think. To worry. He was trying to soften me up. At last some stubbornness, some measure of resolve, flooded into my system.

Just then the door burst open and in came Thomas. Behind him trailed DS Templeton.

'Sorry to keep you, Twm,' said Thomas.

'Would you please explain what I am doing here?' I asked, calmly.

'Oh just a little chat. Nothing to worry about.'

'I'm beginning to think I might need someone in here with me before we talk.'

'A lawyer?' asked Thomas, surprised. 'And why would you need a lawyer? You haven't done anything wrong, have you?'

'Somehow I think I'd just feel a little … safer.'

'Okay, we can go ahead and call your solicitor if you like. That's your right. But you and I both know that's going to keep us here all night. And we're busy men, you and me, aren't we? A few quick questions and we'll be out of here before you could drag a decent brief from his local bistro on a Friday evening.'

Behind him Templeton shrugged in agreement.

'Besides, the police force in Porthcoed has a special relationship with the *Gazette*,' continued Thomas. 'And this relationship works both ways, doesn't it? You help us out, we help you out. Big story for you, this one.'

'This isn't just a story for me. I've known Bren Blake since I was at school. Her husband is my boss.'

'Humph,' repeated Thomas, to emphasise that I'd brought up the subject and he hadn't. 'And when did you last see Humph?'

'I haven't seen him since you turfed me out of his house yesterday,' I replied. 'Well, he's been in here with you, hasn't he?'

'And when was the last time you spoke to Humph?' asked Thomas.

'He rang me earlier tonight.'

'What time?'

'I don't know. Earlier this evening.'

'Where from?

'From his house.'

'And?

'And what?'

'And what did he have to say?'

'He told me you'd let him go and he asked me to come round. And that's where you found me when you turned up, if you remember. We'd just got there.' No need to mention the encounter with Harris, I told myself. Keep that one to yourself.

'A bit odd that Humph invites you round but isn't at home when you arrive, don't you think?' asked Thomas.

'I don't know. Maybe he popped out for a bottle of Scotch. For all I know he could be sitting there right now wondering where the hell I am.'

Thomas's face froze and he looked up at Templeton. 'Okay, boss, I'm on it,' said Templeton, who left us.

'So, Thursday afternoon … yesterday … when I found you with Humph at his house … "gardening".' A disdainful grin. 'What did he have to say to you then?'

'We just chewed the cud, you know. Newspaper talk, that sort of thing.'

'And no sign of Bren. Did you ask him where she was?'

'He said he thought she might be at her sister's,' I lied. 'In Abergerran.'

'He "thought"? He didn't know?'

'Yeah. No. Look, it's not my business what goes on between them.'

'What *went* on between them, you mean. Bren is dead, remember? Brutally murdered. When did you last see Humph at the *Gazette*?'

'Wednesday morning.'

'You were out of the office on Wednesday afternoon?'

'Me? No, not for any length of time.'

'So Humph was out of the office on Wednesday afternoon, then?' asked Thomas, contriving a quizzical expression. 'The editor not at work on the afternoon of production day? That's a bit odd, isn't it?'

'Yeah, maybe.' I didn't like the way this was heading but I had no choice at this point but to agree with him.

'And did he let anyone know that he'd be out of the office? Did he tell anyone where he was going?'

'No. I don't think so.'

'So no one's seen nor heard from Humph Blake between Wednesday morning at the *Gazette* and Thursday afternoon at his house?'

Only Grumpy and Mara, I thought. 'As far as I know, no.'

'Okay, Twm. That'll do for now. See? Just a quick chat. Nothing to worry about after all.'

'Are you sure it's Bren?' I asked, getting to my feet. 'Has anyone identified the body?'

'I'm afraid I can't comment on an ongoing inquiry,' replied Thomas, deadpan. He stood to one side, and gestured towards the door, now being held open by the returning Templeton. 'I expect City CID will slap a press release on the fax at some stage tomorrow if you ask them nicely.'

So much for the special relationship, I thought, as I walked between the two of them.

Chapter 27

Mara and I left the station together. It had started to rain.

'Pub?'

I nodded and we set off towards the nearest watering hole, the Royal Crown.

'So what did he ask you?' I said, stopping and turning to Mara.

'Me? Nothing,' she answered. 'They didn't want to talk to me.'

'He didn't interview you?' I stopped still in my tracks, surprised. 'Why not?'

'I don't know.'

Prompted by an impatient look from Mara, and the continued fall of rain, I set off again.

The Crown was crowded, smoke-filled and stuffy. Standing in the crowd Mara brushed back her fringe, a shade darker and more responsive to her fingers now it was wet. She took a sip from her Guinness.

'Well, what was I supposed to do, volunteer a statement?' she asked above the din of conversation. 'I don't know Humph Blake or his wife. I've only met him the once and that ended badly.'

'I'm just trying to work out where Bryn Thomas is coming from with this.'

'You know, Twm, if you and I are going to work together on this you need to tell me what you know about Angharad Sullivan's murder that I don't. What's the deal with Humph Blake exactly? His wife has just been found dead and he's doing a pretty good impersonation of a man with something to hide if you ask me.'

She looked into my eyes, trying to weigh up my response. The trouble with two journalists talking, I decided, is that each would rather ask the questions than answer them. And I felt I'd already answered more than I'd wanted to.

'Okay ... okay,' I decided, reluctantly. 'But not in here. Drink up.'

CHAPTER 28

We left the pub and stopped at Aarav's corner shop just before it closed to pick up a bottle of whisky. We climbed the rickety staircase, Mara closed the flat door behind us and I slipped into the bathroom, emerging with a towel.

'It's clean,' I said, offering it to her. 'Promise.'

Mara smiled, put down her shoulder bag, tilted her head to one side and with both hands began to rub her long fringe with the towel. I was struck by the intimacy of observing this simple act. I'd seen it before. I'd watched Alys Roberts dry her hair this way many times and the memory unnerved me.

'I'll get a couple of clean glasses,' I said when Mara turned her eyes to meet mine. 'I'm sure I can find two somewhere.'

In the lounge I reached down to switch on the lights at the socket and the stereo flicked on. I bumped the CD to track eight on John Martyn's *One World* album, 'Small Hours', and sat on the edge of the sofa. I placed the two glasses on the low coffee table in front of me and opened the bottle with a click and a twist. Mara followed me in and folded the towel neatly across a radiator. As she sat beside me, I caught the heavy musk of her damp hair.

'Did you want ice or water with this?' I asked and was met with raised eyebrows.

'Oh, I forgot. You lot have your arcane rules with whisky, don't you? Have I suggested something unforgivably vulgar?'

'Straight up is fine if it's a blend,' she replied.

'Oh it's a blend all right.' I showed her the label on the bottle. 'Salary won't stretch to single malt, I'm afraid.'

I poured the whisky neat and ran her through events as they had unfolded since Humph had taken me over the road to Grumpy's on the Wednesday morning and told me about the missing five grand. I held back on Humph's version of what had happened back in 1968, his relationship with Delilah Sullivan and my meeting with Annie Léchet. Just for now.

'So apart from my spectacularly brief meeting with him at Grumpy's on Thursday morning, no one can vouch for Humph's whereabouts between Wednesday lunchtime and Thursday afternoon when he crowned you with a pot of pansies?'

'No.'

'And Humph was in police custody here in Porthcoed from Thursday afternoon right through until late this afternoon?'

'That's what he said.'

'When did he say he first noticed that Bren had gone missing?'

'Humph told me he came home on Tuesday night and found a mess near the potting shed and no sign of Bren.'

'And they found Bren's body on the stadium site in the city sometime this morning. Friday morning. Did DI Thomas say anything about how or where they discovered the body?'

'You mean was Bren killed on Thursday night and dumped where her body might easily be found by the construction team the next day, or had the body been hidden, meaning she could have been there since Tuesday or Wednesday night? No, they didn't say.'

I visualised the truth behind these words in silent disbelief then unscrewed the top of the whisky bottle and poured us both another two fingers each.

'How did you find out that money had gone missing from the *Gazette*?' It was my turn to ask a question, and I wanted some sort of a quid pro quo from Mara before I decided whether or not to open up on the subject of Delilah Sullivan.

'I got a tip-off,' she answered. 'Anonymous. A letter to the newsroom with a Porthcoed postmark.'

'When?'

'Just over a week ago.'

'That would be after you contacted Ivan Harris's people looking for an interview but before you came down here?'

'Yeah.'

'And you already knew who Humph was because of your involvement in the Eddie Lennox case?'

'As I've already said, his byline was on all the *Record* trial stories back in 1968,' answered Mara. 'I trawled through them after Eddie got in touch.'

'Did Lennox ever mention Humph to you?'

'No.'

'And what was your reaction to this tip-off about Humph and the money?'

'Let's just say that given the circumstances it intrigued me,' she replied.

'But it wasn't just you asking Humph about the missing money that pissed him off, was it?'

'What do you mean?'

'I mean there was something else you said to him that made him storm off from your meeting in Grumpy's, wasn't there?'

Mara looked down at her whisky and then back up at me. 'I told him I knew about something dodgy from his past.' That tallied with what Humph had told me and was what I had hoped to hear.

'You threatened him?'

'I needed him to sit and talk with me.'

'And what was this secret of his that you'd uncovered?'

Mara swept back her fringe once again and smiled.

'You didn't have one, did you?' I said. 'It was all just a bluff.'

'Call it an educated guess. I had my suspicions, because I'd been digging into Humph's story. When I found out he'd left the *Record* and come back here suddenly after the Lennox trial, I thought that was odd. A big story like that is usually a ticket to Fleet Street, but he runs straight back home to the *Gazette*?

It seemed to me he had something to hide. But he called my bluff pretty quickly and told me to do one. That's one of the reasons I need your help.'

This time Mara reached across the table towards the bottle of Scotch and splashed a stronger measure into both tumblers. In the low light of the room I tried to locate the thin pale scar I'd seen beneath her eye, but was diverted by a single loop of her hair curling down over her forehead.

'Why *did* Humph come back here after the Lennox trial?' she asked, turning abruptly and catching my glance.

'It's complicated. Humph had a relationship with Delilah Sullivan.'

'Delilah?'

'Delilah was a name that Angharad gave herself, an in-joke between her and Humph. They met just after he arrived in the city in the mid-sixties. He was pretty smitten with her. But they burned out around a year before she married Ivan Harris. He had some trouble getting over her, though. Drank.' I picked up my glass.

'And he held this back from the police?' Mara asked, reclining into the deep cushions of the sofa.

'He told me that when Delilah went missing he decided to keep it to himself because he wanted to be allowed to work on the story. When her body was found he expected the police to get round to asking him about his relationship with her but they never did. Then when Lennox was charged and tried, he felt it was too late. But when his editor found out after the trial it cost him his job. Apparently.'

'And you believe him?'

'Well, yeah. When he told me I believed him. What else was I going to do?'

'But you're starting to wonder about him now, aren't you? You're not sure that he came home on Tuesday night and found signs that Bren had been taken?'

'I don't know what I think. But I just can't believe that Humph Blake is capable of murdering anyone, let alone the two women he loved most in his life. I think maybe he was just a young reporter who made an error of judgement back in the sixties and got somehow trapped by it.'

'Which is why he returned to the *Gazette* when he did?'

'I went to talk to Annie Léchet today,' I said.

A puzzled look from Mara.

'She owned the hairdresser's that Delilah worked in. She and Delilah were close. She also knew Humph. She's a bit of a fan. She told me Humph knew his career at the *Record* was over after the Lennox trial because city police had something over him.'

'The fact he didn't come clean about his relationship with … Delilah?'

'Maybe.'

'And by police you mean Bryn Thomas?'

'You knew he was working there, too?'

'He was one of the first responders at the stadium site after her body was discovered. He gave evidence at the Lennox trial.'

That answered that question.

'According to Annie Léchet,' I said, 'Bryn Thomas was part of a corrupt element in the city force at that time. Taking money from criminals.'

'And yet here he is, all these years later, part of the investigation into another death at the stadium. The plot thickens …'

She reached forwards for the bottle again. 'Small Hours' faded and the room fell silent, but for the pouring of whisky.

'Are you trying to get me drunk, Miss McKenzie?'

'Are you telling me you can't hold your whisky, Mr Bradley?'

Mara looked at me for a moment and then placed the bottle, half-empty now, back down on the table. She reached across, raising her right hand towards my face, softly brushing a wisp of my hair back behind my ear, then her fingers reached round to the back of my head. Gently, looking firstly into my eyes, and then down to my mouth, she pulled me towards her and kissed me. The first kiss was fleeting, a brief brushing of lips that fired off a nerve inside me. I responded with my right hand, drawing her back firmly in my direction. The scent of her damp hair, something like nutmeg and honey, filled my senses and I kissed her deeply.

'Is it okay with you if I stay the night?' she whispered after a little while.

'I think maybe you'd better.'

CHAPTER 29

'What happened here?' I asked, my finger gently tracing the line of the faint scar beneath Mara's eye as we lay in bed in the light of the morning.

'My scar, you mean?'

'Yes.'

'Car crash,' Mara replied, after apparently thinking it over. 'When I was just a girl.'

'Bad?'

Her pale complexion coloured slightly. 'Bad enough,' she said, aware that I had glimpsed something she didn't like to show. Then she changed tack. 'So, what happened with your father?'

I'd forgotten that I'd even mentioned my father to her.

'You don't mind me asking?' she said, picking up on my reaction.

'My father has a wandering eye,' I replied after some thought of my own. 'Before he retired he worked as a university lecturer. Up in the north. A lot of young female students on his radar.'

Mara's eyebrows asked for more.

'My mother gave him a few chances but when it became clear that he wasn't going to change she left him and we came down here.'

'Do you still see him?'

'We haven't really had much to do with each other for quite a few years now. Not since Mam died.'

'Maybe you should, Twm.'

'Maybe I should.'

'So, Humph,' she said, after a minute or two of loaded silence.

'What about him?' I asked, aware of a familiar tightening within.

'Seems like he's filled a bit of a gap in your life.'

'For fuck's sake, why does everyone throw that glossy magazine-style psychobabble at me?'

'I'm just saying,' Mara replied, 'that maybe your perspective on Humph is … a little skewed.'

'What exactly does that mean?' I asked her, sitting up straight. Mara did the same.

'It doesn't exactly look good for Humph. You've got to see that. There's a pile of circumstantial evidence stacking up against him. You say he's in debt. There's money missing from the paper. Then he goes missing around about the time his wife's body shows up, in exactly the same place where his first love, Delilah, was dumped. And where is he now?'

'But I know Humph …'

'Do you? Do you really know him? Or do you just believe in him because you need to?'

'I think you'd better go,' I said.

Mara looked at me for a moment to see if I was being serious. What she saw in my face must have made her mind up for her, because she got out of bed and took her clothes to the bathroom to dress. A few minutes later I heard her shut the flat door behind her.

CHAPTER 30

At a news conference at the city police headquarters that Sunday evening the chief inspector leading the murder inquiry revealed that the body found at the stadium site had been formally identified by her sister as Brenda Blake. An appeal was made for witnesses in the streets around the stadium at the time of Bren's murder, which was estimated as some time on the Wednesday night – just when Humph had gone missing. Bryn Thomas, seated on the top table, confirmed that officers in Porthcoed were working in conjunction with City CID to ascertain the whereabouts of newspaper editor Humphrey Blake, who they were very keen to rule out of their inquiry. It was police speak for 'We think he did it.'

On the Monday, I arrived at work to find the *Gazette* building under siege by the news media. That morning the *Record* had been the first to draw a parallel with the death of Angharad Sullivan in 1968, and now 'The Stadium Murders' were a great story in anybody's book. The *Gazette* was right at the centre of the storm. Even Ted Buckett, whose news agency had been earning good money from Humph and the *Gazette* for nigh on ten years now, was among the throng at the gate as the press turned cannibal.

On my way inside I was door-stepped breathlessly by Mike James-Jenkins, the WTV Hairdo. 'Twm Bradley, have you spoken with Humph Blake? Have you heard from him, Twm? What can you tell us about Humph being a suspect for his wife's murder?' I shot him a look and forced my way through the crush by the main door, where I was asked for my pass by one of two unfamiliar, beer-bellied security guards, and into reception.

Teg's hair had turned raspberry over the weekend, no doubt in anticipation of the TV cameras. 'Head office have sent in the cavalry,' she explained, flicking her eyes towards the corpulent sentries. 'Yes, I know, lovely, but if that lot look like storming the building we can always wedge them together in the doorway.'

In the newsroom it was all hands on deck. There was no way we could avoid reporting on Bren's death so, as the week passed and our deadline neared, Coma and I decided to play a straight bat. I wrote a measured, non-hysterical piece reporting the established facts and paying tribute to the life of a much-loved local schoolteacher. We did not report the matter of the missing *Gazette* funds turning up in Bren's bank account, as the police had yet to publicly reveal this. Our thinking was that Bryn Thomas had been acting on a tip-off when he had searched the newsroom for the *Gazette* accounts book. It seemed likely, given that Mara had also been tipped off. Apparently Bryn hadn't yet been able to prove that any money was indeed missing. Whatever Humph had apparently done to brush over the tracks in that respect was proving most effective. I was glad of this and yet a little troubled by it too.

From Mara I heard nothing all week, and by the Friday I presumed she had returned to London. I had been stung by her assertion that I was anything other than detached from the furore surrounding Humph, but as the week went on I began to concede that she had perhaps hit a raw nerve and that I had reacted badly. For both professional and personal reasons I found myself wondering time and again where she was and what she was doing.

One week turned to two and still the hunt for 'The Stadium Murderer' dominated the news. Each day I checked Mara's paper to see if she had broken cover on the story, but there was little to read on the subject apart from the occasional piece with a 'Staff Reporter' byline, which normally meant it was verbatim Press Association or news agency copy. Ted Buckett filling his boots, no doubt. In general it seemed the London papers weren't as interested in the murder now as their local counterparts, with the notable exception of one down-market Sunday red top, which asked whether there was a possible UFO angle. The *Western Morning Record* reported on 'the circumstantial evidence linking our man at the 1968 murder trial and the murder of his own wife three decades later, and his subsequent disappearance'. Mike the WTV Hairdo squeezed every last drop of drama from his nightly live pieces to camera from the street, either outside Humph's house or the *Gazette* building or the stadium site. In truth there were only a few facts that he could safely report without appearing to accuse Humph of either murder or double murder.

As time progressed the *Gazette*'s approach to the story became more problematic and was the subject of increasingly heated daily discussion in the newsroom. On the one hand we had an angle on the story like no other paper: the wife of our editor had been murdered, he himself was missing and of course there was his link to the 1968 murder trial. This placed quite an onus on the *Gazette*, the small, local newspaper that it was, to be seen to break new ground on the story before other bigger, better-financed media outlets, and the *Gazette*'s arrival on the news-stands each Thursday would now be hotly anticipated.

Amid such a weight of expectation Coma and I tried stoically to retain a measure of professional journalistic detachment and continued to report just the established facts alongside any new developments. A brief official statement that I had to practically prise out of head office offered a surprisingly lukewarm defence of Humph Blake's character and gave assurances that the Bentall Newspaper Group was bending over backwards to help police with their inquiries.

I attended police press conferences in Porthcoed and in

the city, and Coma cautiously approached Bren's sister to ask if she wanted to head off the increasing media interest in her by speaking exclusively to a friendly voice at the *Gazette*. She agreed and Coma drove over to Abergerran with Smudge Tucker to interview her. We ran her emotional tribute to Bren over two pages inside the paper. Ted Buckett stole every quote, repackaged them, and made a fortune selling the story in London.

By the third week, however, the dissenting voices around the *Gazette* conference table had begun to gather momentum. Both Coma and I had stressed our concern for Humph's own welfare, expressing our fear that for all we knew he, too, may have come to some harm. But first Smudge Tucker and then Albie Evans argued that the *Gazette* – by which they meant Coma and I – needed to get its head around the idea that Humph had in all probability murdered Bren, most likely while pissed, and then done a bunk. It fell to us, Smudge insisted, to try to track him down and bring him to justice. 'It's a huge story, boys, and we have the inside track.'

Emotions were running high – even the normally reticent Germolene Twins were making themselves heard among the raised voices – when the door to the conference room opened and in walked Helen Snow.

Helen Snow's reputation both within and beyond the Bentall Newspaper Group was legendary. Five-foot-six of pure Yorkshire grit in a tight-fitting business suit, Helen had made her name as a tabloid queen at the *News of the World*, where she had specialised in Westminster kiss-and-tells. It wasn't exactly clear why she had left the paper – some said it was at the personal request of a recent Home Secretary – but she had since reinvented herself as Bentall Newspaper Group's regional editor-in-chief. And now here she stood in the *Gazette* conference room, reduced but delighted, if her smile was any indication, to find herself knee-deep in another scandal.

'Which one of you is Coma Jenkins?' asked Helen, lighting a long, thin cigar.

'That would be me,' volunteered Coma.

'What sort of hillbilly name is Coma anyway?' she replied, blowing smoke at him in more ways than one.

'It's just a nickname,' said Coma. 'Had it for years now. It's just kind of stu …'

'Sit down, Coma, I didn't ask for your life story. Right, for those of you who have had your head up a sheep's backside for the past ten years, my name is Helen Snow and I'm here to run this pathetic excuse for a newspaper while the boys in blue are out trying to nick your editor.'

Chapter 31

It soon became clear that life at the *Gazette* was going to be quite different under the rule of the Ice Queen, as she was quickly dubbed. Smudge Tucker had worked with Helen in a previous existence on the *News of the World*, so the two of them re-bonded easily. But the blunt tabloid mentality that Helen Snow introduced into what had always been a friendly provincial newsroom soon ruffled feathers, and I found myself a shoulder for a steady succession of staff members to cry on. Each in turn fell foul of our new caretaker editor, who clearly subscribed to the theory that a happy newsroom was an inefficient newsroom. She took no prisoners. First Coma, then Nigel and Aled, as I now knew them, and finally Albie Evans came to me to share the injustice of her treatment of them. George Mellor, on the other hand, hit upon the tactic of following Helen around like a slobbering lapdog, gladly accepting both approbation and praise.

Helen kept her distance from me to begin with, though I suspected she would come at me sooner or later, as she had done with Teg. Instinctively sensing the presence of another alpha female in the building, Helen had made a beeline for the front desk on her first day to goad Teg into a public confrontation. But Teg was a smart cookie and had known not to indulge her.

Around a week after the Ice Queen had burst into our lives, I sensed a cold wind was finally headed in my direction when I was summoned into the editor's office down the corridor, a stationery cupboard no more.

'So, Bradley,' she said, perched on the edge of her desk, picking specks of lint off her dark grey trousers, 'the word is that you're the one reporter around here with a full set of balls.'

I didn't respond, which was just as well because she kept on talking.

'You're going to be my point man on the Humph Blake story. I want you to come off diary, dig up whatever dirt you can find from his past and nail him. If this newspaper doesn't take ownership of this story and bring its own editor to justice then I will personally see to it that Sir Norman Bentall shuts it down for good.'

I followed Teg's lead and kept my powder dry. Helen had clearly discovered that I was close to Humph, and she was enjoying the prospect of pitting me against him. She was also creating a classic win-win situation for herself. If I brought in the story, she would take the credit for it and her professional rehabilitation would be complete. If I didn't, then she'd ingratiate herself with Bentall by cutting overheads in the shrinking local publishing market. I realised, however, that the task she was setting me could also work in my favour. I wanted nothing more than the freedom she was giving me to stay on the story full-time, so I accepted her offer, and backed myself to find Humph before Bryn Thomas did. I just hoped I would find him innocent.

Chapter 32

The one lead I still had on Humph was flimsy: the racing formbook he'd hidden in my desk. In truth I didn't expect it to lead anywhere other than back to Dai Whitehouse's bookie shop, but I couldn't overlook the fact that Humph had gone to some trouble to put it in my possession before he'd disappeared. It seemed like the act of a man reaching out for help and this gave me a measure of hope. So I unwrapped the book from the *Sporting Life*, which I tossed into a bin beside my desk, and crossed the road to Grumpy's.

I sat in the window and sipped a creamy black coffee from what Grumpy assured me was an expensive new Italian espresso machine. 'My cousin Meidrim lives in Seattle, Twm,' said Grumpy. 'Says posh coffee's gonna be huge.'

I opened Humph's formbook. Coma was right. Humph's handwriting was awful. But then I'd rarely met a reporter with good handwriting. In my own case the process of acquiring a shorthand speed of 100 words per minute for my journalism qualification seemed to have permanently altered the muscle memory in my fingers. In just four months at the start of my career the longhand I'd spent my whole life perfecting had been beaten up and left for dead by a new and arcane set of squiggles. These days even the act of writing a message in a greetings card filled me with dread.

There was nothing much of interest in the first half of Humph's book. Over a number of years Humph had recorded his successes and failures, mostly failures, in a confusing jumble of ticks, crosses, underlinings and deletions. I kept turning the pages, hoping for illumination, only to be presented with yet more messy blue or black ink. I was beginning to resign myself to the fact that there was nothing of value to be found when, towards the last few pages of the book, one particular scrawl jumped out at me.

Alongside a reference to a horse by the name of Forza Aspa was a note which he had underlined. What had immediately caught my attention was that unlike the rest of the book this note was written in shorthand. Unfortunately it appeared to be in Pitman shorthand and I, along with most journalists of my generation, had been taught Teeline. Many of the signs looked familiar, but I just couldn't make it out. Pitman was a phonetic system of shorthand whereas Teeline, not invented until 1968, was based more on spelling. I needed another journalist of Humph's era to help me make sense of the note, so I drained the last of my coffee, complimented Grumpy on his new espresso machine and headed back to the *Gazette* to find Coma.

'Yeah, it's Pitman all right,' said Coma, pushing his half-glasses up his nose. 'The trouble is that it's not always easy to read someone else's shorthand, unless they are especially neat.' Coma turned to me with a look that suggested that was more than could be expected from Humph.

'Well, can you have a go?' I asked him. 'Anything you can make out might be helpful.'

'Okay, well let's see.' Coma turned back to the formbook. 'Yes, the first two words are "*Sporting Life*".'

My heart fell.

'Then, strangely enough, the next bit looks like a series of numbers,' continued Coma. 'I say strange because he's written them in Pitman rather than in plain digits. Why would he do that?'

So that they weren't readily apparent to someone reading the book, I said to myself. Suddenly I was interested again.

'The numbers are "twenty-three", "seven", "ninety-seven" and "twenty-five". Yeah, that's it. I'm pretty sure. Does that make any sense to you?'

'No,' I replied, searching my brain. 'Unless ...' I crossed the newsroom from Coma's desk to my own, and retrieved Humph's copy of the *Sporting Life*, the one in which he had wrapped his formbook, from my waste-paper basket. I unfolded the paper and examined the masthead on the front page. There it was: 'Wednesday 23rd July 1997'. Twenty-three, seven, ninety-seven. I unfolded the paper and turned to page twenty-five. Halfway down the page I saw a headline: 'STADIUM SYNDICATE ACQUIRES DERBY PROSPECT'.

'Any luck?' asked Coma, who had followed me over to my desk.

'I think so,' I said. 'Thanks, Coma. I'm just going to ... I'll see you later.'

CHAPTER 33

It wasn't the headline in the *Sporting Life* that had sent me walking out of the newsroom towards the lift, leaving Coma hanging. It wasn't even the story, which was about Ivan Harris leading a small international consortium of businessmen in buying a promising young racehorse. It was the photograph.

There, among a small group of people in an unsaddling enclosure, stood Ivan Harris. But that wasn't it either. It was the figure standing next to him which really caught my attention. The unmistakeable figure of my father.

He had aged since I had last seen him, his hair more salt now than pepper. He still looked in pretty good shape, though. It seemed late middle age had even added a touch of gravitas.

The caption confirmed it. The consortium was namechecked from left to right: '*Giancarlo Azzotti, Mr and Mrs Andrea Bianchi, Mr and Mrs Ivan Harris and Dr Thomas Bradley.*'

Alone in the lift, which descended with its usual moans and groans, I could feel my heart beating in my chest. The sight of two people from what I had imagined were two quite separate areas of my life standing together was a shock. And this was no fleeting racecourse encounter. My father was actually part of a syndicate with Ivan Harris. How had they met? What did this mean?

My thoughts flashed back to that last, doomed, conversation with Mara when she had steered the subject around to my father. At the time I had taken her interest in my background as a distraction from talking about her own, but now I was beginning to understand that it was something else. She had clearly discovered this link between Harris and my father and had been gently prying to see if I was aware of it too.

With a clunk, and then a ring, the lift reached the ground floor and the door slid open. I stepped out, ignoring a friendly greeting from George Mellor who was waiting to step in, and crossed the foyer to the front desk.

'Teg, can I use your phone?'

'Of course you can, lovely,' she replied. 'Make yourself right at home ... and then put ten pence in the charity box.' She gave it a little shake.

I pulled out my wallet, found what I was looking for and dialled. The phone rang three times before my call was picked up.

'Mara? It's Twm.' There was a brief silence on the other end of the line, which I filled. 'I need to see you. Where are you?'

'I can't speak now,' she replied. 'I'm about to go into a meeting.'

'I know that my father is involved with Ivan Harris.'

Teg's face lit up with surprise before she managed to compose herself and return to her duties, unwilling to be caught prying any more than was absolutely necessary.

'Look, I'm actually heading back down there later today,' said Mara. 'I'll be arriving in the city at just before five ...'

'I'll meet you at the station,' I interrupted her. 'We can have a drink, maybe, and then catch the train back to Porthcoed together. You are coming to Porthcoed?'

'Yeah. Look, I really have to go. Okay? I'll see you this evening.'

Chapter 34

I took a sip from my coffee and gazed through the window of the café into one of the half a dozen elegant Victorian shopping arcades that snaked through the city centre.

'The land on which this arcade was built was once covered in slum housing,' I said.

'Really?' replied Mara. 'You wouldn't know it now.'

'It was something my father told me. He knows stuff like that. He'd always bring me here whenever we visited the city when I was a boy.'

Mara stirred the foam on her cappuccino and then looked in my eyes. 'I wasn't sure if you knew,' she said.

'I didn't. I only found out this morning. I guess I should apologise. You know, for the other weekend.'

'I wasn't sure who Dr Thomas Bradley was at first. Then when I came across you I wasn't sure if you were related.'

'In this part of the world it's always safer to assume two people with the same surname are related. Isn't it like that in Scotland?'

'So you were named after him?'

'Not really. Twm is sometimes used as an abbreviation for Thomas, but not in my case.'

'And he's a hydrologist?'

'Yeah. A lecturer in the geographical sciences department. He took early retirement.'

'So what do you make of him working for Ivan Harris on the new rugby stadium, then?'

I stared at Mara open-mouthed.

'You told me you knew about Harris and your father,' she said.

'I knew from the photograph that they'd bought a racehorse together. I didn't realise he was working for Harris.'

'What photograph?' asked Mara.

I explained about Humph's formbook and pulled the newspaper from my bag. 'When did my father start working for Harris?'

'June last year.'

'Around the time this picture was published, then.'

'So Humph knew about this a year ago, but he didn't say anything to you?'

'Humph knows I don't have much of a relationship with my father. He also likes to keep his cards pretty close to his chest, as you've probably spotted by now.'

'He's kept that photo pretty close to his chest,' said Mara. 'He keeps it tucked away for a whole year, and then suddenly he goes to a lot of bother to put it safely in your possession? What's changed?'

'He's up to his neck in trouble, that's what's changed. There's money missing from the newspaper he runs, and the police think he killed his wife.'

'And you don't think he killed his wife?'

'You know I don't,' I said, accepting the picture back from Mara. 'I think he's left this as a line for me to follow to prove his innocence. Humph's been on Ivan Harris's case ever since Harris came back to Porthcoed. He's been writing editorials about what Harris has been doing at the Buzzards for the past year.'

'Humph's been investigating Ivan Harris?'

'Why not? Think about it. A year ago, almost thirty years after Delilah Sullivan's murder, Ivan Harris returns to Porthcoed. Now Humph's patch. It can't just be a coincidence that Eddie Lennox is released from prison around the same time, too, seeking justice. All of a sudden old wounds from Humph's *Record* years in the sixties are reopened. Maybe he starts re-examining the Delilah Sullivan murder. Maybe he starts digging into Ivan Harris, the miracle witness at the Lennox trial who we now know was not above being violent to Delilah himself. Maybe Humph starts to get somewhere, which is why things start going wrong for him.'

'So the missing five grand was arranged as, what, a warning? Back off or else?'

'Could be.'

'Or else what?'

I shrugged.

'You don't mean Bren? You think Bren was killed because Humph was getting too close to the truth?'

'I think maybe Humph has gone into hiding to save his own neck,' I said.

'Leaving you a trail of breadcrumbs that leads towards Ivan Harris?'

'Towards Ivan Harris and my father. That's the bit I don't get. What has my father got to do with all this?'

'Don't ask me,' said Mara. 'Ask him.'

CHAPTER 35

Talking with my father was not a prospect I relished. Meeting up with him face to face was even lower down my wish list now that I knew he was a chum of Ivan Harris's. As it turned out I had more pressing business to attend to, though I wasn't looking forward to that much either.

Some weeks after Bren's death, presumably after all the forensic work on her remains had been carried out, Bryn Thomas finally forwarded a curt, two-par fax to the *Gazette* newsroom announcing that City CID were allowing her body to be released to her family.

Bren's sister and her husband arranged a service at Porthcoed Crem and, as the day approached, the debate around the *Gazette* conference table was whether Humph would show up.

'Can't see it myself,' said Coma. 'I mean if you've done a bunk from the police you're not suddenly going to walk into the Crem in broad daylight ten minutes before the funeral. Doesn't make sense.'

'He'd be in the b-back of Bryn Thomas's car and down Porthcoed n-nick before the curtain fell on Bren's c-c-c-coffin,' agreed Albie Evans.

'I've seen it before,' said Helen Snow. 'A man kills his wife in a drunken domestic, goes on the run but can't resist the urge to hang around the funeral. He's arrogant, cocky, and flirts with the danger, thinking he's too smart to get caught out.'

'We are still talking about Humph Blake, here, aren't we?' offered Smudge.

'Twm,' said the Ice Queen, 'I want you and Smudge at the Crem half an hour before kick-off. You two,' she added, turning to the Germolene Twins, 'borrow Mummy's Sure Shot and spend the afternoon patrolling the grounds around the Crem. If Humph Blake comes within half a mile of his wife's funeral I want his face on the front page of the *Gazette*.'

'What's a Sure Shot?' whispered a worried-looking Nigel as we filed out of the conference room.

Chapter 36

Attending the funeral of a friend with the expectation of seeing an even closer friend arrested for her murder is just one of the surreal things that can happen to you when you're a newspaper reporter. I'd been lucky in my career so far in that the line between my private and professional lives had rarely if ever crossed. But in a small community like Porthcoed – 'close-knit' as the Hairdos loved to say – it was always going to happen eventually. For me, ever since Humph's mini-confessional over a cup of whisky-spiked tea at Grumpy's, the line had now completely disappeared.

I agreed with Coma Jenkins, of course, that Humph Blake was the last person we could expect to see at Porthcoed Crem that day. But as I walked through the tree-lined car park with Smudge Tucker, our sudden appearance scaring a squirrel up a nearby tree trunk, there was just a touch of curiosity in my mind. The idea of Humph missing Bren's funeral was unthinkable, and because I was convinced now that he had nothing at all to do with her murder, it seemed quite obvious to me that he simply had to be there. Would Humph, perhaps in fear of his own life, give himself up in the hope of a fair trial as the price of a final farewell to Bren? Stranger things had happened.

But as the tyres of the long, black hearse carrying Bren hissed gently to a halt on the tarmac outside the main entrance to Chapel Number 2, and I saw the fresh, polished wood of her coffin, the dark thought crossed my mind that there was at least one other good reason why Humph might not show up. The possibility existed that whoever had killed Bren had also caught up with Humph. My mood wasn't helped by the recollection that Chapel Number 2 had been where my mother's funeral had taken place. And I hadn't been back here since.

'I hate these places,' said Smudge. 'My old man died at one last year. Keeled over on a job just like this one. Can you imagine that? One day he was standing outside the crem with his camera, a week later he was the one inside the box.'

'Your dad was a snapper, too?'

'Yeah. Fleet Street, for the most part, though he did a long stint up on the *Glasgow Herald* back in the day. Fond of a pint and a smoke, he was, and that's what did for him in the end.'

Smudge interrupted our conversation by firing off the shutter of his camera with a series of shots. It was not a sound that went down well at a time and a place like this, but that was just how it went for a reporter and photographer. Decency often took second place behind professional obligation and commercial reality, and I had long ago become inured to the sort of looks now being aimed in our direction. At least that's what I thought until I saw Bren's sister, her eyes swollen, being helped out of a dark saloon by her husband.

'Okay Smudge, I think we've got it now,' I said, and Smudge tilted his camera back to check its settings.

The service passed without interruption and the mourners, including the majority of the *Gazette* staff, shuffled quietly out of the chapel. As I filed past Bryn Thomas I caught his eye. No words passed between us but his expression was clear enough. Humph had been a no-show today but that wouldn't save him.

Refreshments were on offer at a nearby hotel but, after popping in to pay our respects, most of the staff made for an unofficial wake at the Railway, where Smudge dropped me off on his way back to the darkroom in the *Gazette* building. We huddled together around the bar while Coma said a few words about Bren, and then we raised our glasses in her memory.

'Get a bit of that inside you,' said George Mellor, sharing

the contents of a large glass of whisky into Nigel and Aled's half-pints of Coke. 'But don't let old Merve Powell behind the bar spot you, all right? He may be cross-eyed but he's been this pub's darts champion ten times in the last eleven years.'

I chatted to Teg, who had turned out for the occasion in a figure-hugging black dress with a plunging neckline, her seasoned cleavage half-hidden by a glitter-studded pink scarf.

'She was a great girl, Bren,' said Teg, her smile revealing the gap between her top two teeth. 'I knew her since she was a child, you know. She adored Humph. Would have moved mountains for him.'

'She put up with a lot,' I answered. 'Playing second fiddle to a newspaper for thirty years can't have been easy.'

'Try being the wife of a man who's married to God,' said Teg.

'I'm sure the late Reverend Rowlands knew which side his bread was buttered.'

'I know all about the missing five grand,' said Teg, right out of the blue. 'Humph always fancies himself as a man of intrigue but there's nothing much goes on at the *Gazette* without me knowing about it. Is it gambling debts, do you think?'

'Well, he's a few grand down with Dai Whitehouse, but there's something much more complicated going on. I think what Humph got himself mixed up with at the *Record* thirty years ago is somehow coming back to haunt him.'

'He was never the same when he came back from there,' said Teg. 'That Delilah girl broke his heart.'

'You know about him and Delilah Sullivan?'

'Like I said, there's nothing much that escapes me at the *Gazette*.'

'But how did you find out?'

'Humph told me. Though I'm pretty sure he doesn't know he did.'

I gave her a quizzical look.

'I found him slumped over his desk in the newsroom one night about a year after he came back to Porthcoed. I got on the phone to Goronwy and while I waited for him to come over and help me get Humph home to Bren, I fed Humph hot coffee and he pretty much spat it all out.'

'It's not like Humph to let the booze loosen his tongue.'

Teg shot me a look. 'You are kidding me, now, lovely, aren't you? An old blabbermouth like Humph Blake?' She sipped from her gin. 'Do you think he's okay, wherever he is? Is he safe?'

'Yes, I think he is. Humph's no fool. He'll be holed up somewhere trying to get a handle on what's going on. And when the time is right he'll step out of the shadows and sort everything out.'

'I know you're doing your best to clear him, lovely. And I want you to know that whatever you need, I am here for you. You just ask Teg, all right?'

'Thanks. I will.'

Just then I noticed Helen Snow walk in with Smudge Tucker. She walked up to the bar, jumped up to lean across it and, much to Merve's surprise, grabbed hold of the clapper and rang the time bell. The room fell silent.

'Right, you lot. You've said your goodbyes. Now I want your backsides back at work. Norman Bentall's not paying you to stand around and drink beer.'

The lull continued for a moment or two longer as the gathered company absorbed her words, but then glasses were drained and placed on the bar. Gradually the crowd thinned out.

'Oh hurry back, Humph, love, for fuck's sake,' said Teg in a voice loud enough to turn the Ice Queen's head. 'Save us from this cold-hearted bitch.'

'Whatever Smudge here is drinking,' Helen Snow barked at a more than usually bewildered-looking Merve, 'and I'll have a large vodka and tonic.'

CHAPTER 37

The pool car had been driving itself down the narrow country lane when I was brought sharply back to my senses. Out of nowhere a white van filled the windscreen. I yanked the wheel over, stamped on the pedals and the van missed me by inches. I sat still for a moment, shook my head and realised that in the half hour since I'd left Porthcoed I'd been lost in my thoughts. I checked the mirror and pulled off again. I hadn't seen my father for some time and already I could feel the tension creeping up the back of my neck.

Eventually the lane opened up and the Channel came into view, a dismal patchwork of brown and grey under hurrying cloud cover. The grass-topped cliffs on this stretch of the south coast were a local landmark and this headland was a popular spot for walkers. But not on a cold, wet day like today. Gravel crunched beneath the tyres as I pulled up in the empty car park opposite the graffiti-shuttered ice cream kiosk. I turned off the ignition and took in the view. On a good day you could see clear across the water to the opposite coast. All I could make out in that late morning murk was the small silhouette of a container ship labouring against a westerly wind, pushing inch by inch towards the open sea.

On my left, at the other end of a bumpy dirt road, rose a lighthouse, defiantly clean and white against the dirty sky. I'd recently written a story for the *Gazette* about its impending automation, which would leave North Foreland in Kent as the last manned lighthouse in the UK. For 166 years lighthouse keepers on this stretch of headland had withstood everything that nature could throw at them, but their time-honoured profession was now being washed away by a threat few of them could have foreseen. The rising digital tide.

Even the lighthouse itself looked unlikely to last forever. The rugged limestone cliff on which it was perched was shot through with layers of shale which crumbled without warning, causing massive chunks of rock face to slip down onto the beach some 100 feet below, drawing the lighthouse ever closer to the edge. Scratch the surface of life, and you often find a dark truth hiding underneath.

Small pebbles of rain began to drum on the tin roof of the car, snapping me out of my thoughts once again. Then the shower blew over as swiftly as it had arrived. There was movement to my right and I turned to see the figure of a man rising head-first into view on a footpath scored into the brow of the hill. I recognised the tall, thin frame and its loping gait.

By the time my father appeared at the passenger window I'd had a few minutes to ready myself for the conversation I was about to have with him, but I still felt unprepared.

'Are you going to let me in?' he asked, tugging at the door handle. I leant across and pulled up the lock button which I must have caught while clambering over the gearstick. 'I'm a bit muddy, I'm afraid,' he said, as I gathered up the rubbish strewn across the passenger footwell.

There was a blast of damp air and my father folded his long frame through the passenger door before yanking it shut. We had never quite come to terms with the etiquette involved in a father greeting his adult son, so in a way the lack of any room for manoeuvre in the pool car did us both a favour.

'So, how are you, Twm?'

'I'm fine. How are you?'

'Grand. Just grand.' Tom Bradley had left Yorkshire thirty-five years ago but Yorkshire hadn't quite left him. I could see the physical change in him, though. His skin was older, dotted here and there with small brown liver spots, and, as I'd

135

noticed in the photograph of him with Ivan Harris, his hair had thinned and greyed. On the whole, however, it seemed that age had merely underlined his rugged good looks.

'I didn't realise you were living down south now,' I said.

'Yes, I seem to spend a fair bit of my time down here these days. I'm renting one of those new flats, you know, on the Wharf?'

'In the Bay? Very trendy.'

'So … I've left the Land Rover outside the pub down the road. Can I buy you a pint?'

'Okay,' I said and reached for the ignition key.

I parked beside the Land Rover and we went inside. The bar was empty and an unseasonal but nonetheless welcoming log fire crackled in the grate to our left.

'Gents, what can I get you?' asked an Australian barman.

'Have you got anything in the way of a pale ale?' asked my father, scanning the line of taps on the bar. After tasting a golden ale from a local brewery and taking it upon himself to order two pints without consulting me, my father lifted both glasses off the bar and gestured towards a table next to the fireplace.

'Good to buy local,' he said. 'And when it tastes this good, why would you drink some fizzy piss from a giant vat in the Midlands?'

By the time we'd sipped the head from our pints and decided against ordering from the bar-food menu, we'd exhausted our small talk. Yet my father persevered in his rusty paternal manner.

'So, how's the job? Any big stories on the go? I liked that piece you did on the lighthouse keepers a few weeks back – 'A DYING BREED' wasn't it? Good stuff.'

'You got hold of the *Gazette*?'

'Oh, I get a copy sent through the post each week. I like to keep an eye on what my son's up to.'

I took another pull from my beer.

'Yes, well, I've been quite busy of late,' he continued, filling the silence. 'I'm working as a consultant on the new national stadium project. Fascinating job. Big pressure, though. Wouldn't fancy being responsible for getting the damn thing built on time, I can tell you.' As an afterthought he added, 'Though that's strictly off the record.'

'Dad, I think we can share a pint without me making it about work.' A lie.

'So it's "Dad" again, now, is it?' he replied testily. 'How come I've heard nothing from you these past few years since your mother died? Not a phone call on my birthday or a bloody card at Christmas?'

'Can we just not do this?'

There was a prolonged silence during which we sipped at our beer, slowly reaching an unspoken agreement to put this brief glimpse of the uncomfortable truth behind us.

'So, you've been working on the stadium then?' I asked, after a suitable pause, hoping my redirect wasn't as transparent as it seemed to me.

'That's right,' he answered willingly. 'I was asked to get involved by a man from your neck of the woods actually. Bloke called Harris who runs the construction firm. You know of him?'

'Ivan Harris?'

'Yeah, that's him. He's the guy who has to make sure it's all going to get built in good time. And he's the one who'll get hung out to dry if it doesn't. Huge pressure.'

'And is there some suggestion that it won't be ready?' I saw the calculation in his eyes. 'Well, it's nothing I won't have already read in the *Record*, is it? They're all over the will-it-or-won't-it be ready in time controversy.'

'Oh, the stadium will get built in time for the tournament,' my father answered. 'But that's only half the story.' He rose from his chair. 'Another?'

'Let me …'

'No, son, I've got this. Save your cash.'

I was still digesting his throwaway comment when the door opened and two men walked in. Tall and athletic, their ill-fitting suits could barely contain their muscle-bound frames. Together they looked like High Street nightclub bouncers, totally out of keeping in a country pub at lunchtime. The nearest of the two of them glanced at me and they both walked over to the narrow bar, positioning themselves either side of my father. He lifted his head to look at each man in turn. From where I was sitting it looked like the three men exchanged some sort of greeting. Then my father returned to our table empty-handed.

'Twm, listen, how about we have that other pint next time? I've got to dash.'

'Er … yeah, okay. Is everything all right?' I asked, turning towards the men at the bar. 'Do you know those guys?'

'It's grand, son. Look, I've just got to dash. I'm expecting an important fax. Need to get back to the flat. Great to see you. I'll give you a ring, okay?'

And with that he was gone.

Chapter 38

Confused by my father's abrupt departure, I looked again at the two men by the bar. They were now facing me, their backs leaning against the bar, each with an orange juice in hand. The taller of the two smiled. I nodded, stood up and threaded my way between two wooden chairs towards the door.

The Land Rover had gone from the car park. I really wasn't in the mood for the indignity of climbing over the passenger seat of the pool car but I had little choice. Ruffled by the exertion, I slid my key into the ignition and turned it. Click. I tried again. Another click. The battery was dead. 'Sodding pool car piece of shit!' In frustration I hit the steering wheel with the bottom edge of my hand.

At that moment I heard the door of the pub slam shut. In the rear-view mirror I saw the two men walking towards my car. I bent over to flick the bonnet open, then climbed out of the car. I had the bonnet propped open and was examining the battery when I heard a voice beside me.

'Problem with car?' Eastern European.

I straightened up but found myself having to look up even further to see the cauliflower-eared face of the man who had spoken.

'We give lift,' he smiled.

'That's very kind, but I'm sure it's something quite straightforward.' I looked back down at the battery and saw that one of the leads had come away from its terminal. The pool car was unloved and mistreated but the nut on its battery terminal hadn't unscrewed itself. 'Yep, there it is. Must have shaken loose somehow. Thank you. Very kind of you but I'll be fine.'

'Be careful,' he said, gently kicking the front tyre of the pool car. 'Old car. Not safe to drive, maybe.'

Both men walked away towards a black BMW parked at the top of the pub car park. I reattached the lead, wound down the nut until it was finger tight and slammed down the bonnet, then wiped my oily hands on a patch of wet grass at the side of the car park. The pool car's engine spluttered into life at the customary third time of asking and I drove towards the exit at the bottom of the car park. I was turning the wheel to swing left, back towards Porthcoed, when I saw the black BMW had blocked off the lane in that direction. It showed no sign of budging. There was a momentary stand-off before I spun the steering wheel right over the other way and pulled out onto the lane heading back towards the headland, the lighthouse and the cliffs.

'Okay, Twm,' I said out loud, realising I'd opted to drive towards a dead end. 'Interesting decision.'

I worked slowly up through the gears and then checked the rear-view mirror. The BMW was following forty yards behind me. If this was a car chase, it was nothing much to write home about. The speed dial in the pool car had yet to touch 35 mph before I pulled up to allow an elderly man to cross the lane towards the graveyard gate of a small church. We exchanged polite nods and I pulled away again. All the while the BMW lurked at a distance behind me.

Apart from a crescent-shaped lay-by on the left-hand side where the residents of a small row of council houses parked, and the odd blocked gateway into a field, there was nowhere for me to go but down the narrow winding lane towards the cliff car park. And with this fast approaching, I was running out of time to make my decision. At the cliff-top parking area I had two choices. I could take the dirt road to the left of the kiosk towards the lighthouse, ditch the car and head towards a friendly lighthouse keeper. Or I could pass the kiosk on the right, drive down onto the grass and then swing back around the kiosk and onto the lane towards the pub. If I timed it just right, I could get ahead of the BMW. Suddenly it was decision time. I opted for Plan B and hoped the BMW would follow suit.

The car park came into view, still deserted. I dropped my right foot onto the accelerator and pushed it towards the floor, trying to steal a few more crucial yards from the BMW. I veered right of the kiosk, leaving the tarmac and bouncing down onto the flat expanse of grass alongside the cliff edge. The turf was wet but firm enough to offer some traction. I swung the wheel to the left and drove parallel to the cliff edge, a good ten feet away from it, waiting to see if the BMW took the bait. It did. So far, so good. But then the powerful BMW started to pick up speed on the grass and closed in beside me, trapping me next to the cliff edge.

Looking ahead I saw that the cliff edge curved around in front of me. If I didn't change direction soon I was heading for the drop. I swung the wheel to the left and rammed the side of the BMW, which did little but nudge me back onto my original heading. In desperation I stood on the brake pedal. Nothing. I heard the Eastern European voice in my head. 'Not safe to drive, maybe.' Had they cut into the brake pipe when they'd disconnected the battery lead? At this point the BMW rammed into me, sending me even closer to the drop, before it turned away towards safety. As a last-ditch hope I grabbed the handbrake, and pulled, and the pool car went into a spin.

The world really does slow down at times like this, giving you just enough time to grasp the absurdity of the situation you find yourself in. Just a few minutes ago I'd been sitting in a cosy pub with a pint of beer. Now I was at the wheel of an out of control car, a mere spectator spinning toward a 100-foot drop. I heard a large crack from beneath the car, which jolted violently and straightened, rapidly losing momentum. Instinctively I reached for the driver's door handle, flicked it and felt myself tumble out onto the grass as the pool car, with one last scream from its engine, toppled over the cliff edge and fell out of sight.

Chapter 39

'So let's get this straight. You drove from the pub after a lunchtime piss-up with your old man, during office hours, and now the *Gazette*'s only pool car is in bits at the foot of a fucking cliff?'

There was no way I was going to be allowed to explain to Helen Snow what had really happened. She had her own agenda at the *Gazette* and would bend any truth to her own advantage.

'I'm fine,' I said. 'Thanks for asking.'

'Don't you get smart with me, Bradley. What you've just done would have cost you your job on any other newspaper. Gone. Just like that.' The Ice Queen perched on the edge of the desk in her office and paused for effect. She lit up a small cigar and exhaled. 'You're just lucky, sunshine, that you currently have me for your boss and I'm a little more understanding.'

What she really meant, of course, was that the *Gazette* was her last chance in the Bentall Newspaper Group, and no bad news from her time here would be allowed to reach head office. One too many scandals had brought her as low as caretaker editor of a small provincial paper, and for Helen Snow it was career redemption or bust from here.

'Now you owe me, Twm Bradley. And when you show up for work each morning I want to see gratitude written all over your face for the second chance I'm giving you here. More than that, you're going to get me a result on the Humph Blake story and soon. I don't care if you have to tramp right around the *Gazette* circulation area on foot, now that you've totalled this rag's only pool car, you are going to bring me his head on a plate. Am I clear?'

Chapter 40

'What happened, lovely?'

After Helen Snow, a lunchtime drink in the Railway with Teg was more like the warm embrace I needed. What had almost happened down at the lighthouse had shaken me up.

'Apparently, as I was heading towards the cliff edge the pool car hit a low wooden barrier. It took out the barrier but the collision slowed down the car just enough for me to fall out of the door. Someone from the lighthouse heard the commotion and their arrival scared off the BMW.'

'Imagine that,' said Teg. 'Six months of having to clamber over the handbrake into the driver's seat and in the end it was driver's side door opening that saved your bacon.'

The thought brought an unexpected smile to my face.

'That's my boy. Nothing a good laugh can't put right. Goronwy, bless his soul, always used to say to me, "Teg, my love, what doesn't kill you makes you stranger".'

'Stronger, you mean?'

'I think Goronwy got it right, don't you?' she beamed. 'And you're really okay, are you?'

'I'm bit shaken up, Teg. A few aches and pains. But that seems to be par for the course these days.'

'And you say you were chased down the lane? How exciting!'

'Well, I wouldn't call it a chase exactly ...'

'How fast did you go?'

'It wasn't so much the speed exactly ...'

'So who was in the car behind you, then?' she asked.

'A couple of thugs. Eastern European. They must have cut into my brake pipe and by the time I got down to the headland all the fluid had drained.'

'Does your father know what happened?'

'I don't know. I haven't said anything, and I don't want anyone else to, Teg, okay? I'm going to sort that out myself.'

'It's okay, lovely. You can rely on Teg.' She sipped at her gin, leaving a fresh smudge of lipstick on the rim of her glass. Then she reached across the table and took my empty whisky glass.

'Let me get you another one of these,' she smiled. 'For the shock.'

Teg, uncanny as ever, had got right to the heart of what was bothering me. Had my father known what was going to happen? Walking back to the flat later I tried to shake the idea out of my head but succeeded only in drawing a sharp lash of pain from my neck and shoulders. I decided to drop into the corner shop for a bottle of Scotch and some paracetamol.

'You're getting to be my number-one whisky customer, Twm,' said Aarav, taking my cash and ringing the till. 'Keep going like this and I'll have enough money to fly to Delhi for Auntie Prisha's ninetieth next year.'

'Keep the change,' I replied, dropping my wallet back into my jacket pocket, 'and give Auntie P my love.'

At the foot of my rickety staircase I found Mara.

'There's a story on the wire about a car going off a cliff yesterday down on the coast,' she said.

'Yeah, I heard something about that, too,' I replied, reaching for my key. 'Drink?'

'You don't think two o'clock in the afternoon's a bit early for the hard stuff?'

'And I thought you were Scottish.'

We climbed the staircase and I let us both in. After a few drinks Mara insisted on drawing me a hot bath and, after I'd slipped in, she insisted on joining me.

* * *

'I'm pretty sure there's a strong connection between sex and the prospect of death,' I said as we lay entangled in my duvet. 'I might ask Coma if he'll take a lifestyle feature for the *Gazette*.'

She sat up. '"Coma"?'

'It's just a nickname. Apparently not long after he joined the *Gazette* as a cub reporter, many moons ago, he fell asleep covering his first ever council meeting. His real name is Richard.'

'Ah, the cruel wit of the newsroom.'

'I thought I was history, Mara,' I said. 'That's in as much as I actually thought anything. For a while there I was just a bystander, watching myself go.'

'Yes,' Mara replied, 'I know ...' and for a moment or two I felt the intense heat of her gaze before she finally looked away. 'One thing seems clear,' she continued before I had time to speak. 'Humph Blake was onto something when he pointed us in the direction of your father. If you talking to your father leads to two men trying to force you off a cliff, then someone must think your old man has an interesting tale to tell.'

'Ivan Harris, you mean?'

'Could be. Apart from you, who else knew you were going down to the lighthouse?'

'Apart from my father? Just you.'

'I'll choose to ignore that,' she said. 'Did you manage to find out anything from him before he left?'

'He told me there was phenomenal pressure on the stadium project and that Ivan Harris is pretty exposed, all of which is common knowledge... but there was something else. Just before the two guys walked into the pub he said something odd. When I asked him if he thought the stadium would be finished in time for the tournament he said it would, but that this was "only half the story".'

'And what do you suppose he meant by that?' asked Mara.

'I never got to find out.'

Chapter 41

Mara was in the shower early the next morning when I heard the rickety staircase start to rattle. I looked at the alarm clock beside the bed. Half six. Way too early for the postman. I got up to open the door of the flat and found the towering figure of DS Josh Templeton standing in front of me, a covered basket in his arms.

'With DI Thomas's regards,' he said, handing me the basket.

'What's this?' I asked.

'It's Humph Blake's cat.'

'Oh, Christ. What's she got to do with me?'

'The cat was found half-starved by Mr Blake's neighbour, who brought it into the station. Bryn thought perhaps you'd like to take care of it until … well, let's just say the cat is going to need a temporary home, shall we?'

'Can't the neighbour look after it? This bloody cat hates me.'

At that moment a door opened behind me and Mara appeared in the hallway beyond the kitchen wrapped in a towel.

'Ah, Miss McKenzie,' said Templeton, deadpan.

Mara paused to rub her wet hair with another smaller hand towel, then disappeared into the bedroom.

'Well, I'll leave you both to it,' he added. 'Thanks for looking after the cat, Mr Bradley. Very public spirited of you.' He smiled and turned back down the stairway.

'What's all that about?' asked Mara.

'I think Bryn Thomas is messing with me. Maybe also doing a little snooping on you and me. Maybe he even expected to find Humph tucked up on the sofa, I don't know.'

'Aren't you going to open the basket?'

'I'd rather not, to be honest with you,' I replied, reaching for the coffee.

'Ah come on, it's only a wee cat,' said Mara, undoing a small leather buckle on the edge of the basket and taking the purring cat into her arms. 'Oh, she's gorgeous,' said Mara. 'What's her name?'

'That,' I said as Mara stroked her head, 'is Modlen. Don't let her anywhere near your throat.' Right on cue, the cat stopped purring, and bared her teeth in my direction.

Half an hour later Modlen was tucking into a saucerful of tuna while Mara and I ate breakfast.

'I'm heading back to London today,' said Mara. 'I've got to show my face in the office but I'll be back in a day or two.'

'You're not going to leave me here alone with her?'

'Feed her, water her and put her out at night. It's not hard, is it? So, what about you? What are you going to do?'

'Find an animal shelter …'

'You can't. Think about Humph. She's all he's got left.'

Her words brought me up short. I realised I'd begun to regard the fact of Humph's disappearance as the new normal. The cold reality was that Humph was out there somewhere on the run from the police, accused of killing his wife. Even if I could somehow prove his innocence, the life he'd known at home with Bren was over. Was he alone, I wondered? Was he scared? The thought blew like a cold draught down my back but redoubled my determination. 'It's not complicated, Twm,' I heard Humph telling me. 'Get out there. Use your feet. Meet people. Look them in the eyes and ask them questions.'

'I think I'm going to pay a visit to Jacqui Harris, this morning,' I said.

'You reckon that's a good idea, right now, knocking on Ivan Harris's front door?'

'I caught sight of a press release on Coma's desk last week. Jacqui Harris is fronting a children's charity day at the Rec next weekend. And I think that's something the *Porthcoed Gazette* ought to cover, don't you?'

Chapter 42

The Harrises' terracotta-tiled villa, with its sage-green shuttered windows, rooftop belvedere and a triple-arched portico, would have looked more in keeping next to a swimming pool in Marbella than halfway up Deri mountain.

Both Mara and Coma had warned me off Ivan Harris but recent events had heightened my interest in this man, to say the least, and I knew I'd never get a better insight into his domestic life than through the charity story. I was greeted at the Harrises' front door by a pale and charmless maid whose clipped accent took me straight back to the car park of the pub near the lighthouse. She led me down a corridor and through the Harrises' entirely white sitting room towards a large sliding window, open in the warm morning sunshine. We walked across a patio and down some steps to a sun terrace alongside a large oval-shaped pool.

We found Jacqui Harris next to the water, lying face down on a massage table in just a bikini bottom, her deeply-tanned back being gently pummelled by a muscular Pacific Islander whose tattooed forearms glistened with oil.

'Reporter from newspaper,' said the charmless maid before disappearing back into the house.

'Thank you, Lakepi,' Jacqui said to her masseur. 'That'll do for now.' She sat upright, her elegantly tapered spine exposed beneath the soft-looking skin, then slipped on and buttoned up a long white linen blouse before rising gracefully and turning to greet me. I had expected Ivan Harris's wife to be bold and brassy but Jacqui Harris was a natural beauty, dark-skinned and slender, with chest-length curly dark brown hair and eyes like black olives.

'It's Mr Bradley, isn't it?' she asked. Her accent had travelled much further than the dozen-odd miles from her hometown of Abergerran, acquiring a softer, more cosmopolitan tone on the way.

'Yes, that's right. Twm.' We shook hands. 'Your maid, Mrs Harris, she's eastern European, am I right?'

'Romanian, to be precise,' replied Jacqui Harris. 'One of the perks of my husband owning a rugby club,' she added, as the masseur followed the maid inside, 'is that I get to borrow the backroom staff occasionally.'

'Very handy,' I replied.

'So, you're here to talk to me about the children's fun day at the Rec next weekend?'

'That's right,' I said.

'It was Ivan's idea. He said he wanted me to get more involved with the club. Help build the community profile of the Buzzards a little. The children's charity is close to my heart. Has been ever since my son died.'

'Oh, I didn't realise. I'm so sorry.' I'd done no research, of course, so this came as news to me and my reaction was genuine.

'It wasn't something that was widely known,' said Mrs Harris. 'But then that's the point of this conversation. He was just ten months old. It was a cot death. Please, sit down.' She slipped a pair of black Raybans down from the top of her head and gestured to a pair of sunloungers.

As we sat opposite each other I reached into my shoulder bag for my notebook and pen. 'For the story,' I explained. 'Is that okay?'

'Yes, of course,' she replied. 'I've spoken with Ivan and we feel that if talking about what happened to us can in some way help bring a bigger focus onto the syndrome then it's the least we can do.'

'It must have been a very difficult time for you. What was your son's name?'

150

'Alex. We named him after Ivan's father. It was a tough time but I got through it with Ivan's help. And we both had a lot of help from the charity that we're trying to put front and centre next weekend. With their help we were able to work through the shock, and the pain, and the loss, and begin to move on.'

'So, how long ago did this happen?'

'Oh, it was not long after we married.'

'And when was that, exactly?'

'Let me see now. About eight years ago, I suppose. Ivan and I met in rather odd circumstances. I drove my Mini into the back of his Jag one morning on the High Street in Abergerran. He was furious,' she laughed, and reached for a packet of Silk Cut cigarettes and a lighter. 'He said it was a vintage model from the 1960s or something. It just looked like an old banger to me. Especially after I'd rearranged the back end of it.' As she laughed her poise slipped a little, just enough to reveal a trace of her hometown accent.

'Anyway he calmed down and we swapped each other's details for insurance purposes. Two days later he showed up at my flat with a bunch of flowers and asked me out. We were married a little over a month later.'

'A whirlwind romance?' I asked, recalling that Annie Léchet had described something similar with Harris and Delilah Sullivan. 'How romantic. But there's quite an age gap between you, isn't there?'

'Twenty-six years to be exact,' she replied. 'Let's just say I was in need of someone who could take me in hand. Not exactly a father figure as such, just an older and wiser head if you like. Ivan was worldly-wise. He'd travelled and made a success of himself, worked his way up from humble origins. And he really swept me off my feet.'

'You are the second Mrs Ivan Harris, is that correct?'

'Ivan was married briefly when he was much younger. His wife died in very tragic circumstances.'

'Yes, I read about that. It must have been awful for him. A big murder trial. He was the key witness, I think?'

Jacqui Harris looked at me as if to work out quite how the interview had strayed so far off piste.

'Have you met my husband, Mr Bradley?'

'Er, yes,' I answered. 'Both professionally and ... socially, if that's the word?'

She smiled to concede the point. 'He does have a bit of a reputation as an old grouch, but he's had a tough life. Having met him you will know that he's a survivor, Mr Bradley, a strong-minded man who has got where he is today very much on his own merits. People say he's a tough nut. Yes, he can be brash and his business style is aggressive, but you should see him when he's at home and work is finally over for the day. He's a big pussycat really.'

I pushed away an unwanted thought of Modlen defiling my flat and continued to press. 'I expect he's under a bit of pressure right now, what with the race to get the new national stadium built?'

'It's an important project that takes a lot of his time. We don't get to see each other as much as we'd like. But it's business, Mr Bradley, and to Ivan business can also be a pleasure.'

'I hear rumours that there are problems with the build?' I wasn't expecting any particular answers to this line of questioning, merely hoping that Ivan Harris would hear from his wife that I had pushed on certain subjects, namely his marriage to Delilah Sullivan and trouble with the stadium project.

'I wouldn't know anything about that, Mr Bradley. You'd be better off directing such a question to my husband.'

'And I'd really appreciate the chance to do that, Mrs Harris, but he's not an easy man to tie down to an interview. Perhaps you could put in a word on my behalf?'

Her smile was non-committal. 'I'm afraid he's away on

business in Italy at present. And now, if you have enough information on the charity day, I'm afraid I must ask you to leave. I have a preparatory meeting to attend at the Rec.'

'One last question for the article, if I may? With such a busy and stressful life I was wondering how you and your husband seek to unwind. Do I understand you were involved in buying a racehorse last year?'

'That's right,' answered Mrs Harris, visibly relieved at what appeared to be a less threatening question. 'Both Ivan and I love the buzz of a racecourse and being part-owners of a thoroughbred has been such fun. Do you go racing, Mr Bradley?'

'No, I don't really have the time, I'm afraid,' I replied. 'But my father does. I think you may know him. Dr Thomas Bradley?'

'You are Tom's son? Of course, how silly of me. I can see it now. How is Tom? I haven't seen him for ages. Do give him my love. Now, I'm sorry but I must insist that we finish. I really do have to dash.'

'Yes, of course. I'm grateful to you for your time.'

Though I hadn't noticed her being summoned, the charmless maid had reappeared at my side, ready to escort me off the premises. As we stepped back up towards the house from the sun terrace, my eyes were drawn further up to a window in the belvedere. There for a moment, before it withdrew into the shadows, I saw the face of Ivan Harris. Not in Italy.

'I must say I do love your accent,' I said to the maid as she led me back through the all-white lounge. Silence. 'I was wondering if you had family playing for Porthcoed RFC. A brother or a loved one, perhaps? Six-three, cauliflower ears. Bit of a thug?'

She opened the front door for me, expressionless and without blinking.

'Lovely to chat,' I said. 'See you soon.'

CHAPTER 43

'I thought we agreed you weren't going to go rattling Ivan Harris's cage?' said Coma after I filed my interview with Jacqui Harris.

'I just needed to show him I'm not scared and I'm not backing off,' I told him.

'You don't know for sure that what happened to you down at the lighthouse had anything to do with Ivan Harris,' insisted Coma, removing his half-specs to rub them with his hankie. 'Why would a high-profile man like Harris, who, let's face it, has got rather a lot on his plate right now, bother with the likes of you?'

I was about to answer that when Coma started up again. 'Anyway, I thought you'd come off diary to sort out Humph? The Ice Queen will have my guts for garters if she hears you've been writing a lifestyle feature.'

'Shove one of the Twins' bylines on the story, then,' I retorted. 'It's actually a half-decent tale.'

'I don't know what she's like now but Jacqui Harris was a nice kid,' said Coma, who also hailed from Abergerran. 'Poor as church mice, Jacqui's family were. And now she's sunning herself by a swimming pool up on Deri mountain. She's done well for herself. But I'm warning you, Twm. Just you be careful messing with the likes of the Harrises.'

To avoid the prospect of bumping into Helen Snow and having to report on my lack of progress with Humph, I stepped across to Grumpy's for a sandwich. The blue sky of the morning had long gone and as I watched rain drops slide down the misted glass of the café windows I reflected on Coma's words. He was right, as usual. In terms of getting hold of

Humph, working out what had happened to Bren, and trying to prove that Ivan Harris had anything to do with any of this, I was nowhere. I needed to go back to my father. Unlikely as it seemed, he was still the best lead I had.

I knew in my bones that the two men in the BMW at the pub near the lighthouse had been Harris's men, so acting on my hunch I negotiated the roadworks on Station Road once more and, after seeing no sign of Helen Snow in the newsroom, parked myself at the Internet Terminal. My initial check through the playing roster of Porthcoed RFC – on the club's brand new website – failed to turn up any familiar faces among the overseas players Ivan Harris had bought in. But then a thought struck me. I walked back across to my desk and picked up the phone. I checked my contacts book for the number I needed, and dialled it in.

'Karl? It's Twm Bradley. I need to pick your brains again.'

'Hello, Twm, how are things? Still working on the Eddie Lennox story?'

'Sort of. Karl, tell me, have the Buzzards released their playing roster for the new season yet?'

'Funny you should ask that. I was just on the phone to Ken Thomas. I got a press release from the club on Monday morning announcing the arrival of two more players. But when I went down to watch training this morning there was no sign of them. I asked Gwyn Shell about them, and he referred me to Ken, and Ken has just got back to me saying there was a problem with their visas and the club has had to scrap both their contracts. They've gone to a club in Italy instead.'

'Where were they from?' I asked.

'They were Romanian. One was a lock forward, a big, tall unit. The other was a flanker. A lineout specialist and a ball carrier. Neither capped by Romania yet but both highly regarded.'

'Did the club release any images of these players?' I asked.

'You'd need to ask Smudge Tucker. I'm a words-only man … a dying breed, I'm reliably informed.'

I thanked Karl for his time and looked across the newsroom to Smudge's unoccupied desk. Just then Albie Evans walked by.

'Albie, seen Smudge?'

'He went off towards the d-darkroom. About t-ten minutes ago.'

'Okay, thanks Albie.'

'By the way, Twm, Helen Snow was l-looking for you. Said it was urgent. Looked p-pretty p-p-pissed off, though come to think of it that's p-pretty much her d-default expression, isn't it?'

'Is she still around?'

'I haven't s-seen her.'

While Albie returned to the newsroom I walked round the corridor to the dark room. Above the door a bulb glowed red. I knocked. From inside I heard a crash, as if a metal tray had dropped onto the floor.

'Smudge? It's Twm,' I said leaning closer to the door. 'You all right in there?'

After a moment or two the red light flicked off. I heard the bolt on the inside of the door slide open, and out came a flushed-looking Ice Queen.

'Well, thanks, Smudge,' said Helen Snow, tidying her hair. 'I think we'll go with the first two shots you showed me.' She turned to look at me. 'Twm,' was all she said, by way of a greeting, before walking past me and heading down the corridor. Apparently she no longer needed to see me urgently. I entered the windowless darkroom, now lit from the ceiling by two rows of strip lights. The room was muggy and warm, and smelled of a variety of chemicals of which Helen Snow's perfume was by some distance the most noxious.

'Sorry, Smudge. I didn't realise you were in the middle of developing something.'

'Mate, the red light was on,' said Smudge in frustration. 'What d'you want?'

I asked him if I could see the latest pictures sent over by Porthcoed RFC.

'Did you try the picture library?' asked Smudge, referring in rather grandiose terms to his photo filing system, which was contained within half a dozen 1950s-era office filing cabinets, in an order that only Smudge himself could hope to navigate with any success.

'These would only have come over from the Buzzards this week,' I explained. 'Two new signings. Romanians.'

'Oh yeah,' said Smudge. 'I remember. I binned 'em.'

'You binned them?'

'Yeah. Phone call from the Buzzards, Monday night. Said they'd been sent out in error.'

'I thought you lot never binned anything?' I asked. It was common knowledge that snappers kept everything. When I'd started at the *Gazette* the then-picture editor had even insisted on taking a shot of me. I'd imagined it was for a picture byline but had been told by a straight-faced Humph that it would be squirreled away in case I ended up dead in a car crash or in trouble with the law.

'Sorry, mate,' shrugged Smudge, pushing past me.

Back in the newsroom I resisted the urge to delve into Smudge's waste-paper basket, as a quick glance into it was enough to turn my stomach. Cigarette butts, chip paper, worn-through socks, half-empty curry containers ... unmarried newspapermen like Smudge tended to live at their desk. Besides, the mysterious disappearance of Porthcoed's two new Romanian forwards was enough to convince me of the identity of my two assailants.

CHAPTER 44

Mara was due back in Porthcoed that evening and we'd arranged to meet at the Railway. There was no sign of her when I showed up so I sat on a stool by the bar, ordered a pint of Guinness and chatted to Merve. An hour and two pints later Mara tapped me on the shoulder.

'Two more of these please, Merve,' I said. 'And something for yourself.'

'Cheers, Twm. I'll bring yours over.'

Mara and I moved away from the bar and sat at a table.

'So how was the delectable Mrs Harris?' she asked.

'Really quite likeable as it turns out,' I replied. 'I just can't figure out what these good-looking younger women see in Ivan Harris, can you?'

'Well, maybe there's something, I don't know … animalistic about him,' said Mara, who then read the quizzical expression on my face. 'Not my cup of tea. But some women go for that testosterone overload thing.'

'Helen Snow seems to,' I said. 'I stumbled across her and Smudge Tucker having a sweaty fumble in the *Gazette* darkroom this evening.' I turned to see Merve hovering right behind me, a pint of Guinness in both hands and one eye apparently on each of them. I saw him briefly process the image I had conjured, then place the drinks on our table.

'So what did you manage to glean from the second Mrs Harris?' asked Mara.

'She and Harris lost a child. Cot death.'

'Hence the charity thing. That's awful. Anything about Harris himself?'

'Not really. Jacqui said he was away on business in Italy, but on my way out I saw him peeping out of an upstairs window.'

'Keeping an eye on the missus?' asked Mara.

'Maybe. But what Jacqui said about Italy got me thinking. You remember Humph's formbook? And the picture in the *Sporting Life*?'

'Your father with Harris?'

'Yeah, the syndicate that bought the racehorse. The horse had an Italian name, as did at least two of the people in the picture with Harris and my father.'

'Is that such a big deal?'

'One way to find out.'

Chapter 45

It took me around an hour on the Internet Terminal at the *Gazette* the next morning to find what I was looking for. I began by searching the name of one of the Italians in the photo caption but 'Andrea Bianchi' seemed just too common a name around the world among both men and women. With the possibilities seemingly endless, I turned my attention to 'Giancarlo Azzotti' instead. After a couple of dead ends the search engine highlighted the name halfway down a web page in Italian. I scrolled down to the bottom but saw no images of the man standing alongside Harris and my father.

Scanning the page more closely I found several references to '*Acciaio S.p.A*'. So I opened up another tab and entered '*S.p.A Italian*'. Two consecutive pages of entries for spa holidays from Milan to Bari left me none the wiser, so I added the word 'businessman'. This did the trick, turning up an entry on the term '*Società per Azioni*' which confirmed my guess: 'This translates as Public Company in Italian'. I cleared the search box and typed in '*Acciaio*': it was Italian for steel.

I clicked back on the original tab, found the name Giancarlo Azzotti once again and then copied and pasted the two Italian words which followed it – '*amministratore delegato*' – into the search box. Mr Azzotti, it transpired, was the chief executive officer of a steel manufacturing firm, Acciaio S.p.A, based just outside the city of Verona in northern Italy.

I looked down at my notes and sensed I was missing something obvious. What was it? Of course. I picked up the *Sporting Life* again. The syndicate's horse was called Forza Aspa. Aspa was an acronym for *Acciaio Società per Azioni*. I typed in '*forza*'. I already knew it was a term commonly chanted in sports stadiums, as in '*Forza Azzurri!*' or 'Come on the Blues!' It translated literally as 'force or strength'.

Finally I cleared the search box once more and typed in both names at the same time: 'Andrea Bianchi, Giancarlo Azzotti'. This brought up the picture of the syndicate, though this version was attributed to an Italian publication, business-related by the looks of it. I searched some more but got no further clarity on the identity of Andrea Bianchi before I was distracted by one of the Germolene Twins waiting to use the Internet Terminal.

'Can it wait, Nigel?'

'I'm Aled. And no, it can't. Coma wants me to print off the agenda for tonight's full meeting of the town council.'

'You can do that?' I had meant to cast doubt on the digital readiness of Porthcoed Council, but from the look Aled shot me, it was clear that he had taken my comment personally. The truth was that he and Nigel were by far the most computer literate of the paper's staff. 'Okay. Look, it's all yours.'

I grabbed my jacket and headed out of the newsroom, down the stairs and past Teg, who was offering the facts of life to yet another punter expecting to be able to place a small ad for free. Out on Station Road I turned right. I needed the library once again.

* * *

Copies of the *Western Morning Record* dating back for the past three years had not yet been microfiched and were filed chronologically, a month at a time, on large metal rods held in racks beneath a large wooden work surface next to the far wall of the library. What I was looking for dated back at least two years so I decided to start my search earlier than that. I navigated my way to a file labelled 'JAN 1996' and slid out the corresponding metal rod. It was heavy and, as the *Record* was a broadsheet, it was bulky too. I needed both hands to swing it up and over the work surface, and the whole thing landed with more of a bang than I was anticipating. I turned and smiled apologetically at the library assistant who was grimacing in my direction. The top copy of the *Record* was a New Year's Day edition. A Monday. As I was after a Thursday Business section I had to flip over several copies. This took longer than expected as each regional edition of every day's paper had been filed. I leafed through the 'Business' pull-out but found no trace of the story I was looking for. My fingers were already black with newsprint. The romance of old-school, humdrum journalism.

Eventually I found what I was looking for in the Business section dated 15 February, 1996. The only way I could copy the story, short of jotting it down in shorthand, was to drag the bundle of papers, heavy metal rod included, to the photocopier, flip open the lid and attempt to place the story face down in the middle of the glass. There was no way I was going to be able to close the photocopier lid but as the whole bundle covered the entire top of the photocopier this didn't seem to matter. I fumbled under one corner of the paper file until I found and pressed the copy button. The machine burst into life and its light passed under the expanse of the glass and back again. I leaned across to the printout tray and saw to my frustration just a portion of the story I wanted emerge on a sheet of A4. Lifting another part of the huge newspaper bundle to search for the Paper Size Selector button I bumped it up to A3. On my third try I got it right – headline, picture, byline and all three columns on one printed sheet. I lifted the paper bundle off the photocopier and, ignoring the inky smudges I'd left all over what had been a pristine white machine, walked back to the work surface and filed the metal rod back into its rack.

'How many?' asked the library assistant.

'Er … three. Two A3, one A4.'

'That's 18p, please.'

I handed over some coins. 'Can I have a receipt please?'

The library assistant looked at me with disdain.

On my way out of the building I stopped at a phone box in the foyer and dialled Mara's mobile telephone. I heard her pick up.

'Mara, it's me. I think I know ...'

I got no further because an arm reached in front of me and disconnected the call. I turned to see the familiar face of Humph Blake.

CHAPTER 46

Humph looked drawn, as if he'd aged a decade in the month since I'd last seen him, but otherwise he was clean-shaven and smartly dressed. He'd even had a haircut, I noticed. This wasn't a hounded man sleeping rough. He took the receiver from my hand and placed it back onto the wall-mounted cradle.

'Humph. Where the hell have you been? Are you okay?'

'Of course I'm not. Bren's dead and the police want to lock me up and throw away the key. Look, we can't talk here, it's too public. Come with me.'

He led me back inside the library to the library assistant's desk. She greeted my return with a sour look but her face lit up when she saw Humph.

'Donna, I need a favour.'

'Humph, of course. What can I do for you, love?'

'I need somewhere quiet where I can talk to Twm here. Have you got a back room or an office or somewhere where we won't be disturbed?'

Donna led us to the back of the main library reading room, to a door marked 'Staff Only'. She unlocked it with a key from a large bunch she carried with her and we followed her in. The room was dark and windowless. The overhead lighting flickered on to reveal a table and chairs, a fridge and a stainless-steel sink unit complete with a kettle.

'It's the staff rest room, but I'm the only one on duty for another two hours so you'll be safe in here for now. Humph, is everything all right, love?' asked Donna. 'I was so sorry to hear about Brenda.'

'Thanks, Donna. It's been a shock, but look, I really need to speak to Twm. Would you mind?'

'Of course,' said Donna. 'She was a lovely lady, Brenda. It's so sad to think she's gone.' She scanned me up and down once more before leaving and closing the door behind her.

I had so many questions for Humph that I really didn't know where to begin. I started with, 'How did you know I was here?'

'I followed you from the *Gazette*.'

'Really?' I made a mental note to be much more observant in future. 'Where have you been?'

'I've been staying with a friend.'

'Humph, what's going on?' I asked.

'It's … a bit of a mess,' he replied, scratching at his moustache with his finger. He pulled a chair from under the table, sat down and gestured for me to do the same. 'When Bryn Thomas released me from the station that Friday I went home and rang you, if you recall, to ask you round. But just after we spoke I got a call from a stringer I know in the city. He said he'd been monitoring police radio transmissions and had picked up some chatter about a woman's body being discovered at the national stadium site. He told me that he'd heard someone say that ID found with the body suggested it might be Bren.' He paused, ashen-faced, as if reliving the reality that he was describing. 'I just knew it was. And I realised immediately, thinking back on Bryn's line of questioning about Bren being missing, that it was going to look like I killed her. Something to do with the missing *Gazette* money. I knew I had to disappear and quickly.'

'The police say Bren was killed on the Wednesday night, Humph. No one saw you from the time you left me at Grumpy's on the Wednesday morning to when you met Mara there early the next day. Where were you on Wednesday night?'

'I was at home. Waiting to hear from Bren.'

'But you can't prove that.'

'Twm, can't you see? Someone is trying to fit me up … for murdering my own wife.'

'But who on earth would want to kill Bren? And why at the stadium? What has all this got to do with Delilah Sullivan?'

'I'm still trying to work it all out myself,' answered Humph. 'But it's next to impossible for me to do that without showing myself, which is why I need your help.'

'That day you hit me with a plant pot you said you thought Bren "had been taken". But you didn't act like a husband worried sick about his wife. Why not?'

'I made that up,' said Humph, sheepishly. 'I was jumpy as hell because of what had happened with the *Gazette* cash and I was embarrassed that I had hurt you. What I told Bryn was true. Bren and I had a row. She stormed out of the house. Whenever she does that ... whenever she did that ... she usually rings a day or so later from her sister's. I thought she would ring, but she never did.' Humph composed himself and looked at me squarely in the eye. 'Twm, will you help me?'

After a pause I nodded.

'Thank you. Now, did you get my formbook? I had to bung George Mellor a tenner to fix that drawer of yours in a hurry.'

'Yeah, I did, but it was touch and go for a minute. Bryn Thomas came across it while he was searching the newsroom. Thankfully Coma managed to put him off the scent by telling him it was just you and your horses.'

'Smarter than he looks, old Coma. And he'll need to be with Helen Snow in my chair.'

'Humph, why didn't you tell me that my father was working with Harris on the stadium build?'

'Because at first I didn't know exactly what it was that I'd found out. I've been digging into Ivan Harris's affairs ever since he came back to Porthcoed. As I've already told you, we have shared history, Ivan and me. I've never trusted him and, with a man like that, attack is the best form of defence. I'd just turned my attention to his involvement in the national stadium project when I opened the *Sporting Life* in Grumpy's one morning and happened upon that picture. I was always going to tell you.'

'I've worked out the Italian connection, I think,' I told him. 'That's why I'm here. I remembered a fuss in the *Record* a few years back when they found out that the new national stadium was going to be built with Italian steel, at a time when local steelmakers were being laid off. I've just printed out the story.'

'The Italian thing is as far as I managed to get, before, well …'

'I'm so sorry about Bren, Humph. She was a wonderful woman, always so kind to me.'

Humph wrestled his thoughts back to what he needed to say. 'Twm, you've got to follow the Italian lead. Ask your father. I don't know where it'll take us but I do know that something is up in Harris's world and I'm guessing it's connected. I haven't been able to prove it yet but my suspicion is that Harris has money trouble. Big time.'

'You're kidding? Have you seen his house? He's got a rugby ball-shaped swimming pool for Christ's sake. They've got servants, the lot …'

'I'm telling you, nothing is quite how it seems when it comes to Ivan Harris. Contrary to all impressions he's only spent a few thousand quid on the Buzzards since he arrived.'

'What about all those foreign signings?'

'Eastern Europeans and Pacific Islanders? He pays them peanuts. They only come over to try and get a break in the British game. He hasn't spent a cent on the Rec since he took it over. He'll cover it with houses the minute he gets the chance. Most of the money he's spent has been on PR, trying to make himself look rich and successful, so that he could cosy up to the governing body and get the new stadium contract.'

'Just what is it about the stadium, Humph? First Delilah, now Bren?'

He paused and in his eyes I could see the struggle going

on inside him. 'I'm not sure, yet. But the one constant is Ivan Harris and so we need to find out exactly what is going on in his world right now. There's more to his relationship with the Italians than meets the eye. I'm sure of it. You have a way in to all that now, with your father. You've got to find out what he knows.'

'Last time I tried that I almost ended up driving off a cliff,' I told him. 'With a little help from a couple of Harris's thugs.'

'Really? Christ,' said Humph, letting the idea sink in for a moment. 'But doesn't the fact that both of us have been getting that sort of attention lately suggest that we're on the right lines?'

'Listen, what are you going to do now?' I asked Humph. 'You can't just swan around Porthcoed in broad daylight. Practically everyone in this town is on first-name terms with you. How long do you think it would take Bryn Thomas to track you down?'

'Don't worry about me. Here, make a note of this.' He read out a telephone number with a dialling code for the city. 'You can leave a message for me there. Call when you come across anything new. But follow the Italian lead, Twm. The Italian lead, your father and Harris's money. And don't trust anyone. Coma and Teg, but nobody else, okay?'

At that point we shook hands and then Humph hugged me, very much for the first time in our relationship. He turned and walked to the door. He opened it a fraction and looked outside.

'Okay. You go first. I'll wait a few minutes before I leave.'

'Look after yourself,' I said.

'I'll be okay,' Humph replied. 'You just mind how you go.'

I walked back through to the foyer of the library, nodding briefly to Donna, who ignored me. I considered calling Mara again from the payphone, but common sense told me to distance myself from Humph as quickly as possible – for his sake. At the top of the library steps I studied the street, suddenly self-conscious. I saw no shadowy figures lurking in a doorway with a newspaper, and the only parked cars I could see were empty. So I pulled up the lapel of my jacket and set off down the steps in the direction of my flat.

CHAPTER 47

Mara arrived at the flat later that evening. I was about to reveal my encounter with Humph when she told me she'd had a call from Eddie Lennox. 'He's on his way down here.'

'Why's he coming here?' I asked.

'He's going to be interviewed by WTV. A guy called Mike something?'

'Jenkins-Jones. Fuck. How did he get on to Lennox?'

'I don't know. But it needn't be a problem.'

'What's their angle?'

'A documentary, from what I could tell. Fallen ex-City star's bid for redemption. It's about the pardon.'

'When did you find out about this?

'Just now. I just took a call from Lennox. He asked me if it was okay and I said it wouldn't harm his case.'

'It might not harm his case but what about our story?'

'Just think about it for a moment. Lennox says he's the victim of a thirty-year-old miscarriage of justice. After Bren's death everyone from WTV to *Match of the Day* is going to be crawling all over him. He was a big football star in his day. But he's promised me that I am the only newsprint journalist that he's going to talk to. And it's up to me if I want to bring you in on that.'

'So you're going to meet up with him?'

'*We're* going to meet up with him.' She walked into the bathroom, adding from behind the door, 'Tomorrow morning at his hotel near Central Station.'

Opening the fridge door I made up my mind not to tell Mara about my meeting with Humph. I'd tell her about the Italians but no more.

'You want a beer?'

'No thanks,' said Mara, over the sound of running bath water. 'I've been drinking far too much ever since I came to this town. You're a bad influence on me, Twm Bradley.'

* * *

Later, as I was cooking us some pasta, Mara asked me about my aborted call to her mobile. I showed her the cutting I'd copied at the library and filled her in on what I had discovered about Giancarlo Azzotti and the Italian steel contract for the stadium.

'Is that such a big deal?' asked Mara. 'Harris needs cheap steel for the new stadium so he goes to a cheap Italian steel firm. And to seal the deal he entertains the CEO on the racecourse and they buy a thoroughbred. That's standard business etiquette for the likes of Ivan Harris, isn't it?'

'Etiquette is not a word that can be associated with Ivan Harris,' I replied, trying to separate two fused strands of spaghetti in the steaming pan. 'There's just something not quite right about it all,' I added. 'What's my father doing with these guys, for starters?'

'He's a hydrologist, you said. An expert in groundwater working on a big construction project next to a river using Italian steel. Is that such a surprise?'

'Also I couldn't identify this Andrea Bianchi guy. Who is he and what's he got to do with it?'

'Someone at the Italian steel firm, maybe,' said Mara. 'Local mayor perhaps?'

I turned off the hob ring, drained the spaghetti water into a bowl of washing up and slopped the steaming pasta into a dish on the sideboard. I placed the dish on the table next to a pot of pesto and then noticed my chair had been taken. 'And you can fuck off, cat.'

'Don't be so mean. She's probably hungry.'

I swooped on Modlen from behind. She made a lunge for me, but I had her safely at arm's length. At the door of the flat, open in the warm evening air, I dropped her gently onto the top step, hopped back inside and shut the door. 'Let her eat mice.'

Chapter 48

We took an early train into the city and at 9.30 a.m. found Eddie Lennox in the hotel bar. On the table beside him stood two glasses, each empty but for a slice of lemon and half an inch of melting ice. Lennox was drinking from a third glass which was half-full.

I had seen pictures of Lennox in his prime but in the face of the man who reached over to shake my hand there was very little resemblance to the good-looking sixties fashion icon. Just the familiar lop-sided grin beneath that long, straight nose, which like his ears was now exaggerated with age. What little hair Lennox had left was shaved down to a ring of grey stubble around the back of his head, with just the shadow of some sideburns on either side. The skin on his clean-shaven face was leathery, pallid and wrapped tightly across his cheekbones. Only his eyes, remarkably blue and vivid, hinted at something out of the ordinary about this man, otherwise just another slightly seedy late-middle-aged man in a dark suit in a city-centre hotel.

'Tom, pleasure to meet you,' said Lennox, who remained seated but shifted the glass to his left hand to extend his right. His Scots accent was still strong.

'It's Twm,' Mara corrected him.

'Twm. Forgive me,' said Lennox, transferring the glass back to his dominant hand to take another drink. 'It's a fair few years since I've been in this town. A lot of mixed memories, y'know?'

'You must have many good memories of your time here, Mr Lennox,' I said.

'Eddie, please. Call me Eddie. Can I get youse two a drink by the way?'

'No thanks, Eddie, we're fine,' said Mara as we sat down with him.

'The darling of the Bob Bank in the mid-sixties, so I read?'

'Aye, I had some good times here,' he said, and the deep creases on his face which suggested a lifetime of frowning were rearranged into a smile. 'It was a different era. Have you seen the moolah they earn today?'

'Not in the third division, they don't.'

'City will be back. Mark my words, Tom. They've got another good Scottish manager now. He'll see them right.'

The barman arrived with a fresh glass just as Lennox was gesticulating with his hand and the barman's glass went flying, smashing on the floor and sending ice and glass in all directions.

'Fer fuck's sake, ye clumsy wee bast …'

Lennox's brief outburst ended almost before it had begun but it had been volcanic enough to render the young barman temporarily speechless. After busying himself retrieving the remains of the tumbler, he stood up and managed, 'I'm so sorry, Mr Edwards, your arm swung round just as I …'

'It's Lennox, okay? Eddie Lennox. Look, forget that. Just get someone to bring me another drink, will ye son?' Lennox's tone was genuinely apologetic now, which only served to emphasise his outburst. A thirty-year stretch inside had done little to tame the infamous Lennox temper, I told myself. But then I supposed it wouldn't have made me a barrel of laughs either. 'Sorry, Tom. Where were we?'

'As I explained on the phone, Eddie, Twm is helping us with the story,' said Mara.

The barman returned with another drink.

'It may be a story to youse two. To me it's been my whole life. I had my best years taken from me. Nothing can bring back my football career. The only thing that matters to me now is clearing my name and if I have to spend the rest of my days doing that I will.'

'And we can help you,' Mara assured him.

'I wanted to ask you some questions, Eddie,' I said. 'Is that okay?'

'I've answered more questions than you've had hot dinners, son. Water off a duck's back. Do your worst.' He drained his glass, turned in the direction of the bar and raised his voice. 'Hey pal, can I get another wee drink here?'

I glanced at Mara. She replied with an almost imperceptible shake of the head as if to say, 'Don't worry about it. It's not a problem.'

Eddie turned back to face me. 'Ask away, son.'

'Thanks. Can you start by telling me how you met Angharad Sullivan?'

Chapter 49

Angharad who?

Ha! I'm just pullin' yer shank, Tom. Sorry, son, it's hard to keep a sense of humour sometimes. It's just a game I play, you know. No hard feelings? Okay. How did I meet Angie Sullivan? We met one day not long after I arrived at City. I found myself having my barnet done by this wee mixed-race girl in a hairdresser's salon. She was a pretty young thing, I can tell you. She made me laugh by kidding on I was that famous rugby guy, y'know. That was Angie.

When did I first learn that she was still married? It was her boss, French bird, who told me. Not long after I met Angie. I think she was warning me off. She said Angie had had a tough time with her husband and she'd been hurt by the break-up of their marriage.

But it takes more than that to scare me off, son. It was the 1960s. You probably read about those days, eh? Free love and all that? Young people like Angie and I did what we wanted. Indulged ourselves. I asked Angie out and we dated a few times. She liked the nightlife, and I took her round the clubs. She was a bit of a wild one, if you know what I mean.

Then one night, in the Morocco, Angie and I had a falling out. She came across me having a bit of a fumble with another wee girl and she stormed out. I went out after her but I lost her. We were both fair hammered, you know? I ended up going back inside but the wee girl had disappeared as well. So I must have consoled myself with a few more bevvies and the next thing I know I'm waking up back at my digs lunchtime the next day with the police hammering on my door. As I told them, after Angie left it was all a bit of a blur.

The prints on her shoe? I don't know. Maybe I picked up her shoe for her sometime. Girls liked to dance barefoot, back then, you know?

I'd never met Ivan Harris before he stepped into the dock and told a jury a pack of lies that ruined my life. Why? I've spent many a long night trying to figure that out, Tom. I didn't even know the man. All I can think is that he was jealous of me. Good-looking, famous football star going out with his wife. I can understand that, y'know? We're none of us perfect.

Aye, he stole my life from me. But you eat yourself alive if you think that way. I have a wee bit of a temper, Tom. Always have had. It's what made me a great player, my old gaffer at City used to say. Chip on both shoulders. But I had to learn to survive inside. I spent my first few years in the big house fighting anyone and everything until I realised that I had to change if I was going to make it back out into the world again. So I changed. I learned to hold my temper. I found God, son. I hated Harris, of course I did, but in the end I found it easier to forgive the man. It's all gone, now, anyway, hasn't it? Pish down the lavvie. What can I do to get it back? City aren't exactly gonna pick up the phone and offer me a contract now, are they?

Who? Blake? No, I cannae remember anyone by that name. He was the guy from the local paper? Okay. No, Angie never said anything about him. Friend of hers, was he?

Them? Oh, they got in touch a couple of weeks back and asked me to do something for a documentary. I need all the publicity I can get. I'm trying to get my conviction overturned here and Mara's cool with it, aren't you darlin'?

Chapter 50

Our meeting was broken up by the arrival, earlier than agreed, of Mike the Hairdo, his producer and a two-man camera crew. After a rather stilted round of introductions, Mara and I left them to it.

'What did you make of Eddie, then?' Mara asked me as we crossed the road into one of the arcades, on our way to Risoli's café this time.

'He's a charmer, your Mr Lennox, isn't he? Does he always have vodka for breakfast?'

'He's not my Mr Lennox,' answered Mara. 'And let's just say he's still adjusting to life on the outside.'

We ordered two coffees and perched on two tall stools next to a narrow, chest-high shelf on the opposite wall to the counter.

'Remind me how you got to hear about Lennox?'

'He found me,' said Mara. 'There's a Scottish guy on our sports desk, a pal of mine. He was a pal of Eddie's back in the sixties and he tipped me off that he was being released and said he'd probably talk to me.'

'I don't buy convict Eddie's Road to Damascus-style prison conversion, do you?' I asked. 'Seems to me the temper that landed him in this mess is alive and well.'

'He's a complex character. Old school, vain ... but, ask yourself, how would you feel in the same circumstances?'

'Oh, I have,' I replied. 'So you believe he was set up, then? That he had nothing to do with Delilah Sullivan's murder?'

'He's no angel, but I just don't think he killed her.'

'So who do you think did?'

A cry of 'One cappuccino, one black,' took Mara off to

the glass-topped counter. She returned with the coffees, two napkins, a couple of sachets of sugar and two spoons.

'You didn't answer my question,' I said.

She smiled into her coffee and continued to stir in a sachet of sugar. 'I try to keep an open mind,' she said. 'I find it doesn't help to have a pre-conceived idea about these things.' She licked her spoon before placing it on her saucer.

'Whatever happened to the good, old-fashioned journalistic hunch?'

'It's just the way I work,' she said.

Something about Mara's reluctance to share her thinking with me pulled me up slightly. It was a reminder that whatever had passed between us we were still reporters from two different news outlets working on the same story. And old habits die hard. I'd already chosen to keep my meeting with Humph from her. She was apparently choosing to be cagey with me. I made a mental note that a quick audit of who shared what between us might be in order and drank my coffee.

CHAPTER 51

'So who was the piece of skirt on the train with you?'

I'd been summoned to the Ice Queen's lair shortly after arriving for work on the Monday morning. After our recent encounter outside the darkroom it was clear Helen Snow was revelling in an early opportunity to level the playing field with me. She wasn't one to let anyone hold an advantage over her for long.

'I didn't see you,' I said.

'Too loved up, by the looks of it. So who is she?'

'No one you'd know, and to be honest I don't think it's any of your business who I spend my time with.'

'It bloody is when you're on works time, matey,' she spat back at me. 'We've already had words about this, you and I, but I'm beginning to think you're not listening.' She leaned across her desk to retrieve a dummy layout of that week's *Gazette*, which she waved in front of me. 'Where's your story, Twm?'

'I'll file a lead on the latest in the police investigation today. There's a press conference this afternoon. We can update on Wednesday.'

'If I want police handouts I'll send one of those pimple-faced kids from the newsroom,' she said. 'You seem to be forgetting that there's a lot riding on your investigation; not least my reinstatement into the good books of Sir Norman Bentall, which is going to happen with or without the continued existence of this backwater rag, do you understand? But what do I get from you? A jolly to the seaside with your old man, where you manage to total a pool car, and a morning out in the city with your floozy.'

She walked back around the desk to her chair where she sat

down. When she spoke again it was in a measured tone, which was no less threatening.

'Now you listen to me, Twm Bradley, and listen well. You can forget all about police press conferences and start getting the job done like a proper news reporter. You've got one more week to pull the rabbit out of the hat on this Humph Blake story or I'll have you covering every charity knitting evening and silver wedding anniversary in this pathetic little town.'

She leaned forwards towards me. 'And if I find you're holding anything back from me I'll see to it that you never work in another newsroom on either side of the border. Do you understand?'

* * *

'You all right?' asked Coma as I returned to the newsroom.
I nodded.

'I tried my best to keep her at bay, but …'

'I know you did. Thanks. I had it coming though.'

'Just what is happening with Humph? Are you getting any closer to finding him?'

I turned and scanned the newsroom, which was empty but for either Aled or Nigel on the telephone halfway across the office. I still wasn't completely sure which was which. At least two other telephones were ringing on the desks in between him and us so I figured I could get away with it in a soft voice.

'I saw Humph on Friday,' I said and Coma's eyes lit up. 'But that's between you and me.' Coma nodded. 'He's okay. In better shape than I expected, to be honest. But he knows the amount of trouble he's in.' Before Coma could interrupt I added, 'He said he's been investigating Ivan Harris's business affairs for some time now. And it looks a little like Harris has been trying to take him out as a result. Humph's convinced that all is not well in the Harris camp, and he thinks it might have something to do with the national stadium project.'

'What are you going to do? We can't keep fobbing off the Ice Queen. She's a sharp one, this girl.'

'I know that, but there's no way I can work all this out in the time she's given me.'

'How long has she given you?'

'A week.'

'Can't we throw her some kind of a bone?' said Coma after a moment of thought. 'Put our heads together and come up with something to keep her quiet?'

'Like what? Humph didn't exactly want to pose for a picture.'

'Well, I'll do what I can to hold her off, but I can't promise …'

'Thanks. Look I've got to run but I'll keep you posted, I promise.'

'Twm, before you go. Your father called the office. He's phoned a couple of times today. Asked if you'd call him. Soon as you can.'

Chapter 52

I caught a train back into the city. It was a week to the day since I'd last seen my father but this time I was ready for him. Nothing sharpens the mind like adrenaline and one way or another I'd had my fair share in recent days.

Passing unchallenged through the ticket barrier, which always annoyed me, I scanned the long foyer of Central Station for Mara. She'd said she had some business in the city first but offered to come along with me to confront the old man, and I'd liked the idea of arriving at his door with someone he didn't know. It would knock him nicely off balance. I'd managed to get an earlier train than planned and there was no sign of her anywhere so I joined a short queue at the coffee stall. I'd just reached the front of the queue when in the corner of my eye, through the glass panel doors of the station, I noticed a white saloon car pull up in one of the few drop-off spaces at the front of the station. Through two panes of glass I made out the dark silhouettes of the driver and passenger, both female. There was something about the passenger that looked familiar and that must have been what had caught my eye.

'Can I help you?' The stallholder's voice turned my head back to the job at hand.

'Er, black coffee, please. And a cappuccino. Both small.'

Glancing back to my left again I saw the passenger door of the white saloon car open and out stepped Mara. She stood upright for a moment, and then leaned back into the car with one hand on the open door. Though it was hard to tell exactly what was going on I knew enough about Mara's body language by now to know that she wasn't happy. Although there was no way of hearing her I was pretty sure she was shouting.

She slammed the car door with a flourish, and turned towards the entrance to the station. Now it was plain for all to see that she was angry. I paid for the coffee and walked over to the entrance to meet her, glad to rid myself of one of the red-hot cardboard cups.

'Problems?'

Mara looked down at the floor as if to compose herself and then lifted her head with a jaded smile. 'It's nothing. Taxi driver hit on me.'

'Really?' I replied, quickly replaying the memory to reassure myself that the near side, at least, of the saloon car had been unmarked and its driver's silhouette had definitely appeared female. 'Not your type, then?'

'Well, as much as I go for your overweight man with dandruff and odour issues, this one had mean eyes,' she joked. 'Not kind like yours. Thanks for the coffee.'

I gestured towards the door and we set off on foot towards the Bay. Mara was quick to move the conversation on so I decided to make a note of the lie and let it go.

After twenty minutes of walking we turned right onto the Wharf, a stretch of new-build apartment blocks leading up the side of the East Dock towards the new headquarters of the city council, which had been erected a decade before as an early sign of the seriousness of the city's intent in the Bay. Around 100 yards further on we turned right into a car park. It took me a while to identify the right apartment block, find the correct doorbell, but eventually I succeeded and my father buzzed us up.

'Twm,' he said as soon as he saw me. 'Are you okay, son? I heard ...'

'I'm okay. This is Mara. She's going to go and make us a cup of tea while you and I have a chat.'

Mara smiled at my father and headed into the kitchen.

'Why did you walk out on me in the pub?'

'I didn't … it's not …'

'We're sitting having a chat. You go to the bar to get another round of beers in. Two heavies walk in, whisper something in your ear and you walk straight out spouting some shit about a fax.'

'I had no idea what was going to happen.'

'So you know what happened, then?'

'I only found out this morning,' he said. He looked at me, thoughts apparently crowding his mind, and then sat down on the front edge of the sofa. I sat on an armchair opposite him. My father shifted his backside slightly and slowly reclined until he was leaning against the back of the sofa. He stared up at the ceiling. After a moment or two he sat forward again, the palms of his hands clamped together as if in prayer.

'I've … I've got myself into a bit of a jam with Ivan Harris,' he said. 'When his people contacted me to sound me out about working on the stadium rebuild I was thrilled. Retirement's been a bit of a struggle. I've felt very isolated. I've been surrounded by people my whole working life, you know? So I jumped at the chance.'

'Why did Harris come to you?'

'Well, I like to think I've built up a bit of a reputation, you know, for the research I've done over the years. And there isn't exactly a limitless supply of people in this part of the world with my particular skill set.'

'What exactly did he want you to do?'

'To understand that, you need to understand the history of the stadium site,' he said and paused again. 'Look, just bear with me a moment while I explain it to you, okay?

'You might know, son, that the stretch of land on which the new stadium is being built has a history of flooding. In technical terms the natural water table on that stretch of land is 4.2 metres above ordnance datum – above sea level, if you like.

'In the early part of the nineteenth century the river didn't flow the way it does now, on the west side of the stadium. It used to flow down the other side closest to the city centre. And, as the river was tidal, most of the land where the stadium is being built used to be under water.

'But then in the 1840s, when they were looking to bring the railway into the city, they wanted a good site for the central station. Isambard Kingdom Brunel, the engineer, took a look at the whole area and decided to re-route the river, reclaiming the land on which the stadium is being built now, and also freeing up the site where Central Station is located today.'

At this point Mara emerged from the kitchen with three mugs of tea, and my father broke off briefly while the niceties of milk and sugar were negotiated.

'Now far be it for me to criticise a genius like Brunel,' he continued, 'but there's been a flood risk on that land ever since. Which is not ideal seeing as it became a sports ground, hosting cricket, rugby and the like. Then during the war a couple of the ground's stands were hit by the Luftwaffe and its drainage system was damaged. In the fifties a big global sporting event put further stress on it, and after that the playing surface of the rugby pitch there quite often became a quagmire. The other home rugby nations regularly used to complain about the state of the pitch.'

He broke off again, to try and foist some biscuits on us. We both declined. 'So ... where was I?'

'A quagmire.'

'That's right. So then in around 1960 the river burst its banks and the old rugby-club ground found itself under four feet of water. That was the beginning of the end. Over the next few years they decided they needed to build a whole new stadium. There were many who wanted to move it out of the city completely. But, eventually, they settled on redeveloping the existing site, and built the new national stadium right alongside the old rugby-club ground.

'They started the North Stand in the late sixties, laid the pitch and played on it while they finished the rest of the build. That first national stadium became world-famous but it didn't last long. Ten years after it was officially opened in the mid-eighties they decided to knock it all down again.'

'Why was that?' asked Mara.

'The governing body won the rights to host the next world tournament,' I answered. 'It was decided that the existing stadium's capacity of fifty-odd thousand wasn't big enough. Not enough corporate facilities. They needed a bigger, shinier stadium to squeeze the most revenue out of the opportunity.'

'And this bigger, shinier stadium needs to be ready by June next year,' said my father.

'June? But I thought the tournament wasn't due to start until October?' I asked.

'The opening ceremony is scheduled for the beginning of October. But in order for the stadium to be able to stage a full house then it needs a safety certificate, and getting a safety certificate is a bit of a process, and a tricky one at that. As part of this process the stadium needs to prove it can successfully stage a series of limited-capacity matches, with the first one around June time. Miss that deadline and there's almost no way back.'

'But can they get the new stadium finished enough to stage a match by then?' asked Mara. 'I mean, from what I've seen it still looks like a bomb site.'

'That ... is Ivan Harris's problem,' my father said.

'So where do you come in?' I asked. He stood up and walked towards the window of the living room, which overlooked the skyline of the city centre towards cranes above the stadium site.

'There was some concern that the amount of preparatory drainage and flood-prevention work needed on the site could not possibly be completed satisfactorily in time for the scheduled building work to begin. As I've explained, it's an area of land that's had a problem with groundwater for a century or more. I was brought in to … advise on this key part of the project.'

'So what exactly is this "jam" you said you've got yourself into with Ivan Harris?'

There was no answer.

'Are you trying to tell me that Harris is cutting corners on the stadium build in order to get the thing ready in time?'

Silence.

'But aren't there laws about that?' I continued. 'Procedures that have to be followed? Building safety regulations, that sort of thing?'

My father simply shrugged.

'You mean Ivan Harris has pulled a fast one on the safety of the build in order to save time and money?'

My father turned to face me. 'He's in deep, Twm. He's promised he'll deliver a stadium in time for the tournament. Can you imagine what would happen if it wasn't ready? Financial meltdown. Not just for him, personally – and he has an awful lot riding on this – but for the entire game of rugby here. And that's just for starters. Never mind rugby, it would be a complete humiliation for the rapidly-growing capital of a newly devolved nation. The stadium rebuild is the shop window for the development of this city as an up-and-coming European capital. It doesn't bear thinking about, but the tournament's organising body is already so worried about the possibility of the stadium not being finished in time that it's drawn up a contingency plan for the final to be played in Scotland. "Fiasco" is the word they're using.'

'So you're implicated in this fix, too?'

'It's not that simple, son,' he replied.

'Don't give me that. You're a part of this, aren't you?

The cover-up. No wonder Harris had his thugs keeping an eye on you. That's what they were doing down at the lighthouse, wasn't it? They were following you, not me. It must have been embarrassing for you that your son was a journalist. And it must have looked suspicious as hell that you should choose to meet up with me for the first time in years at this particular moment in time. No wonder you suggested a quiet little pub in the middle of nowhere.'

'I tried everything I could to protect you,' said my father. 'Why do you think I haven't been in touch with you for the past year?'

'We haven't seen each other for years. So how come you suddenly decided to meet me last week?'

'Well, firstly you didn't ring until last week. But recently I ... I've started to have misgivings about the whole Harris situation. When you got in touch I decided I would meet you, drop a hint or two about the situation and then decide on whether or not to make a clean breast of it.'

'You suddenly developed a conscience, you mean? So how's that going for you? I nearly went over a cliff because of you. Did it not cross your mind that you might have been followed to our meeting?'

'I'm a scientist, for God's sake. I'm not into all this cloak-and-dagger stuff. If I'd known what was going to happen, what they almost did to you, I'd have ...'

'You'd have ... what, exactly? Warned me before you left? Why didn't you?'

Chapter 53

'You have to understand what they've got over me,' said my father, his eyes pleading for understanding.

'And what exactly is that?'

'It's complicated.'

'It always is.'

'It wouldn't have anything to do with a racehorse and a couple of Italian gentlemen, I don't suppose?' asked Mara.

My father twisted round to look at her and then turned back towards me.

'I'm sorry, but who exactly did you say she is?'

'My name is Mara McKenzie, Dr Bradley, and I can speak for myself. I'm a journalist working for a national newspaper based in London.'

'For fuck's sake … Twm, I thought she was your girlfriend. What the hell is going on here?'

'I think you were about to tell *us* what's going on.'

My father wandered over to a sideboard in one corner of the living room and poured himself a large whisky. 'Anyone?' We both declined.

'Before you start taking any of this down we've got to agree that this is all off the record, okay? And then we'll see where we go with it afterwards. Is that agreed?'

Both Mara and I nodded and he returned to the sofa, sat down and began to choose his words carefully.

'Ivan Harris is way out of his depth on the stadium project. Okay, we know he's built everything from flats to factories in his time. The governing body wouldn't hand its golden egg over to just anyone. But Harris hasn't worked with public money before. And he's bringing his own inimitable private-sector approach to the job.'

'In what way?' asked Mara.

'Cheap raw materials sourced from … interesting foreign firms.'

'So what's so wrong with saving some public money by getting a better deal on the steel?' Mara continued. 'Or are you saying the steel isn't fit for purpose?'

'The steel is okay. But it's cheap because the Italian firm Harris is dealing with has let him have it at practically cost price.'

'What do you mean?'

'Well, let's just say it's a loss-leader for them. But the truth is they didn't have much say in the matter.'

'I'm sorry?' I asked him.

He shrugged.

'You're kidding,' I said. 'The mafia?'

'Call it that if you want to. I don't have the first clue about that sort of thing but I do know that the guy who is behind all this comes from a background of European-wide organised crime.'

'And that would be Andrea Bianchi?' I asked. My father looked surprised but nodded.

'So what's in it for Ivan Harris, apart from cheap steel?' asked Mara.

'And what's in it for the steel firm?' I added.

'Don't underestimate the value of what Harris has saved on the cost of steel on this project,' my father said. 'If he pulls off this stadium project, on time and either on or under budget, he's laughing. And so is the steel firm. There are sporting stadiums all across the world that are coming to the end of their natural lifespan around now, and thanks to his Italian-based connections Ivan Harris could be building new stadiums with Italian steel for the next twenty years.

'But there's a catch. The trouble for Harris lies in the penalty clauses he signed with the governing body when he took on the stadium project. If he overshoots the agreed budget on the build, or misses the deadline for completing it, he is financially liable. And Harris is already massively overstretched financially. He purposely overstretched in order to clinch the stadium contract. He's all in on this. And if he can't pay the Italians, he's as good as dead.'

'None of this explains why you walked out on me that day at the pub.'

'At the bar that afternoon Harris's guys told me they were under orders to warn you off. Nothing serious. They promised me they wouldn't do anything to harm you. Just give you a scare. I decided I needed you to back off a bit for your own safety so I left them to it. I'm so sorry, son, but you have to believe me when I say that I was trying to protect you.'

'So where does the racehorse syndicate come into all this?' asked Mara.

'It wasn't something I wanted to do but it was made plain to me that if I didn't accept an invitation to become part-owner of this horse it wouldn't go well for me.'

'It was Harris's way of visibly connecting you to the Italians,' said Mara. 'So that if it went tits-up you'd be implicated too. It was his insurance that you would stay onside.'

'Either that or they're all fitting me up as some kind of fall-guy to protect themselves,' my father replied. 'That wouldn't surprise me in the least.'

'If it is true that you have had second thoughts about your involvement in this, and you want to help put the situation right, we're going to need some hard evidence,' I said. 'What proof can you give us that Harris has taken short cuts with safety?'

'I have nothing in my possession that can prove it,' he replied. 'And I can't imagine that Ivan Harris will have left any sort of a paper trail on something like this, can you?'

'But is there anything you can get your hands on?'

'Give me a few days,' he said. 'I'll see what I can do. Though first I think I'm going to need to sit down with my lawyer.'

CHAPTER 54

Although we had much to discuss, Mara and I hardly spoke on the train back to Porthcoed. The carriage we were in was crowded and noisy and I for one didn't want to shout about what I'd heard. The train pulled into the station and we filed through the barriers, out of the station into the night air.

'Do you want to get a taxi?' Mara asked.

'I'd rather walk,' I replied and we set off towards my flat.

'Bit of a turn-up,' said Mara, biting her lip to avoid too much of an ironic smile.

'My father being linked to a criminal conspiracy involving Italian organised crime, you mean?'

'Well, yes. There's that. I was thinking more about Ivan Harris...'

'I'd have put money on Harris being involved in something like that,' I told her.

'So where does this all fit in with the Stadium Murders, do you suppose?'

I glanced back at Mara and shrugged my shoulders. 'My head is so full of information right now I'm just struggling to take it all in.'

As we turned the corner onto Terrace Road we saw flashing lights in the distance. I began to smell smoke. Something tightened deep inside my stomach. At the corner shop Aarav was standing on the pavement.

'Twm,' he said, looking relieved. 'You're okay? I'm so glad.'

'Yeah, why?' I asked. But then I knew. I left Aarav and ran the hundred yards towards the car park at the back of the doctors' surgery, where two teams of firefighters were directing hoses up towards my flat, which was well ablaze.

'Woah, son, that'll do,' said a heavily-clad fire officer, sticking out an arm to block my path, and then guiding me away from the heat.

'That's my flat,' I told him. 'What happened?'

'Was there anyone in there, do you know?' he asked me.

'No. No one,' I said.

'Just a cat,' said Mara, who'd caught up with me.

I sat back on a low brick wall and watched as the flat, and almost everything I owned in the world, burned. Mara sat beside me, her arm across my shoulders, knowing better than to speak.

'Some good news, son,' said the fire officer, returning after a short while with his arms in a cradle. 'We've rescued your cat.'

* * *

We spent the night at the Railway, where Mara had kept a room. I didn't sleep, in spite of the whisky Merve foisted upon me in sympathy. At first light I rose from the bed, dressed in silence in the only clothes I now possessed and let myself out. I needed some air.

By 6.30 a.m. I was standing at the back of the flat. The rickety staircase was charred black, warped and had finally come loose from the building. The back door and all visible windows were either missing or else tarry rectangular shadows. I turned away and after a short while found myself outside Grumpy's.

'You look like you haven't slept a wink,' said Grumpy, unlocking the door.

'Just bring me a strong black coffee, will you?'

'Okay, okay. Someone got out the wrong side of the bed this morning,' he muttered, disappearing back behind the counter.

Two hours later I was still sitting at the window, watching the road crew churning up dust on Station Road. How long had they been at it, I wondered. It seemed like forever. By now the café had filled up but I remained detached from the chatter all around me until a figure slid across the bench on the other side of the table.

'Twm?'

I looked up to see the swarthy face of Smudge Tucker, his curly black hair swept back towards the shoulders of his well-worn leather biker's jacket.

'I heard about your flat. Gutted, mate.' I saw a familiar flash of gold among his nicotine-stained teeth.

I stared at him in silence.

'Sorry. Bad choice of words. What are you going to do?' he asked.

'I'll find somewhere. I think Merve's got a room at the Railway for now.'

'I'm afraid I've got some more bad news for you. It's Humph. He was arrested last night in the city. He's being held pending charges. Bryn Thomas is on his way over there right now.'

'Where did they find him?' I asked.

'He was staying in a house somewhere near the park. Doesn't look good.'

I stared at Smudge, almost dead inside.

'And, er, Helen wants to see you. She sent me out to find you. This is the first place I looked.'

CHAPTER 55

'She fired you?' asked Mara.

'She didn't fire me. I quit,' I replied, reaching across for my Guinness and clocking the surprise on Merve's face behind the bar.

'You quit? Why?'

'She took me off the story. Actually sent one of the Germolene Twins to the city to cover the news conference on Humph's arrest.'

'The … who?'

'One of the kids in the office. Helen told me I'd screwed up the story. She said she didn't like being scooped by the *Record*. They got a tip-off and were in on Humph's arrest. I tried to tell her we're a weekly newspaper not a daily and that happens, but she didn't want to know.'

'She's all heart, this Helen Snow, isn't she? Talk about kicking someone when they're down.'

We both stared at our Guinness.

'I know this isn't a good moment, but I've got to head back to London again,' continued Mara. 'A meeting with Lennox and his legal people. And then I've got to fill in for a colleague at the paper for a while. I'm not going to be back for a few weeks.'

I smiled at her. 'It's not a problem, Mara. You've got a job to do.'

'What are you going to do? Are you going to be okay? Do you need money or anything? Maybe you could come to London with me. You could stay at my flat?'

'Thanks. I appreciate it but there's the insurance to sort on the flat. I've got a few quid saved up. I'll get by.'

'How did it happen … the flat, I mean?'

'Well, it's hard to look past my father's … business associates, isn't it?'

'It couldn't be dodgy fridge wiring or maybe we left a hob ring burning?'

'I expect I'll find out from the fire brigade at some stage.'

'What are you going to do with your time?'

'Nothing's changed, Mara. I'm still on the story. There's Bren's murder to get to the bottom of; Delilah Sullivan's too. Humph is going to need me more than ever now. And that's not forgetting the small matter of Ivan Harris and the stadium project. If nothing else, at least I'm free of the Ice Queen. It's time to go freelance.'

PART THREE

Chapter 56

The truth is that for weeks after the fire I was a mess. I didn't live above a pub, I lived in one. Merve opened a slate for me behind the bar and, when it came to whisky, Aarav's loss was Merve's gain.

The world had caved in on me. After forty-eight hours in a police cell in the city, Humph was charged with Bren's murder and the theft from Bentall Newspaper Group. He was brought before a magistrate and remanded in custody pending his trial. I heard nothing from my father and next to nothing from Mara.

I was in my usual spot at the bar at the Railway late one evening when I looked up from my glass to see the bulky figure of Gwyn Shell, the dome of his head reflecting light from the mock chandelier above him.

'Twm?'

'What do you want?'

'Mr Harris would like a word.'

'Well in that case tell him it's his round,' I said, slapping my hand onto the seat of the spare stool beside me. 'And mine's a large whisky.'

'Mr Harris would like you to come with me. He's waiting outside in the car.'

'Too posh for the Railway, huh? You ought to remind your employer that a working-class man should never turn his back on his roots.'

Shell remained expressionless, though I got the feeling he was none too impressed with my sentiment.

'Just give me a second to down this.' I belted down the last two fingers of Scotch and slapped the glass back onto the bar. 'Just off for a walk with Mr Shell here, Merve, okay?' I said.

'He's a pal of Ivan Harris's, so if I'm not back in a couple of hours you might want to get them to drag the river.'

I left the bar closely followed by Gwyn Shell and saw Harris's vanity plates across the road. Shell opened the Bentley's rear door and ushered me in.

'Twm, I'm so glad you could spare me a few moments,' said Harris from the far side of the plush leather bench seat. As my eyes adjusted to the street light I could just make out the silhouette of Harris's stocky figure in the sodium glow. I sat there in silence.

'How is your father these days?' asked Harris. 'It's been a little while since Jacqui and I last saw Tom. He's in good health, I hope?'

The car rocked and there was a clunk as Gwyn Shell climbed into the driver's seat, pulling his door closed behind him. I stared at his bull neck in front of me, studded on each side with a small cauliflower ear.

'Where are we going?' I asked Harris.

'Nowhere. I just thought we could have a quiet word here in the car. I hear you've had some misfortune? Losing your flat like that. Thank goodness no one was at home at the time. What happened, did you leave a cigarette burning?'

'You tell me,' I snarled at him. 'I expect it was one of your boys who started it.'

'Come, now. Don't be like that. I'm just trying to show some concern for the son of a trusted friend and business associate. In fact, that's why we're here, isn't it, Gwyn?'

I turned towards the front seat to see Shell reaching across to the passenger seat beside him. He grasped a bulky brown A4 envelope and turned to poke it through the gap in the front seats towards me.

'Take it,' said Harris. 'It's for you.'

I took the envelope, opened it and saw in the orange light that it was crammed with fifty-pound notes.

'I expect you'll have some insurance on the place but, you know, these loss adjusters can be right bastards sometimes. One little detail in the small print and they've got you. Not a penny. Sometimes I think they just don't want to pay up, don't you?'

'What is this, some kind of a bribe?' I asked.

'That's not it at all, Twm. You've got me all wrong. This is just an advance on your salary. I need a PR guy. Someone who knows the ropes, locally, and who I can trust to do a sound job, you know what I mean? I hear that you're in the market for a job right now. That is the case, isn't it?'

I opened the side window, grabbed a handful of notes from the envelope and scattered them out into the open air.

'You can take your money and shove it.' I left the envelope on the seat, opened the door and then slammed it behind me.

Harris leaned across the bench seat until his head was visible through the open window. 'Twm,' he said, calmly, 'Just look at yourself. You're turning into a lush just like Humph Blake. Such a shame.'

The driver's door opened and I took a step back, half-expecting Gwyn Shell to come at me with his fists. Instead he began to chase down the bank notes that were blowing down the street.

Chapter 57

'If you ever doubted my affection for you, Twm Bradley, then let this be proof of it.'

'Thanks for coming, Teg,' I said, sitting at the window in Grumpy's. 'I know this isn't exactly your scene.'

'My scene? You wouldn't catch me dead in this place,' she said. 'Unless I'd just eaten one of Alwyn's breakfasts of course.'

'Grumpy's all right. And the new coffee machine has been a bit of a breakthrough for him. Are you sure I can't get you a cup?'

'No thank you,' replied Teg. 'Just breathing the air in here I can feel my arteries furring up. How are you, lovely?'

'I'm okay.'

'You don't look okay,' said Teg. 'You look rough as fuck, to be honest.' She sighed, reached her hands across the table and took hold of mine. 'Never, never, never give up, Twm. That's what that old boss of mine used to say. If you've made an enemy, like Helen bloody Snow, then good. It shows you've stood up for something.'

'What was he like to work for, your old boss?' I asked.

'He was a bugger, I'll tell you. A complete shit. And I adored him. But you don't have to be Sir Winston bloody Churchill to overcome a setback in your life. Pick yourself up, get your chin up off your chest and look the world in the face. And stop going on the piss, lovely. Won't do you any good.'

'It's under control,' I replied. 'Honest.' The truth was that Harris's attempted bung had stung me from my alcohol-soaked stupor.

'Twm, gossip flies like shit off a shovel in a town like Porthcoed. And Mervyn Powell is not the most discreet of men at the best of times. Now what did you want to talk to me about?'

For the next quarter of an hour I told her everything that had happened since Humph, seated at the very same table, had confided in me about the money missing from the *Gazette*. She listened in silence and without expression, and when I'd finished she calmly reached for a compact mirror in her handbag and checked her make-up.

'I've just told you about two murders, an attempted murder, fraud, arson, a conspiracy involving millions of pounds of public money and the Italian mob, and you haven't so much as batted an eyelid,' I said.

'Nothing surprises me in a town like Porthcoed,' she replied. 'It's like bloody Sodom and Gomorrah, this place. And as for Ivan Harris, I'd have been more surprised if you told me he leaves flowers on his mother's grave every Sunday after chapel. Lovely old dear, Mrs Harris. One of Goronwy's regulars, she was. Used to come over from Abergerran, special like. But that's not what you want to hear, is it lovely?'

'Teg, I'm going to try to clear Humph's name, and it looks like I'm going to have to take on Ivan Harris.'

'Good for you,' she replied.

I reached down to my shoulder bag and pulled out a bulging green wallet folder. 'I want you to take this and keep it in a safe place, and … well … if anything happens to me I want you to give it to Coma, okay?'

'What's in it?'

'It's an old formbook of Humph's, a few newspapers and some notes I've made on everything I've just told you.'

'And you don't want to give this to your pretty young Scottish friend?' asked Teg.

'No.'

'Protecting your scoop, eh?' grinned Teg. 'You're Humph

Blake's boy all right, aren't you? Well, don't you worry. I'll look after this until you come and get it back off me. Okay?'

'Thanks Teg.'

'And remember, anything you need – anything at all – just come and see Teg, all right? I've got friends in low places, if you know what I mean.' She leaned over the table, planted a pink lip-shaped heart on my cheek, straightened her hair and left.

CHAPTER 58

My father had promised to hunt down something that might help us prove Harris's safety fix on the stadium, but so far I'd heard nothing from him. My phone calls were going straight to a recording machine and when I'd gone back to the Bay to see him his doorbell had gone unanswered. I wondered if he'd had a change of heart and was trying to avoid me. Whatever the reason for his reticence, I hadn't liked the way in which Harris had asked after his health.

I travelled back to my father's apartment block once again and this time pressed each of the buttons around his in turn until the security door to my left buzzed. I pushed my way into the building, jogged up two flights of stairs to my father's floor and knocked on his door. Nothing. After a moment or two I banged on it with the edge of my hand.

'Dad?'

Behind me I heard a scratching and a click as a chain was unhooked and the door across the corridor opened to reveal a young woman in a hijab and a long cloak. She was holding a little boy around two years old.

'Can I help you?' she asked.

'I'm looking for my father. Dr Bradley?' I said, thumbing towards the door of his flat.

'Tom's not been around for a while,' came her reply. 'You look like him,' she added, pleasantly.

'Yeah. That's what everyone tells me. Do you mind me asking ... when did you last see him?'

'Oh, it must be three or four weeks ago now,' she said. 'He had a visitor. They left together. Your father was carrying a suitcase. I remember he looked a bit flustered. I asked him if everything was all right and he said he was just running late for the airport.'

'I'm sorry, I don't know your name. Mine's Twm. Twm Bradley.' I showed her my now outdated *Gazette* ID.

'I'm Basma,' she said. 'And this is Yusri.'

'He's a good-looking boy,' I said. 'Basma, can I ask ... what can you remember about this man who was with my father? It's just that I haven't heard from Dad for a while and I'm a little concerned. Have you ever seen this guy before?'

'No. He was around forty, I'd say. Well-built but not tall. He had no hair. Shiny head.' She smiled, revealing a perfect array of pure white teeth.

After a moment Basma added, 'I have a spare key if you want to get in? Tom asked my husband if we could keep a spare just in case, you know.'

'Thanks, Basma. That would be great.'

'Would you mind holding Yusri for me?'

It was only a minute or two before she returned but by then I had already managed to reduce the boy to tears.

'I'm so sorry,' I said. 'Kids don't seem to like me.' She took Yusri back into her arms after handing me the key.

'He's normally very good with strangers,' Basma said, jiggling her son and gently admonishing him in a sing-song tone. 'Yusri, this is Dr Tom's son.' And then to me again, 'He loves your father.'

My smile must have begun to wear thin because Basma apologised for keeping me and said she would leave me to it.

'Thanks,' I replied. 'I'll drop the key off before I go.'

I turned and slid the key into the lock, twisted and pushed. The door gave way and I went inside. I didn't know what I was looking for; I'd only ever set foot in the flat once before and as far as I could tell everything looked pretty much as it had done then. A bachelor pad. I scanned the coffee table and the wall-mounted shelves, hovering briefly over objects familiar from my childhood home. A William Selwyn watercolour; a polished World War One shell casing; a three-cornered, thick cut-glass ashtray. I crossed to my father's desk, the focal point of the room. I pushed away the shade of an angle-poise lamp and leaned over the desk to shuffle through my father's papers. Was there anything that might hint at Harris's stadium fix? Judging by the first few handfuls of correspondence, no. But then he'd hardly have left something like that strewn across his desk in plain sight, I told myself.

I sat down at the desk and started opening drawers. From the second drawer I pulled a desk diary for the current year. I turned to the date of my visit to the flat with Mara and leafed forwards from there. The following Tuesday was marked 'Italy' with a return on the Friday. Otherwise there was nothing of obvious interest. I tucked the diary away in my shoulder bag to scan through later and examined the room around me again. The windowsill in front of the desk was dusty and crowded: a stapler, another ashtray, this one half-full, a small wooden carving of three monkeys – see no evil, hear no evil, speak no evil – that I had brought back from my backpacking year as a peace offering between us and was surprised to find here. Soon my eyes settled on something reflective half-hidden behind the gathered curtain. The edge of a silver photo frame. I stretched forward and picked up the picture. A racehorse. The racehorse? In the bottom left corner of the photo, was a handwritten dedication: '*To Tom, my thoroughbred. J xx*'.

Chapter 59

I was expecting to hear the charmless maid's harsh tones on the speaker next to the gates, but instead the tinny voice belonged to Jacqui Harris. I spoke my name and she buzzed me through. By the time I got to the front door she was waiting for me in a white silk full-length robe, barefoot.

'Twm,' she said. 'Did we have an appointment?'

'No, but I need to speak with you. May I come in?'

She gestured me in. 'I've been meaning to write and thank you for the feature on the charity day,' she said. 'It was sensitively written and I'm grateful, because, well, it's a deeply personal issue for me. I noticed, though, that they put another reporter's name on the piece?'

'Ah yeah. Just a news-desk mix-up,' I assured her.

She led me through the house to the all-white living room, where she placed herself at one end of a long sofa, her long, tanned legs folded elegantly beneath her. She nodded across a low coffee table to another sofa beside a redundant log burner. I sat opposite her and was reminded again of how attractive Jacqui Harris was. Natural and assured. Delicate but in control.

'No staff, today?' I asked.

'No. Just me. Us,' came her reply.

'Your husband is not at home?'

'He's very rarely at home these days and I expect that to be the case until the stadium is up and running.'

'He's in the city?' I asked.

'Yes. But, as I told you last time, he's also in and out of Italy.'

I came right out with it. 'I need to talk to you about my father.'

She reached forward across the low, clear glass-topped table between us to retrieve her drink. If it was a ploy to unsettle me with a glimpse, through the parting in her robe, of her full left breast, it worked.

'Can I get you something?' she smiled.

'No. Thank you.'

'And how is Tom?' she asked, nonchalantly.

'I don't know, Mrs Harris. Perhaps you can tell me.'

'Jacqui, please. Just Jacqui.' I suspected this was as much a feint as the flash of her nipple. 'I'm sorry. I'm not sure I'm following you.'

I pulled the framed photograph from my shoulder bag. 'I think we can cut the pretence here. This is your handwriting, I take it?'

She glanced briefly at the photograph, smiled, then leaned forward to place her glass back on the table, this time clasping the two sides of her robe together to safeguard her modesty. She then stood up and walked towards an ornate white sideboard, out of which she pulled a decanter of colourless spirit.

'Drink?' she asked, bringing the decanter and a bottle of tonic water back to the table.

'I've only just had breakfast.'

She ignored my dig, fixed her drink and sat back down on the sofa. 'Yes, that's my handwriting,' she said. 'But I'm still not sure what you are suggesting.'

'I'm suggesting that my father may be in trouble. He hasn't been back to his apartment for weeks now and he's not answering my calls.'

Jacqui Harris sipped at her drink, her natural calm starting to look just a little laboured.

'The last time he was seen he was leaving his flat in the Bay with Gwyn Shell and talking about running late for a flight,' I continued. 'Have you heard anything from him in the past few weeks?'

'Should I have?'

'Mrs Harris, it's pretty clear that you and my father are having an affair. Can we just get past that?'

'He called,' she replied suddenly. 'From Italy. He flew there for a meeting some time ago but I've heard nothing from him for weeks.' She took another sip of drink. 'It's not like Tom.' And, after another moment, 'What makes you think he may be in trouble?'

'My father has some delicate information which your husband and his Italian colleagues would probably rather he kept from me.'

'Information about what?' she asked.

'Information concerning the stadium build.'

Jacqui Harris reached towards the table, flicked the top of a wooden box and fumbled inside for a cigarette which she lit with a heavy-based ornate lighter. 'You don't think they'd hurt Tom, do you?'

'No, I don't. I think he's potentially too useful to them. But you know these people better than I do.'

'Andrea Bianchi is a dangerous man. I wouldn't put anything past him.'

'I don't know about Bianchi,' I said, 'but I am aware that your husband has a violent nature. Or is that just reserved for the women in his life?'

She stared at me, a fire in her eyes, but didn't answer.

'My father and I need your help, Jacqui. I need you to tell me everything you can about Andrea Bianchi, and about your husband's relationship with him. Most of all I need to know when Ivan is due next in Italy, and where exactly he will be staying.'

CHAPTER 60

Verona is one of those airports where, if you arrive on one of the cheaper airlines, a bus meets you at the foot of the airstair. This at least allows you a moment to savour the feeling of solid tarmac beneath your feet and test the temperature of a new city. During the ninety-minute flight from London I had read in the airline's magazine that the average for October in that part of north-eastern Italy was fourteen degrees Celsius. In the night air it took me only a second or two to decide it was a hell of a lot warmer than that.

The bus dropped me and my fellow travellers outside a dimly-lit glass-walled arrival hall where two immaculately turned-out customs officers were waiting in kiosks to check our passports. As the queue shortened in front of me I felt the familiar mix of impatience and tension, but before long my passport was handed back to me and I realised I was at liberty in a foreign land.

The taxi ride into Verona's *centro storico*, its old town, took around twenty-five minutes and cleaned me out of a good chunk of the Italian lire I'd brought with me. The cab driver dropped me off at a Spanish tapas bar, where I was of immediate interest to a bored-looking couple dining al fresco. I opened my wallet, unfolded a piece of paper and re-read the address. I took a step back to inspect the tall wooden double doors on the building next to the tapas bar, hoping to find the right number. There it was. I consulted the row of doorbells to the right of the doors, selected the one marked 'Alena House Suite' and pushed.

After two or three minutes in which I remained a subject of interest to my new friends at the tapas bar, the huge door rattled and an upright rectangle in the right-hand half of it opened inwards to reveal a fair-haired woman of around thirty-five. 'Signor Bradley?' she asked and I smiled. 'Welcome in Verona. I am Francesca. Please come inside.'

I stepped over the threshold into a high-ceilinged stone portico and Francesca closed the door behind us. She then ushered me through a tall and ornate wrought-iron gate, which she also swung shut behind us, and beckoned me towards an inner courtyard open to the night sky.

'You had a good flight?'

'I did. Thank you.'

Francesca beamed enthusiastically and gestured towards a small set of stone steps leading to a lift and more stairs.

'The lift is small. I will walk. Press number one.'

The tiny lift's concertina doors unfolded until they met in the middle and, as I was silently sprung upwards, I watched through the glass-sided panel as Francesca climbed two flights of the staircase that wrapped itself around the lift shaft. We reached the first floor simultaneously, which left me feeling mildly embarrassed for having blindly followed Francesca's instructions.

The staircase and lift gave way onto a narrow balcony, which ran around three-quarters of the open courtyard one floor below. Notoriously fearful of any altitude above six feet, I gripped the ageing iron balustrade with my left hand, persuading myself it was no less safe than my own rickety staircase had once been. In this way I followed Francesca to a door which was revealed from behind a pair of heavy-duty, dark green shutters. She inserted a key, twisted it and pushed open the frosted-glass door.

Francesca showed me around the one-bedroomed apartment with business-like efficiency, ran me through the house rules, explained which keys opened which door and the iron gate, and then smiled graciously, wishing me a pleasant stay in the city.

'Teg asked me to send her love to you and your mother,' I said, dutifully recalling the instructions I'd been given, and hoping the idiom wouldn't let me down.

Francesca beamed delightedly. 'My mother will be happy to hear this. They are such good friends. Now I will leave you. You have my number if you need to call?'

'Yes, thanks,' I nodded and watched as Francesca retrieved her helmet and bag from a corner of the apartment and left.

The three-roomed suite, which consisted of a kitchen-diner, a bedroom and an en suite shower room, was tall-ceilinged and beautifully baroque. With the palm of my hand I pushed the mattress of the double bed – it yielded softly – and walked around it to the window, opening first the window itself, and then a pair of external shutters. I felt the warm, still air and heard the hubbub of the city. Below me a Vespa kicked into life. I looked down in time to see Francesca, astride her scooter, flick back her long blonde hair and slide the helmet over her head. She leaned forward onto the handlebars, pulled out into the street, and disappeared around the corner to my right.

I fetched my sports bag from the kitchen floor, dropped it onto the foot of the bed and began to unpack. If I needed a reminder of how far off track my life had slipped then here it was. There I was, standing alone in a stranger's apartment in the middle of an Italian city I'd only heard of from a Shakespearean tragedy. Laid out in front of me were all the possessions I had left in the world, and these were just about enough to cover the bottom half of a double bed.

Had I been surprised about my father and Jacqui Harris? Very little surprised me any more. I'd suspected their relationship the moment I read the inscription on the photograph of the horse in his flat window and to Jacqui's credit she hadn't denied it. When I'd suggested to her that my father might be in danger, it had become clear that her feelings for him were serious. She'd explained to me that they'd met on the day the photograph with the Italians had been taken and that Ivan Harris's busy schedule had allowed them plenty of opportunity to follow up on the immediate attraction between them. They'd been seeing each other for a year now. That was a surprise. This was much longer than my father's usual dalliances. Maybe late middle age was having a mellowing effect on the old man.

Jacqui had agreed to tip me off before Harris's next Italian trip, which she said would almost definitely be to Verona where, on the one occasion she had accompanied him there, they'd been lavishly entertained by Andrea Bianchi and his glamorous wife Caterina: front-row seats in Verona's 2,000-year-old Roman arena for an open-air opera, a private visit to Juliet's balcony and a trip by helicopter to nearby Venice, staying overnight at the Gritti Palace Hotel. Back in Verona, a day-long tour of the historic piazzas and modern shops of the old town had been arranged for Jacqui and Caterina while Harris and Bianchi had travelled by car to meet Giancarlo Azzotti at his steel plant twenty miles to the east of the city.

She'd told me as much as she could remember about both Bianchi and his wife. 'Caterina told me they had a villa somewhere not far from Verona,' she'd said. 'Outside the city somewhere, but I couldn't tell you exactly where.'

I picked up my spare clothes and folded them into a drawer, unpacked the contents of my toilet bag in the en suite, and then turned in, listening to the sounds of the street below and wondering what the next day would bring.

Chapter 61

My first night in Italy was restless and I was woken at 6.30 a.m. by the tinny moan of a Vespa. I managed to drift off again but thirty minutes later the tolling of a nearby church bell put paid to any further sleep.

I climbed out of bed and fiddled sleepily with the coffee machine in the kitchen, trying to follow Francesca's brief instructions from memory. I unfolded a street map of the city, sipped my black coffee, which put Grumpy's much larger new machine to shame, and tried to find my bearings.

Verona's old town stands on the river Adige, which curls around it on its eastern, northern and western sides, with a bridge on each axis. A medieval wall which runs along the bottom of the Piazza Bra, the city's largest square, marks its southernmost boundary. The old town is compact and criss-crossed with narrow streets, and from the map it looked like you could walk through it from top to bottom in just fifteen minutes.

I showered and left the apartment. On the street I dithered briefly then set off towards the right-hand turn where I had seen Francesca disappear the night before.

It was still early but the air, even in the morning shadows of Verona's cobbled streets, was already warm; an Indian summer had settled over northern Italy. As I walked through the old town I met few if any cars, with the natives seemingly preferring to either cycle, walk or ride a moped through the rabbit warren of byways that cut through this elegant twelfth-century quarter.

My plan was by necessity simple. It was also something of a long shot. Not long after Jacqui Harris had agreed to help me, she'd rung to tell me when her husband was due next in

Verona. On a pretext, she'd called his office to check where he was staying, swearing her husband's PA to silence so as not to spoil some marital secret she was supposedly cooking up. I would rise, lie in wait outside his hotel and then tail him. My hope, perhaps naïve, was that sooner or later he would lead me to my father. Failing that, I expected at the very least to learn a little more about Harris and his Italian connections and so get a little closer to the truth.

By 7.45 a.m. I had installed myself under a parasol at a street café opposite Harris's plush hotel just off the Piazza Bra. I'd ordered an Americano in hesitant Italian from a waiter who'd answered in perfect English, and begun my stake-out of the hotel entrance behind a pair of sunglasses and a baseball cap. I was sipping on my third coffee, and feeling decidedly edgy, when at last I saw Harris appear in the doorway. To my horror he looked straight in my direction before heading off on foot towards the square, though I was confident he hadn't recognised me. Twm Bradley, late of the *Porthcoed Gazette*, was the last person he expected to see outside his hotel in Verona that morning.

By now the sun was well up in a cloudless blue sky, and Verona's old town was buzzing with life. The size of the crowd made me feel less conspicuous as I tailed Harris, but it also made him that much harder to spot. I thought I'd lost him halfway across the open square but, as I skirted round the arena, I caught a glimpse of him striding purposefully through the throng. For a Brit in Italy he was smartly dressed, in a pair of white chinos and a pale blue shirt open at the neck. His sandy-grey hair also acted as a useful identifier from the rear. At the entrance to the amphitheatre there was an amusing moment as he was briefly accosted by two Roman gladiators, dressed in full armour-plating to lure tourists inside for an arena tour. As he reached the far end of the square, I saw him disappear into a darkened backstreet. I held back for a moment or two, as the street was considerably less populated than the piazza, and then I went after him.

For the next ten minutes or so I followed Harris with some ease as he threaded his way through the old town, all the time heading north. In time we passed the street on which I was staying and, after referring to the map, it occurred to me he was heading towards the Ponte Pietra, the bridge at the top of the old town. The major landmark of note on that side of the river was the Castel San Pietro, a medieval fortress set high on a hilltop overlooking the river and the city. The only other obvious destination was the ruins of the Roman theatre below the castle. Both were clearly popular with the tourists, but then Ivan Harris was no tourist.

As I reached the arched gateway of the Ponte Pietra, I could see Harris at the far end of the bridge. He waited briefly for a gap in the traffic before crossing over the road and then he set off up a street on the left. I consulted my map again. He was heading away from the Roman theatre and, I decided, towards the funicular railway that went up to the castle. I had to think on my feet. There was no way I could travel in the same carriage as Ivan Harris without giving myself away and if I waited for the next one I might lose him altogether. Ahead of me, midway up a steep street, I noticed a set of steps which looked like they rose to the castle. I set off in the warm sun hoping my hunch was right.

The sweat was dripping off me by the time I had joined the large crowd of tourists milling on the elevated terrace next to the fortress. There was no sign of Harris so I paused by a low wall to catch my breath and cool off for a moment. I gazed down through a gap in a row of giant cypress trees towards the river Adige, flowing fast and white beneath the bridge but sedate and blue further downstream. I lifted my head and looked out over the clay roof tiles and church towers of Verona and lost myself momentarily in the view.

But then I felt a tap on my shoulder and jumped briefly out of my skin. My startled reaction brought a gracious apology from a young Japanese man holding his camera expectantly in my direction. He pointed to himself and his girlfriend, grinning widely. I nodded my understanding, took his camera and backed slowly away from the wall on which they set about posing, framing themselves against the backdrop. I had the viewfinder to my eye when I heard an unmistakable Porthcoed accent right behind me. To increasingly quizzical looks from the Japanese couple I continued clicking until the voice behind me receded and the camera was practically snatched from my hand by its owner.

Looking to my left I saw Ivan Harris walking away from me, his arm over the slender shoulder of a dark-haired woman in a white linen dress. For the next twenty minutes or so I played a tense game of cat and mouse with Harris and his companion, circling in and around large groups of tourists, trying unsuccessfully to get a glimpse of her from the front without giving myself away. In time the pair of them came to a halt and took one last look at the vista across the city before starting to retrace their footsteps. I followed them as closely as I dared until, without warning, Harris stopped walking and the woman turned to look at him square in the face. As she lifted the large sunglasses from her eyes and closed in for a long and lingering kiss, I got a clear look at her at last. I delved into my bag for a copy of the photo just to make sure, but there was no mistaking the alluring features of Caterina Bianchi.

CHAPTER 62

You had to admire Ivan Harris's nerve. It was one thing doing business with an Italian mobster like Andrea Bianchi, quite another doing the business with his wife. And in his own backyard. The chocolate-haired Caterina was yet another unlikely catch for Harris, exotic and effortlessly chic. Older than Jacqui Harris yet still much younger than Harris. How on earth did he do it?

Their tender embrace over, the pair walked on, turning down onto the same steps that had brought me up to the castle. I gave them two minutes' head start and then set off after them. Around halfway down towards street level the path split into two, with one set of steps heading left towards the Roman theatre, and the other right towards the Ponte Pietra. There was no sign of them so on a hunch I turned left. I reached street level just in time to see them climbing into the back of a taxi, which pulled away at speed. I stood by the side of the road for a minute or two trying to flag down a cab but it was too late.

Dejected at being shaken off so easily, I trudged back across the bridge into the old town and towards the apartment. The heat of the sun had grown fierce so I showered for a second time and then lay on the bed, listening to the sounds of the street through the open shutters. So much for Plan A, I thought, and contemplated an ignominious return home on the next plane back to London. But then another thought flashed across my mind. I leaned across the bed, rummaged around in my shoulder bag and produced my father's desk diary. I flicked it open to the date of his most recent visit to Italy and, this time, started working my way chronologically backwards, looking for something, anything that might shed light on where he might be.

I'd gone back as far as mid-January when I turned a page and a piece of paper the size of a small receipt fell onto the bed. I picked it up and unfolded it. The print was faint but I could just make out what it said:

NAVIGAZIONE LAGO DI GARDA
Biglietteria di PESCHIERA.
Da PESCHIERA a BARDOLINO.

I swung my legs off the bed and took four steps to an antique wooden hatstand near the kitchen. On a shelf below the mirror Francesca had left a selection of tourism flyers. I shuffled through them until I found one advertising Lake Garda. A map on the back of the flyer indicated that Peschiera del Garda was a small town on the southern shore of the lake, around thirty kilometres to the west of Verona. A ferry service operated between Peschiera and Lazise and Bardolino, two small towns on the eastern side of the lake. I looked again at the ticket. It was dated June 1997. Why would my father keep a ticket from June 1997 in a desktop diary for 1998?

It could have been something or nothing. Either way it was enough for me to dismiss any thought of going home. I looked at my watch. It was too late to make the trip that day but, if a second morning stake-out at Harris's hotel should prove fruitless – Jacqui had said Ivan was booked in for just the one night – I resolved to go the next day.

* * *

To save money I started my journey by foot. It was a sticky, fifteen-minute walk from the Piazza Bra to Verona's Porta Nuova railway station where I caught a lucky break. The train to Milan was waiting on the platform and it was air-conditioned. I'd had no such fortune perched in the café across the road from Harris's hotel and had settled my bill after two hours with no sign of my quarry.

Fifteen minutes after the train had pulled out of Verona I stepped down from the cool carriage onto the stifling-hot platform at Peschiera del Garda. I made my way out of the station and followed my nose to a jetty on the lakeside, only to be told by the gateman of a nearby holiday park that the ferry operated from a different jetty around a mile away. I doubled back for half a mile, crossed a flower-decorated road bridge and entered the centre of the former fortress town through one of many stone arches in its fortified wall. After another couple of hundred yards a road sign pointed me towards the correct jetty and the ticket office, which was closed. A printed note on the door, in German, Italian and English, announced that the office would open ten minutes before the next departure.

I waited until a crowd had built up around the ticket office: families with young children; a young couple with bicycles; an elderly couple with a disabled middle-aged man in a wheelchair, possibly their son. German seemed to be the prevailing language, though I also heard American voices. The office opened, we queued politely for our tickets and then looked on as our ferry appeared out of the distant haze covering the lake, growing steadily larger. After some noisy manoeuvring and an exchange of dock lines between the ferry crew and the ticket-office attendant, a walkway was stretched across to the boat and those on board disembarked. Within ten minutes the crowd on the jetty had taken their place, the dock lines had been exchanged once more, and the ferry was heading back out onto the water.

Although the forty-five-minute crossing promised some much-needed cool air on the upper deck, I remained standing next to a bulkhead inside the hot and musty cabin. I waited ten minutes for any urgent duties the crew might be called on to perform and then stopped the first crew member who walked past me. He was a ruddy, pock-faced man, aged around forty. I asked him if he spoke English.

'A little,' he replied.

From my bag I produced the photograph of the racehorse syndicate and pointed to my father.

'Have you seen this man?'

He studied the image briefly and then shrugged his shoulders, gesturing with open hands.

'Maybe,' he said. 'Maybe no. Is many, many men every day.'

But then he took the picture from my hand and studied it more carefully in the light of the cabin window.

'This man,' he said, pointing to Andrea Bianchi. 'Signor Bianchi. He have a ... big villa in Bardolino. Signora Bianchi,' he added, his eyes alive with the passion that gave his countrymen their national stereotype. 'She is a very beautiful woman.'

* * *

Twenty minutes after touching briefly at Lazise the ferry arrived at Bardolino. I disembarked and headed down the narrow wooden jetty towards the harbour, which began to my left with a fortified tower, leaning off the vertical as Italian towers occasionally did. On my right a cluster of blue-grey olive trees offered extra shade to a collection of parasol-covered café tables, well-populated in the afternoon heat. In the middle of the harbour front a short, straight street stretched directly away from the jetty, lined with shops, gelato kiosks and cafés. At its far end, my brochure informed me, the church of San Nicolò and San Severo rose impressively behind a porch of four Corinthian columns.

From the harbour, the ferryman had assured me, it was no more than a ten-minute walk to the Bianchi villa, but after twenty minutes in the stifling sun I conceded to myself that

I was hopelessly lost and flopped onto a chair in the shade of a café parasol, from where I ordered a cold beer.

For half an hour or so I watched the world go by. In the soporific heat of the afternoon Bardolino sounded quiet and sleepy, but there was plenty going on. Tourists filed through its narrow streets, pausing to inspect a café menu here or the price tag on a leather handbag there. An elderly lady, dressed more for winter than summer, put down her heavy shopping bags and paused in the shade of a florist's shop to admire the riot of colour on show. Two dogs, each on a leash, dragged their owners reluctantly into the sunlight from the shade on either side of the street.

I picked up my notepad and tried once again to make sense of the directions I'd jotted down in shorthand on the ferry. But to no avail. I caught the waiter's eye, paid for my beer and asked him if he knew the Bianchi villa.

Around twenty minutes later I found myself skirting around the high perimeter wall of the latest in a succession of expensive-looking villas which I decided had to be the Bianchi residence. After a few yards more the intimidating stone wall, topped with broken glass, gave way to a much shorter wall topped with tall iron railings. Hot and bothered once more, I sat on the ledge of the low stone wall with my back against the railings and fished a bottle of water out of my bag. I took a mouthful of warm water and admired the view out over the lake which, on a less hazy day than today, presumably included the mountains beyond.

'Twm?'

I swivelled around. 'Dad?'

'What in God's name are you doing here?'

There behind the railings, tanned and healthy in knee-length blue cargo shorts and a white linen shirt, open to the waist, stood my father. He was unshaven and on his head he wore a battered old straw hat above a pair of aviator sunglasses.

Alongside him two large mastiffs stopped panting and sniffed at me suspiciously.

'What do you think I'm doing? I'm trying to find you. Are you okay? You've been gone for weeks.'

'I'm fine, son. I'm … on holiday, I suppose you could say. I'm staying in this rather elegant villa as a guest of Andrea Bianchi. Although it seems his guests are encouraged to stay until they are invited to leave.'

'Why didn't you phone or write or something? I've been worried sick about you. And so, by the way, has Jacqui Harris.'

He allowed her name to pass without comment. 'I don't have access to a telephone, I'm afraid, and Bianchi's staff seem to prefer it if I don't actually stray any further than the garden.'

'In other words you're being held in this place against your will?'

'Oh, it's all been very pleasant,' he said. 'The young chef here is amazing and Bianchi's wine cellar must be the best I've ever tasted. Even these fellows can be quite good fun when they get to know you,' he added, looking at the dogs. 'I haven't felt this relaxed in years.'

I was about to remonstrate with him further when I heard footsteps approaching on my side of the railings. I turned to see two familiar faces staring down at me from a height. Romanian faces, cauliflower-eared.

CHAPTER 63

I wasn't an expert on wine cellars but it seemed to me that Bianchi's was a little on the cold and clammy side. A night had passed since I had been frogmarched into it by the Romanians to the annoyance of my father, who had been pushed in alongside me.

'You had to come and stick your oar in,' he said, pacing up and down beside a six-foot-tall rack of bottles. 'How on earth did you find me, in any case?'

'I found an old ferry ticket in your desk diary.' He was still thinking that through when I added, 'Just what do you think Bianchi's intentions are towards you? It seems to me you're a prisoner here not a house guest.'

'Andrea has been perfectly civil, son, until you showed up. He's placed a number of his domestic staff at my disposal and I have to say my living quarters are a hell of a lot comfier than this.'

'How did you end up here anyway?'

'Ivan Harris insisted I attend a meeting in Verona, not long after you and your girlfriend showed up at the flat. Just routine, he said.'

'She's not my girlfriend.'

'Anyway, Harris must have told Bianchi about our second meeting at the flat. Apparently I have been under pretty close observation. Bianchi asked me if I'd ever spent any time near Lake Garda. "Lake air is good for the constitution, Tommaso," he said, and he invited me to stay at his villa. Well, he insisted actually.'

At this point several pairs of feet began to descend the stone steps towards the cellar. First through the door were the

Romanians, each positioning himself on one side of it as if guarding a ruck. Then in walked Ivan Harris.

'A family reunion in Italy. How nice.'

'You never told me you had such good-looking sons,' I replied and was rewarded with a gut punch from the smaller of the two Romanians that left me doubled up, breathless, on the dusty cellar floor.

'Ivan is that really necessary?' remonstrated my father. 'And just why the hell have we been locked up in here like common criminals?'

'Maybe I don't like the idea that you've gone back on our little arrangement, Tom,' said Harris. 'Or maybe I just don't like the way you look at my wife.'

There was no comeback from my father. 'Bring him,' Harris said, pointing to me. 'His father can entertain himself for a while longer. Relax, Tom. There must be a corkscrew down here somewhere.'

I was pushed up the cellar steps by the two Romanians, then led along a corridor and into a large, stone-walled reception room dominated by an open fireplace, empty in the heat of the day.

'Sit,' said the taller Romanian, gesturing towards a studded leather sofa, before he joined his compatriot in guarding either side of the door.

On the other side of the room Ivan Harris stood looking through a glass-panelled wall towards the haze on the lake.

'What are you doing here, Twm?'

'Isn't it obvious?' I replied. 'I came looking for my father.'

'But why the sudden concern? I was led to believe that you two were estranged. For some years now, Tom said. Your recent reconciliation couldn't have anything to do with Tom's involvement in the stadium project, I don't suppose?'

'And how is that going for you?' I chirped. 'All going according to plan, is it? Or isn't life quite as simple when you're at the mercy of the Italian mob?'

'Oh my God, not another one,' spat Harris. 'I've had to put up with this sort of shit from Humph Blake for the past twelve months and now that he's finally out of my hair I'm going to get it from you as well?'

'Just because you've managed to get Humph "out of your hair" doesn't mean you'll be able to do the same with me or the people I'm working with.'

'You're taking an awful lot for granted there, if you don't mind me saying. Whatever mess Humph Blake has found himself in, it's his own stupid fault.'

'You honestly expect me to believe that?' I said. 'Humph's been all over you like a rash since you came back to Porthcoed and when it comes to investigative work Humph is no mug.'

'Humph Blake is a broken-down drunk. A brittle, unstable joke of a man.'

'If that's the case then why kill his wife and frame him for her murder?'

'I have no idea what you are on about. I had nothing to do with the death of Brenda Blake, or Humph's arrest for that matter,' said Harris.

'I expect you leave that kind of dirty work to your hired thugs, don't you? Or perhaps to your new Italian friends? Don't forget I'm a witness to how these two Neanderthals tried to force me off a cliff.'

'An unfortunate motoring accident. Things got out of control. But you have no idea how irresponsible and dangerous your behaviour has been in recent weeks. You needed to be warned of the seriousness of the damage that could be caused by your uninformed meddling. Do you have any understanding of just how important it is that the new stadium gets built in time and on budget?'

'Oh I understand how important it is to you. You miss your deadline and you're a dead man. Andrea Bianchi will see to that.'

'You really don't get it, do you?' said Harris. 'Do you imagine for a minute that I am alone in wanting to do everything within my power to get this new, state-of-the-art stadium up and running in half the time it would normally take to build? Has it not occurred to you that there may be other interested parties back home who are not going to just stand by and allow me to fail? You need to grow up a bit, son. This is the real world we're living in, not the sort of moral paradise you journalists like to imagine yourselves at the centre of.'

'It doesn't work that way, and you know it. You and your "interested parties" don't get to make the rules any more than I do. If something happens to me Mara McKenzie will break this story wide open. And if the stadium isn't ready on time you're going to have to get on your knees and beg Bryn Thomas for a nice secure jail cell. There are more important things in this world than money or rugby. The truth, for one.'

'Go ahead and write your story, Twm; whatever you think that is. Just make certain you and your Scottish girlfriend get it right or I'll sue the arse off both your newspapers. I could do with a few million quid around now, let me tell you. But you don't have anything on me, do you?'

'Don't I?' I replied. 'I know a lot more about you than you imagine. I know that Eddie Lennox's legal team would be more than interested to discover how you used to knock Delilah Sullivan about before "someone" fitted him up for her murder. That never came out back in the day, did it? The miracle star witness who had a history of assaulting the murder victim? You'd never survive that.'

Harris screwed his eyes up just a little. 'Who told you that? Humph Blake? No one is going to believe a man under suspicion of killing his own wife. He'd say anything right now to save his own skin. And her name was Angharad, not Delilah, okay?'

'Do you knock Jacqui around, too? Whose side do you think

she's going to be on now that you and Bianchi are a threat to my father? It's a love job, you know. Jacqui's smitten. Practically blushes whenever she thinks about Dr Tom Bradley. And just imagine the entirety of what she knows about you.'

'Jacqui and Tom are welcome to each other …'

'… Because you're screwing Caterina Bianchi now, is that it?'

Harris looked at the Romanians, who glanced at each other before all three turned their eyes at me.

'And what do you suppose a man like Andrea Bianchi is going to do when he finds out that his wife is shagging a business partner of his behind his back? A mob figure like Bianchi won't take kindly to losing face, will he? I took some nice holiday snaps on Monday morning up at San Pietro. And they're already in the mail home. If my father and I don't follow them back to the UK pretty soon they're going to be published in a Fleet Street gossip column and I've already arranged for a copy to be mailed to Bianchi.'

'You're bluffing. You've got nothing on me and, when it comes down to it, neither has your father.'

'If that's the case, then why are you holding us here against our will?' I said. 'That is what you're doing, isn't it?'

There was no answer.

'You really think you're holding all the cards, don't you?' said Ivan Harris, eventually.

I'd rattled him. I knew it. I'd winded him just like his Romanian thug had winded me down in the wine cellar. But, to his credit, once again he regained his composure quickly.

'And yet here you are, you and your father, rather a long way from home and in the secure surroundings of Andrea's villa. Do you seriously think that anything goes on in this neck of the woods without Andrea Bianchi knowing about it? Either involving his wife or otherwise? What sort of man do you think he is?'

'Oh, I think he's a jealous man, and a proud man who

cannot afford to be made to look a fool. Which makes him a very dangerous man from your point of view. But, okay, let's imagine for a moment that for some strange reason Bianchi has no objection to you and his wife screwing around in his hometown. Nobody gets away with the sort of shit you've pulled. You must know that. You say you have important friends back home who will watch out for you on the stadium project. Well, maybe they will. But not forever. Once that stadium is built and the tournament has come and gone these "interested parties" of yours won't care quite so much about you, will they? And when the truth starts to emerge about your safety short cuts, and the murders of Bren Blake and Delilah Sullivan, they'll have no reason to protect you and your good name any longer, will they? They'll chuck you under the first bus to save themselves and you know it.'

Harris finally snapped. 'I didn't kill Angharad,' he screamed. 'And I had *nothing* to do with the death of Brenda Blake. Do you hear me? *Nothing.*'

Chapter 64

Just a few days after my conversation with Ivan Harris in Andrea Bianchi's villa in Bardolino my father and I found ourselves walking off a plane at Heathrow.

We hardly spoke during the flight back. When my father wasn't being cute with the air stewardess he had his head stuck in a paperback that he'd picked up at Verona airport, more than likely for that very reason. I put his behaviour down to embarrassment on his part that, despite his protestations about being comfortable in Italy, I may have actually succeeded in getting him out of a jam.

As it turned out I was fine with being left to my own thoughts. There was much to pick over as I gazed down at the cloud tops, not least Harris's decision to let us both go.

Had I really managed to get Harris running scared of Bianchi, or was it more a measure of Harris's confidence that we had no way of proving that he had bypassed safety protocols at the stadium? I decided I couldn't rely on the idea that I was holding any leverage over Harris just because I'd spotted him with Caterina. Harris knew Bianchi; I'd never met the guy. For all I knew Caterina might have been under instructions to seduce Harris to keep an eye on him and report back. As for Harris's stadium shenanigans, it would simply be a case of his word against my father's and in that eventuality Harris's word would carry far more weight.

Unless … unless I could dent Harris's reputation by proving that he was in some way implicated in the deaths of Bren Blake and Delilah Sullivan. He had to have been. The coincidences were far too great. In 1968 he'd been a foreman with easy access to the stadium construction site, and thirty years later he'd been in charge of building its replacement. More than that, Harris had strong links to both victims – one was his wife, the other the wife of a long-term rival. On both occasions he had a motive. Jealousy in the case of Delilah, and self-preservation when it came to Bren.

But after confronting Harris in Italy I realised that I was less certain about the nature or extent of his involvement in their fate. There had been something in the look on his face when he had angrily exclaimed his denials that had left a mark on me. To my surprise I realised I had believed him. And I didn't really know where that left me. Or Humph.

'This way, Dad,' I said when I saw my father squinting around the arrivals hall for directions to the baggage claim.

'I'm not completely stupid, Twm,' he replied.

We went our separate ways after the customs check. He had decided to head back north for a week or two, possibly to put some distance between himself and Jacqui Harris until things calmed down a little, and so he made off for the Underground and Euston Station. I set off towards the coach stand for the bus, and then a train back to Porthcoed.

CHAPTER 65

Christmas came and went and my investigation got bogged down in the mire. I couldn't get a purchase on Ivan Harris's possible involvement in the Stadium Murders and I was nowhere near a breakthrough on the stadium fix. Harris, it seemed, had succeeded in marginalising me.

My domestic life was faring no better. I found myself in a disagreement with my insurance firm over my claim for the flat and had been forced to stay on at the Railway. My savings were drying up fast, and I hadn't seen anything of Mara since before my trip to Italy.

It was spring when I found a scribbled note from Merve behind the bar: 'Teg rang and wants you to call her. Merve.' I dialled the *Gazette* switchboard from my new office line – the public payphone outside the Railway's ladies' toilet – and Teg answered in her best telephonese. As usual, as soon as she heard my voice she snapped back into her more familiar tone.

'How are you, lovely?' she asked. 'Seems like I haven't seen you for ages. Everything all right?'

'Yes, thanks.'

'Twm, I need to see you. Stuff I can't talk about on the phone, okay?'

'Okay.'

We arranged to meet in the Railway snug at 8 p.m., though it was twenty-to-nine by the time Teg showed.

'I'm sorry,' said Teg, planting the customary red heart on my cheek. 'Bit of a flap on at the *Gazette*. The Ice Queen has announced a round of redundancies.'

This news came as no real surprise since Helen Snow had

warned me that she would get her own career back on track at any cost. I ordered a large Bombay and tonic for Teg and another Scotch for me.

'It's a blatant attempt to impress Sir Norman Bentall by cost-cutting,' said Teg. 'And, in the process, she gets to clear out anyone who hasn't fallen under her spell. Doesn't look good for Coma or yours truly right now, to be honest with you. My guess is that within a month or two either Nigel or Aled will be doing Coma's job and some teenager on work experience will be running the front desk.'

'I'm sorry to hear that, Teg,' I said. 'Maybe Humph wasn't so wrong after all when he said local newspapers were doomed. Are you going to be all right?'

'I'll be fine. Goronwy left me a few quid so there's no need to worry. As long as I can afford a bottle of gin every now and then I'll be all right. Actually, it's Humph that I need to talk to you about.'

'Is he okay?'

'He's fine. Well, as fine as you can be in his situation, I suppose. I went to visit him last week. They're holding him on remand in the city. They like to keep it local if they can. Anyway, I expect you know that in your line of work, don't you, lovely?'

'Any news on a trial date yet?' I asked.

'Nothing yet, but he said he wants to see you. He said he's had plenty of time to think in prison and there's something he needs to talk to you about.'

I promised Teg I'd arrange a visit and we spent the rest of the evening discussing Verona, the slow progress of my insurance claim and the atmosphere of fear and loathing that continued to hold sway at the *Gazette*.

* * *

As it turned out I didn't get to visit Humph. After applying to the prison for a visiting order I heard nothing back. A week or two later I found a number to ring and was told that Humph's visiting rights had been suspended following an altercation between him and a fellow inmate. I tried to imagine any scenario where Humph might end up in a fight with an incarcerated convict and failed.

In the end he telephoned me. Merve extended the handset in my direction but I asked him if there was anywhere more private than the bar in the public lounge to take the call. He showed me into his back office and I waited for the sound of the handset being replaced in the bar before speaking.

'Humph? I heard about your … excitement. Is everything all right?'

'It's fine, Twm. Don't worry. Just a bit of nonsense with an old lag who was mugging off some first timer I'm sharing with.' He was already speaking fluent jailbird. 'Listen, I haven't got long. I've had to blag a phonecard and I don't know how much credit is left on it. I just wanted to say I've been thinking about the *Gazette* cash that went into Bren's account.'

'What about it?'

'Well, with everything else that was going on I didn't really have time to think it through properly but, these days, time is the one thing I'm not short of. And it's suddenly become quite obvious to me.'

'What has?'

'Whoever took the five grand from the *Gazette* must have pretended to be me, as I'm the only one with permission on that account.'

'Well, yes …'

'And so whoever moved that cash had to have had easy access to the *Gazette*'s bank details.'

'You think it was an inside job?'

'It must have been. Until Bryn started sniffing around

I used to keep all the bank stuff under lock and key in the drawer of my desk in the newsroom. Anyone working on the paper would know that and have a chance to take or copy the key.'

'Well, that takes care of the *Gazette* account, maybe, but what about Bren's?'

'Ah … well, you see, I kept the whole lot together in that same drawer. It saves time, Twm, because I'm in the office more often than not and if Bren rings and says she wants something it's all there and I can pop down the road to the bank.'

'For God's sake, Humph …'

'Well, it was under lock and key, and I thought I could at least trust the people I worked with – most of whom I actually gave a job to.'

'So who do you think might have done it?'

'Well, that's just it. I've been working through it in my head and I can only come up with two possibil …'

At that point, agonisingly, the line went dead. I hung up the phone and waited a few minutes for Humph to ring back, but no call came. I picked up the handset, dialled 1471 to get the number Humph had been calling from, but when I pressed 3 to return the call I heard the engaged tone. In my mind I saw a line of inmates queued up to use the phone after Humph, and his phonecard running out of credit. He wasn't going to call back today.

Chapter 66

In my old life at the *Gazette*, Grumpy's had been a welcome bolt-hole from the occasionally stressful confines of the newsroom. These days it represented almost the sole solution to the problem of waking up each morning and having nowhere to go. At my usual seat in the window I drained the last mouthful from a cup of black coffee and tried to bring to mind the taste of the coffee in Italy. There was no comparison and, I knew, little point dwelling on it, so I settled instead for the caffeine kick that I hoped it would bring.

I needed a lift. I'd spent a restless night following my conversation with Humph. In his prison cell he'd reflected on who at the paper might have wanted to betray him, and apparently he'd managed to identify two possible culprits. In my bed above the Railway bar I had tried to do the same but had failed to produce even one. I guess that's what a prison cell can do to you. I asked Grumpy for a second coffee and grabbed a couple of daily newspapers from the rack on the wall. The red tops had already gone, leaving just a couple of broadsheets, but that suited me fine.

I dropped the *Telegraph* onto my table, sat back down and unfolded Mara's paper. My eye was immediately drawn to a puff above the masthead on the front page. Next to a shot of Eddie Lennox in his follicular prime I saw the strapline:

'FALLEN FOOTBALLER SEEKS JUDICIAL REPLAY'.

On an inside news page, above a more recent shot of Eddie Lennox, warts and all, the headline read:

'"I DIDN'T KILL HER": CONVICTED STADIUM MURDERER'S 30-YEAR BID FOR REDEMPTION'.

The story, which carried Mara's byline, marked the latest milestone in Lennox's quest to have his conviction deemed a miscarriage of justice. It contained some emotive quotes from Lennox describing his 'protracted jail nightmare' and included a tip-off from an unnamed source at the Criminal Cases Review Commission saying that it was 'giving serious consideration' to referring Lennox's application to the Court of Appeal.

That evening, as I half-expected, Mara showed up at the Railway.

'Hello, stranger.'

'Hello.'

'Lost, are you?'

'No, I don't think so. Hi, Merve.'

'Welcome back, Mara, love,' said Merve. 'How are you?'

'I'm fine thanks. Thirsty actually.'

'Pint?'

'Yes, please.'

'On your slate, Twm?'

'Help yourself,' I said, as Mara sat on the stool next to me. 'So what brings you back to the old wild west?'

'Oh I don't know. There's a natural break in the Eddie Lennox story, until we hear whether he's been granted leave to appeal his conviction. But my boss did also tell me I had some leave owing and I either had to use it or lose it.'

'That's a bit harsh. And you didn't want to go home to the folks?'

'Maybe I've been missing Merve's Guinness,' she said, forcing a smile. 'Although, let's see … yeah, a multi-million-pound public scandal and the unsolved murders of two women might also have something to do with it.'

I looked up in time to catch a look of astonishment on Merve's face. Aware that I'd caught it he quickly rubbed the skinny black beard on his neck, rearranged the red Paisley cravat emerging from the open lapels of his denim shirt, and topped off Mara's pint.

'How long have you got?' I asked Mara.

'Three weeks.'

'Nice.'

'So, what's news with you?' she asked.

'Much the same. No job, no home, a reluctant insurance company and a rapidly dwindling savings account.'

'Well, thank heavens for your slate, then. Cheers.'

We took our drinks into the corner of the Snug, safely out of Merve's earshot, and Mara asked for a blow-by-blow account of the Italian trip.

'So Harris pretty much challenged us to go ahead and accuse him of corruption?' she asked.

'He's banking on the fact that we don't have the proof.'

'And he's right. So far. Got some nerve, though, hasn't he?'

'He has an interesting notion about a collection of "interested parties"; some sort of guardian angels who he says would never let anything jeopardise the completion of the stadium in the time left remaining.'

'Who do you suppose he means by that?' asked Mara, sipping from her drink.

'Oh, you know. People in high places, I suppose. Faceless bureaucrats, the Deep State – call it what you like.'

'And he actually said he had nothing to do with the deaths of Delilah Sullivan or Bren Blake?'

'Not exactly,' I said. 'He was somewhat emotional at the time, but still he chose his words carefully. What he said was, "I didn't kill Angharad, and I had nothing to do with the death of Brenda Blake."'

'And you believed him?'

'I did. I do. Yes.'

'But surely he's just being cute? By saying that he's practically implying that he *had something to do* with Delilah's death.'

'Something to do with her death, or just to do with the conspiracy which sent Eddie Lennox to jail for her murder? We already know he was the prosecution's miracle star witness.'

'A conspiracy involving who?'

'You tell me,' I said. 'You're the one with the inside track on Lennox. What's Eddie's theory? What have his lawyers told the Review Commission?'

This question heralded an awkward silence, as if both of us recognised that an honest answer from Mara now would require her to do something she had so far appeared unwilling to do: share privileged information with me.

'Come on. Let's go upstairs,' she said and headed off with her drink.

Thinking Mara might prefer to talk in the privacy of my room, which had once been her room, I humoured her. I picked up the small suitcase she'd left for me to carry and followed her up. Clicking the door shut, I found her next to the bed, peeling off her top, cross-armed over her head. The manoeuvre left a few locks of her blonde hair askew. From somewhere behind them her reckless eyes fixed on mine.

'Mara …'

With just her cream-coloured underwear next to the milk white of her skin, she approached me, slipping one hand under my arm and around my shoulder while the other went straight to the part of me that was already burning, tracing its contours, gently squeezing.

'Mara …'

She lifted herself onto her toes and kissed me, challenging my reluctance with her tongue. I felt a familiar spark, then a rush in my chest, which I realised was anger. I pulled back.

'Mara!'

'What?' she replied with playful frustration.

'We can't keep doing this.'

'I don't think you really mean that.' Another gentle squeeze. 'I mean I'm definitely getting mixed signals here.'

I pulled back further. 'I can't keep doing this. You can't keep doing this to me.'

'You haven't objected yet.'

'Mara, will you just stop this for a moment and listen to me?' As I backed away from her she looked on, astonished. 'I can see what you're doing. You're happy to hear everything I have to say but when it's your turn to share, you either clam up or you jump me …'

'That's not true …'

'… and in my mind right now that makes you one of two things.'

'You just watch what you say,' she said, and for the first time I saw a stirring of genuine anger in her. She walked around to the other side of the bed and bent over to recover her skirt from the carpet.

'Either you're just one of those national newspaper journalists who's happy to rip off a small-town hack like me …'

'Or what, exactly?' she said, turning to face me again.

'… or else you're something altogether more sinister.'

'Just what are you suggesting?'

'I'm suggesting that nothing I've heard from you stops me wondering if I'm being played.'

'Look,' said Mara, 'maybe I'm no good at sharing information on an ongoing story. Show me a reporter who is. But I haven't been quite as reticent as you're making out.'

'Remind me what, exactly, you have contributed to our partnership?'

'I told you about your father working for Harris.'

'You confirmed it after I'd figured it out myself.'

'I tried to tell you, but it wasn't an easy thing to say. I promised I would open the door to Lennox for you and I did that, didn't I? You asked me how I got involved with him and I told you. I took you to meet him, I let you question him. I've vouched for you when he's asked me if he can trust you.'

'So how come you clam up each time I ask you for an insight about him or his appeal?'

'But that's not true. I've made it quite clear that in my view Eddie's no angel but I don't think he killed Delilah Sullivan. Twm, I'm a small-town reporter just like you. Go back a couple of years and I'm working on a paper just like the *Porthcoed Gazette*. Go forward a couple and you're working for a national newspaper like mine. We're the same people, you and I. And we're on the same side.'

'If we're on the same side then why did you lie to me at Central Station the morning we went to talk to my father?'

'What do you mean? When did I lie to you?'

'When you arrived at the station you were clearly upset. When I asked you why, you gave me some crap about being hit on by some creepy male taxi driver. Except you didn't arrive in a taxi, and the person who drove you to the station was a woman. Who was she, Mara, and why were you arguing with her?'

Did I imagine a moment of doubt in Mara's eyes for a split second or was she genuinely trying to recall the moment in question?

'That? That was just personal stuff,' she said. 'Personal baggage which I didn't feel like sharing with you, okay? So I shut you down with a white lie because I just wanted to forget about it and get on with the day.'

'And I'm supposed to believe that?'

'Well, that's up to you, but it's the truth. The woman who drove me to the station that day is an old friend of the family. She lives in the area so I've had to meet up with her from time to time. But she's a bit of a controlling cow when she wants to be and occasionally, like that morning, she winds me up. So I told her so in no uncertain terms.'

There was a pause. She dropped her skirt onto the floor again and kneeled on the bed. Resting back on her heels, her hands in her lap, she looked me straight in the eye. 'Twm, has it not occurred to you yet that ...'

'That what?'

'... that I've fallen in love with you?'

'I'm not sure why I should believe anything you say, Mara.'

The silence was thick with emotion.

'Well, I guess that answers my question. Thanks, Twm.'

For a second time in our relationship, Mara dressed hurriedly and closed the door on her way out. But not before I'd caught a glimpse of the tears welling in her eyes.

Chapter 67

The newspaper billboards in Central Station were doing their best to build up the hype surrounding the fast-approaching inaugural match at the new stadium, but there was little need. The moment I walked through the tall doors of the Grade II listed building I could feel a heightened sense of anticipation in the early summer air.

Though the skyline was still busy with cranes, what had once been a mess of concrete and steel was beginning at last to resemble the futuristic-looking stadium that I'd glimpsed in the official artist's impressions. According to the latest update in that morning's *Record*, which I'd bought for the journey from Porthcoed, the pace of construction work had increased dramatically over the past six months. Around a thousand workers were now labouring night and day, seven days a week, to get the stadium ready in time. The *Record*'s article, under the byline of a reporter named Wynne Jones, someone I didn't know, had explained that the June fixture was the first of three over the course of the summer that would allow the stadium to earn a safety certificate in time for the big tournament kick-off in October. The inaugural game would to all intents and purposes be played in the middle of a building site, the article explained, with 25,000 tickets on sale, around one-third of the stadium's capacity.

As I left the station I caught a glimpse of a lower part of the first of the four steel spires that would eventually carry the weight of the stadium roof and become an everyday part of the city's skyline. The stadium, like my investigation into the murders that had taken place there and the corruption that jeopardised its safety, was still a jigsaw missing a significant number of pieces.

As my bus inched alongside the stadium site, I brooded over what had happened with Mara. Had she really said she'd fallen in love with me? And had I really told her I didn't believe her? My feelings toward Mara were contradictory to say the least. Just the act of thinking about her produced the same rush of excitement that I'd felt when she'd walked back into the Railway. And I hadn't felt this way about anyone for quite some time. But there was undoubtedly something about her that troubled me.

I was saved from further introspection by an unexpected glimpse of a familiar figure through the window of the bus. Ivan Harris, sporting a hard hat, was waiting to cross the road. He looked older than when I had seen him in Italy. I wondered how his nerves were holding up. There was no room for error in the run-in to the stadium's all-important first fixture. Any significant construction delay now would be disastrous, while any significant hiccup on the day of the match itself would likely kill off the stadium's chances of hosting the tournament's opening ceremony, opening match or final.

At last the bus started to make some headway towards the castle. A year ago I had passed this way to knock on Annie Léchet's door. What I had learned back then had sown the seeds of an idea that I hoped would help reveal whether Humph had indeed been betrayed by someone at the *Gazette* and, if so, who. This time, as with the last, Mme Léchet had no idea I was on my way to see her. But I was confident I could win her over to my cause.

'Mr … Bradley, isn't it?' she asked at the doorstep, petite and immaculate as I had remembered her. 'Is everything all right?'

'Yes, thank you. I've come to return Delilah's letter, but I was hoping for a few moments of your time if you would be so kind?'

I was led inside the house.

'Can I get you some coffee?' she asked. 'I was about to have some myself.'

'I'd love one. Thank you.'

'Come into the kitchen,' she said. 'We can talk in there while I fill my coffee machine.'

This turned out to be nothing more sophisticated than a large stainless-steel stove-top percolator.

'Allow me to let you into the secret of making good coffee, Mr Bradley,' she smiled. 'You don't need an expensive machine. Just good beans and the right amount of water. I use a French brand of coffee that I can only find in Olly's delicatessen in the city. You know Olly's? I've had this little pot for twenty years but nothing beats it. Tell me, how is Humphrey?'

'I spoke to him not so long ago, on the telephone from prison. He's being kept on remand in the city. He seemed okay, considering.'

'Is there a date yet for his trial?'

'Nothing that I have heard.'

'You will know of course by now that he was staying with me here while the police were looking for him?'

'I guessed as much when I saw his haircut. I know he was grateful for the kindness of a friend. But has this been a problem for you, with the police?'

'My lawyer has warned me that I may face a six-month prison sentence or a fine. The fine, he thinks, is more likely. In which case I will gladly pay it.'

'Madame Léchet, as you may have already guessed, I am trying to help clear Humph of the charges he is facing. To do this I need your help. It's only fair to warn you, however, that there may be an element of risk ...'

Chapter 68

The rotund figure of Coma was the first to show, shuffling into the Railway in his customary beige cotton jacket and light grey flannels, his tie askew, half-specs midway down his nose and a copy of the *Gazette* under his elbow.

He refused my offer of a pint, insisting instead on standing the round. 'I'm a working man, Twm. Though for how much longer is anyone's guess.'

I sat at a table away from the bar and waited for him to join me.

'I saw your lady friend the other day,' said Coma, adding the unnecessary clarification, 'the Scottish one?'

'Oh?'

'She was at the station.'

'Yeah.'

I was saved from a conversation I didn't want by the arrival of Teg, fashionably late as ever. While Coma returned to the bar for a gin and tonic, Teg removed her glossy leopard-skin raincoat and settled in alongside me.

'So, how's that young lady of yours?' she asked. 'Mara, is it?'

'She's fine, thanks. As far as I know.'

'Oh dear. Like that is it? You know you can tell Teg all about it. For you, lovely, I've got two shoulders to lean on, whenever you want.'

'Thanks, Teg.'

This time I was rescued by Coma's return from the bar.

'Here's to those who wish us well,' said Teg raising her gin and tonic. 'And all the rest can go to hell.'

'So. What's this all about?' asked Coma.

'Yes, cut to the chase, Twm, will you? *Sex and the City*'s on tonight.'

I took a deep breath and shared with them Humph's theory about the fraudulent transfer of *Gazette* funds into Bren's account being an inside job. Neither replied and I could tell that each was weighing up likely suspects. I would have given more than a penny for their private thoughts.

'Remember, at this stage this is all just a theory. I still need to prove it.'

'And how are you going to do that?' asked Coma.

'*We* are going to set a trap for the bugger to fall into, aren't we?' interrupted Teg. 'Catch them with their finger in the honeypot?'

'With any luck, yes,' I said, 'and I am going to need your help. A couple of days ago I went into the city to speak to Annie Léchet. She ran the hair salon where Delilah Sullivan worked back in the sixties.'

'Who's Delilah Sullivan?' asked Coma unhelpfully.

'Delilah was a nickname that Angharad Sullivan gave herself.'

'Oh, okay, I'm with you,' said Coma, sipping his pint.

'Now Annie Léchet is also the one who looked after Humph when he was on the run. She's agreed to help us.'

'So what's the plan?' asked Teg.

'Well, it's quite simple, really ...'

'The best ones always are, lovely.'

'Between the two of you, you are going to let it slip that as a freelance reporter I've been to interview Annie, and that she has come up with important new evidence from the time of Delilah's murder which involves Ivan Harris and is likely to have a bearing on Eddie Lennox's appeal. You'll say that I recorded the interview on tape and I've asked Teg to transcribe it.' I reached into my shoulder bag and pulled out a mini-cassette. 'Here, I've already got Annie's "interview" on tape.

You just need to write it up and hide the tape and the transcript where someone is likely to find it.'

'And then, what?' asked Coma.

'Then we're going to sit back and watch and see who takes the bait.'

'But how are we going to know if that happens, lovely?'

'I'll tell you now, in a minute. The important thing is that the Ice Queen doesn't get to hear the contents of this tape or before we know it she'll be splashing a phoney interview all over the front page of the *Gazette*.'

Chapter 69

Teg and Coma agreed to start the ball rolling at work the next day. I waited until early that afternoon and called Teg.

'How did it go?'

'Smooth as you like. The worm is on the hook, I'd say.'

'So we're on for tonight, then?'

'Copy that,' answered Teg. 'Teg out.'

By five o'clock I was installed at my usual window table at Grumpy's. At just after five I saw Teg walk out of reception. I wiped the condensation off the inside of the café window and watched as she crossed the road and sauntered into Grumpy's like Sophia Loren walking into McDonald's.

'Phase two is complete,' she said in a lowered voice. 'Just the Ice Queen, George Mellor, Smudge Tucker and Albie Evans left. It's all down to Coma now.'

By 6 p.m. we'd seen Albie Evans leave. As he normally did at around this time Grumpy switched off the lights of the café, now eerily quiet but for the background hum of a couple of refrigerators, and appeared at our table.

'Twm, you promise you'll remember to turn on the alarm and lock the back door on your way out as I showed you?'

'I promise, Grumpy.'

'And you promise you'll tell me what all these amateur dramatics is about?'

'Goodnight, Alwyn,' chimed Teg impatiently.

With great reluctance Grumpy left his spare set of keys on our table, and left by the front door, locking it behind him in timeworn manner. Teg and I slid back on our benches so that we were less visible from the road. The only light in the room now was the blue glow of an electronic fly killer behind the counter.

At just after seven o'clock we saw the Ice Queen emerge from the *Gazette* building. As a more recent arrival to the *Gazette*, Helen Snow was theoretically beyond our suspicion, though none of us found it easy to regard her, of all people, as in any way innocent. After a few steps down the street she stopped to take a call on her mobile phone. The conversation quickly became animated and didn't appear to go well. Was she pleading? We looked on in silent disbelief as the call ended. Slipping the phone back into her handbag she searched the ends of both sleeves for a paper hankie with which she dabbed her eyes and then wiped her nose. She stamped a heel in frustration, checked her make-up in a nearby shop window and then set off down the street with as much confidence as she could muster.

'Well, well,' said Teg, still in an unnecessary whisper. 'Maybe she's human like the rest of us after all.'

'So that leaves Coma, George and Smudge,' I added after a moment.

Five minutes later Coma appeared. He glanced across the road to Grumpy's and surreptitiously lifted both thumbs in our direction before setting off towards home. A few minutes later the public phone in the corner of the café began to ring.

'Twm? It's me.'

'Hi, Coma.'

'I did as we agreed. I waited until there was just one person left in the building before I left.'

'But Coma, both Smudge and George are still inside.'

'Really? Oh, damn. Should I go back?'

'No. It's too late now.'

'Sorry, Twm.'

Just over an hour later Smudge and George left the *Gazette* building together, heading towards the station. This wasn't an eventuality I had foreseen but it didn't necessarily mean our plan had failed.

Chapter 70

'Sorry I'm late,' said Coma, as he took his seat at our table in the Railway snug. 'Had to stop off at Ernie's for a fishcake for Humph's cat.'

'How is the dreaded Modlen?' asked Teg.

'I don't know what all the fuss was about,' said Coma. 'She's a little sweetheart.'

I'd heard enough. 'Can we please stop talking about the cat? Teg, what makes you think that somebody's found the phoney Annie Léchet interview?'

'Well, as we agreed, I left the tape and the transcript somewhere in the office behind reception where I figured it could easily be found. In the end I settled for the top drawer of my desk.'

'Teg?' interrupted Coma.

'Shush a minute, Coma, let me finish,' said Teg, who was clearly proud of what she had done. 'I arranged the contents of the drawer into an exact pattern, which I memorised, and left a tiny circle of white paper from my hole puncher on top of the little cassette box. Just to be sure, I left the drawer open by the exact width of a tuppenny piece and Sellotaped a strand of my hair to both the drawer and the desk where no one would notice it.'

'You're wasted at the *Gazette*. And?'

'And this morning when I got to work the tape and the transcript were still in the drawer but all my traps had been sprung. I found the drawer had been moved, the hair had been pulled from one end of the Sellotape, the pattern of the drawer's contents had altered and the small dot of paper was lying on the bottom of the drawer.'

Coma's face had fallen.

'Teg, I think maybe I should tell you …'

'Tell me what?' barked Teg.

'Well, last night Helen was in a right stinker of a mood … something about the finances, she said, and … well, before she left she asked me for the latest sales figures from the classified ads and …'

'You went into my bloody office drawer looking for them, didn't you?'

'I did, Teg. I'm so sorry. But as soon as you said that's where you'd hidden the …'

'*Pric pwdin wyt ti*, Coma. *Dim gwerth rhech dafad!*'

From the tone in which it was delivered Teg's outburst needed no translation.

'Well, you should have told me that was where you were going to hide them,' said Coma.

My heart fell. We'd missed our chance. 'It's okay,' I said. 'We should have gone over the plan a little more thoroughly. Leave it with me. I'll see if I can come up with another idea.'

* * *

An hour later I was in Grumpy's, racking my brain trying to work out my next move, when I heard the bell above the door ring and turned to see Coma and Teg. They walked over to my window table and sat down opposite me. Teg was smiling.

'What?' I asked.

'Twm, my lovely, I had a brainwave.' By now both of them were positively grinning.

'Well, is someone going to tell me or what?'

'When I went back to the office just now I got to thinking. I thought to myself, "If I was a conniving little shit and I wanted to sneak into Teg's top drawer without anyone seeing me and make a quick copy of the transcript, how would I do it?"'

'And?'

'And I thought to myself I'd use the fax machine right next to the desk in Teg's office to photocopy it.'

'Okay ...'

'So then I remembered something the fax machine man told me when he was showing me how it worked. He said the machine had a facility whereby you could press a button and it would print out an activity report logging the times that the machine had been used. So I went and fetched Nigel and he worked out how to print out the report and ...'

'And what?'

'Well, the bad news was that the activity report only records the details of transmissions to and from the fax machine. Not the photocopying.' She shot a knowing look at Coma who returned it with interest. 'But the good news is that the printout shows that someone used the fax in my office at 19:45 last night to successfully send a two-page document to a fax number in London, judging by the dialling code.'

'How long was the transcript?' I asked.

'Two pages,' beamed Teg.

'And, no, it wasn't me,' added Coma, enthusiastically.

Chapter 71

I made a note of the fax number and told Teg to hide the fax printout somewhere safe. She also promised to go straight back over the road to shred the transcript and destroy the mini-cassette. After she and a relieved-looking Coma left Grumpy's I went back to the Railway. At the payphone in the corridor outside the toilets I dialled in a number from my contacts book and waited for an answer.

'Twm! Long time no speak. I was sorry to hear about your job.'

My go-to girl for identifying car registration plates, ex-directory telephone numbers and that sort of thing was Marian Evans, younger sister of Albie, the *Gazette*'s production manager. Marian worked on the admin staff at the police station in Abergerran. She wasn't a police officer as such, but she was a lifer on the force and, having worked all around the local area, she was well-connected.

We chatted about the new broom sweeping through the *Gazette* and Marian said that Albie had been 'as miserable as sin' ever since Helen Snow had taken over. After the regulation amount of small talk, I asked Marian if she could do me a favour, and read the London fax number down the line to her.

'Okay, I'll need me a few minutes on that one. I'm going to have to reboot and log back in. Can I ring you back?'

I gave her the number of the payphone and hung up. Hanging around outside the toilets in a pub wasn't my idea of spending quality time. As I waited for Marian to call back I picked over the events that had brought me so low, wondering whether things might have worked out differently if I'd had a sharper eye. It was a pointless exercise, which only served to underline the importance of the call that was coming. Thankfully it was only a couple of minutes, as promised, before the phone rang.

'Yeah, Twm, that's a fax number and it belongs to a firm called Meachen, Schlenther and Lewis. She spelled out the first two names. 'That's a solicitors' firm in Southgate, North London.'

'That's great, Marian. Thanks, as always, for your help.'

'It's my pleasure. It wasn't right what happened to you, Twm. I hope it all works out.'

I pushed my luck a little further. 'Before you go ... I just wanted to ask you about a DS who moved over to Porthcoed CID from Bristol, I think it was, sometime in the last eighteen months or so. Name of Josh Templeton. What's the inside skinny on him?'

'Templeton ... Tall guy? Works for Bryn Thomas?'

'Yeah, that's him.'

'Sorry, Twm. I can't go there. Big red flag, okay? Listen, you take care now.'

'I will. Thanks again.'

I walked back into the bar trying to decipher what exactly Marian had just told me. It was quite clear that Marian's 'big red flag' comment was a warning for me to back off Templeton, but the reason for that was less so. On the one hand she might have been warning me that Templeton was as dodgy a copper as his boss, and to leave well alone. On the other ... had there been just a hint of a suggestion that Templeton was the quite the other thing, an 'untouchable' – an undercover officer from another force sent in to investigate an officer suspected of corruption?

I took a pull from my pint on the bar and then, noticing Merve in full flow with a couple of regulars in the snug, I crept into his office and shut the door behind me. For the conversation that was coming I didn't need the background noise of a local boozer. After a quick call to directory inquiries I dialled the telephone number I had been given.

'Meachen, Schlenther and Lewis. Good afternoon, how may I help you?'

'Oh hello. I'm calling from a newspaper called the *Porthcoed Gazette.*'

'Er, yes. What can I do for you?'

'I sent a fax to your office at around seven forty-five last night. I just wanted to check that it came through all right?'

'Please hold the line.'

There was a click and I was left to listen to an appalling electronic cover of Abba's hit 'The Winner Takes It All' until, after two minutes or so, there was another click.

'Hello? Mr Tucker? Yes, Mr Lewis says he received your fax and he has already passed it on to his client.'

I swallowed hard.

'Oh great,' I said. 'I'm glad to hear it came through okay.' My brain was whirring but I needed just a little more. 'Er, tell me … I'm sorry to ask … it's a little embarrassing, actually, but you see I've forgotten Mr Lewis's first name?'

'It's Frank Lewis.'

'Frank, of course it is. Thank you.' I put down the phone, and reached for my shoulder bag, pulling out the copy of Mara's paper that I had pinched from Grumpy's. I opened it up and turned to Mara's piece, scanning my way through it until I found what I was looking for. Around three-quarters of the way down the story Mara had quoted Eddie Lennox's solicitor, a Mr Frank Lewis.

Chapter 72

I stuffed the paper back into my bag and left the office, walking straight into a serious-looking Merve.

'Listen, Twm,' said Merve, 'I've got a proposition for you. Seeing as you're starting to feel quite at home here now and your slate is well … getting longer, shall we say … how about you start doing the odd shift behind the bar? See if we can't put a dent in what you owe me, eh?'

'Er, yeah. Okay. Great idea.'

'Excellent. Then maybe you can start when we reopen tonight?'

'Merve, I'd love to. Honest I would. But there's something I really need to do this evening. Can we talk about it in the morning, maybe? In the meantime … would you mind if I just used your office phone one more time?'

* * *

The newsroom was dark, with just one desk illuminated by the white light of an angle-poise lamp.

'Hello, Smudge.'

'Twm, you gave me quite a start. What brings you here at this time of night? I thought you were persona non grata?'

'Coma let me in on his way out. I needed a word.'

'Oh yeah? What's up? Need a job reference or something, do you?' He grinned, insincerely.

'Maybe. Merve's told me I'm going to have to start pulling pints to pay off my slate.'

'I've never done that. I'd rather be the other side of the bar, me.'

'Amazing what we'll do for money, isn't it?'

Smudge's eyes tightened just perceptibly and he started shuffling a couple of contact sheets. 'No offence, mate, but I've got these school sports day pictures to sort out before I knock off for the night.'

'I'll get right to the point then. Why did you set up Humph Blake?'

'I'm sorry?'

'It was you who broke into Humph's desk and made that five-grand transfer from the *Gazette* into Bren's account, wasn't it?'

'You what?' he laughed. 'I think you've been spending too much time in that pub of yours.'

'And right after you switched the money you sent an anonymous tip-off to Mara McKenzie and another to Bryn Thomas, didn't you?'

'Are you having a laugh? Why would I do that to Humph?'

'Presumably for the same reason you followed me to the library the day I met Humph there, and then followed Humph back into the city and tipped off Bryn Thomas once more about where Humph was staying.'

He shook his head. 'I think you've lost the plot, mate.'

'Ever heard of a man called Frank Lewis?'

'Not sure I have. Why?'

'He's a London solicitor. Represents Eddie Lennox. Lennox is the ex-footballer I reckon your dad used to drink with up in Glasgow back in the day. Remember telling me about your father outside the crem before Bren's funeral?'

Silence.

'Last night at around a quarter to eight you went into a drawer in Teg's office and then faxed to Frank Lewis's office a two-page transcript of an interview which you thought was of vital importance to Eddie Lennox's appeal.'

'Nonsense,' said Smudge.

'Oh, I can prove it, don't worry.'

'Okay. So what if I did fax something over as a favour for an old mate of my dad's? Nothing wrong with that, is there?'

'Maybe not. But bank fraud? Conspiring to frame Humph? That's jail time, pretty much.'

'So how exactly are you going to nail me for that?'

'You admit it, then?'

'I'm not admitting anything to you. You've probably got a tape recorder hidden in your coat pocket, you bloody boy scout. You have no proof of any of this, Twm. You're bluffing.'

'Am I? Did you ever stop to wonder why Eddie Lennox would want to screw up Humph's life in the first place? He must have quite a grudge against Humph to want you to do a thing like that, don't you think? Bad enough for Lennox to want to kill Bren, do you reckon? What if the police decided to follow that particular line of inquiry?'

I saw Smudge's Adam's apple rise and fall.

'And do you suppose a big drinker like Eddie Lennox will have been careful enough to cover over his tracks? Because it only takes someone to remember seeing Eddie on a train or in the city on the day in question and he's history. And in the hands of a good brief, that's you done for conspiracy to murder. How's that favour for an old mate of your dad's looking now?'

CHAPTER 73

'I didn't have anything to do with Bren, I swear it,' said Smudge, suddenly all out of bravado and looking visibly shaken. 'You've got to believe me. I liked Bren; I could never be a party to something like that ...'

I pulled up a chair and sat on the other side of Smudge's desk.

'So it *was* Eddie Lennox who killed her?'

'I don't know, Twm. Honest I don't.'

'But you suspect it might have been?'

'It's been on my mind ever since. I didn't think Eddie was nuts enough to do something like that. I mean why would he do something like that the minute he got out of nick?'

'You tell me,' I said. 'I'm serious. Tell me. You've got to see this as your only chance. If you can give Lennox to the police and get Humph off the hook, it's going to go much better for you. And I can help you.'

Smudge reached for his cigarettes and lit one up. He took a heavy pull and apparently decided to get it all off his chest.

'Eddie called me just after he got out of prison. He said he was a pal of my father's and that he'd once helped him out of a big jam. I already knew the story from my old man. Anyway, Eddie said he'd found out I was working on the same paper as Humph Blake. He told me that Humph had information that could have prevented him being sent down for the Angharad Sullivan murder. But for some reason Humph had kept it to himself.

'Eddie was bitter. Who wouldn't be after thirty years inside? He told me he was calling in the favour he'd done for my old man. It was just meant to be a shot across Humph's bows. That's all he said it would be. And he'd see me right with a couple of grand for my trouble. So I caved. But once I'd switched the bloody money over, Eddie had me on the hook, didn't he? I'm not a bad guy, Twm. I just made a mistake.'

'Alan Tucker, I am arresting you on suspicion of bank fraud ...'

Out of the shadows at the far end of the newsroom stepped Josh Templeton, and Smudge's face went white. His fiery eyes turned back to mine. 'You bastard, Bradley.'

'This is your only chance,' I said. 'But just so you know, I'm doing this for Humph and for Bren.'

Chapter 74

'Mara, it's Twm. I need to speak to you. Soon. It's about Eddie Lennox and it's something you have to hear. Please, call me. It's important.'

This was the third time that Mara's mobile had gone direct to voice message. I needed to talk to her. I needed to tell her that Smudge Tucker had been arrested and to explain the bogus Annie Léchet interview that had been faxed to Lennox's lawyer. But most of all I needed to tell her about Lennox. I'd called her mobile and I'd rung her office line, but it was starting to look like she wasn't going to call me back. In the end I called her news desk.

'Mara's on leave,' said a plummy male voice surrounded by newsroom hubbub. 'Is there something I can help you with?'

'Do you know where she is?' I pleaded.

'No,' said the plummy voice, 'and even if I did I'm afraid I wouldn't tell you.'

I left a message asking her to call me urgently if she got in touch and read out the number of the Nokia mobile I'd just bought. Things were moving too quickly now for me to stand outside the ladies in the Railway waiting for a phone to ring.

I left the pub, heading towards the *Gazette* and a meeting that Helen Snow had requested. I guessed she'd heard about Smudge or maybe my 'interview' with Annie Léchet, and wanted in. I was just about to turn onto Station Road when a blue Vauxhall Omega pulled up beside me and the driver's window slid down.

'Get in, Twm,' said Josh Templeton. 'Bryn wants to see you.'

* * *

The wooden chair in the centre of the interview room on the basement floor of Porthcoed police station was just as uncomfortable as I remembered it. The room was sparse and depressingly familiar. In the thin daylight from an iron-barred cellar window high up on one side I could make out patches of flaking paint and damp stains on the once-cream walls.

This time, it seemed, Bryn Thomas was eager to speak to me. No more than five minutes after I'd been led downstairs, the door flew open and in he steamed, Templeton trailing in his wake.

'Proper little sleuth you are, Bradley,' said Thomas, who'd aged since I'd last seen him. His hair had continued its retreat from his forehead, with what remained looking visibly greyer. On either side of a nose that still defied gravity, his ruddy complexion now resembled full-blown rosacea, and the copper's trademark yellow-grey shadows under each eye had puffed up into fully-fledged bags. 'Ace reporter saves boss from prison stretch. Your new editor is going to wet her knickers when she hears what you've done.'

'I think you're forgetting that I don't work at the *Gazette* any more, Bryn.'

'Mmm. "Saves boss from prison stretch." That's not entirely true, though, is it, Josh?'

'No, boss.'

'Seeing as you two seem to have struck up such a firm friendship, maybe you'd care to tell Twm why?'

'Smudge Tucker's confession gets Humph off the fraud charge,' I interrupted, 'but Smudge can't deliver Eddie Lennox on Bren's murder. There's no evidence against Lennox. Yet.'

'Which sort of leaves Humph with the same old problem, doesn't it?' said Thomas.

'I'd have thought that depends on the strength of your case against him.'

'Nice try, Twm, but I didn't get you in here so you could go on a fishing expedition.'

'Seriously, though. What have you got on Humph? DNA? A key eyewitness? I hope for your sake it's nothing you're going to have a hard time explaining when Eddie Lennox admits to killing Bren.'

'Just shut the fuck up, Bradley, all right? I'm the one who asks the questions in here.'

As his voice rang round the walls of the interview room it occurred to me that I'd developed an uncanny knack of hitting people's sore spot of late.

'Tell me how you singled out Smudge Tucker,' he asked after a pause.

'I've already told Josh.'

'That's DS Templeton to you,' snapped Thomas. 'And never mind him. I want you to tell me. Now.'

'Humph was convinced that whoever moved the cash must have had access to both Bren's and the *Gazette*'s bank account details. As he kept both in his desk in the newsroom, that suggested it was an inside job. And that gave me the idea of setting a trap.'

'So once you and your geriatric mates decided Smudge was the odd man out, you got on the blower to Josh with the idea of interrogating the poor unfortunate Mr Tucker until he cracked and spilled the beans. Just like that?' The look on Thomas's face underlined the tone of disbelief.

'You're honestly saying you don't believe Smudge set up Humph?' I asked him. 'Why don't you ask DS Templeton? He was there …'

I turned to look at Templeton, who resisted my gaze.

'I think you've cooked this whole thing up, Bradley. You've set up Smudge Tucker as the fall guy to try and get your precious boss off the hook. Well, you may have fooled DS Templeton here, but you don't fool me. Lock him up, Josh. Let's see whether a few hours in a police cell will bring him to his senses.'

'Well, this is a bit of a turn-up, eh Twm?' smirked Smudge Tucker as he was led out of the same cell I was about to be processed into.

'That'll do, Smudge,' said Templeton. 'Just be on your way before we change our minds and lock up the pair of you together.'

'Name?' asked a uniformed sergeant from behind the counter.

'Tell you what, Derek,' interrupted Templeton. 'It's half-twelve, why don't you grab your lunch break while I process this one?'

'Well, if you're sure, Josh?'

'Go on. My treat.'

'I will, then. Cheers.'

The uniform grabbed his copy of *The Sun* and headed towards the canteen. Templeton took his place behind the counter and started filling in a form. 'Okay, Twm, if you could take off your shoes and your belt. And empty the contents of your pockets into this box.'

I wasn't wearing a belt so I left my shoes next to my shoulder bag on the counter. Into the cardboard box I dropped my wallet, my watch, my loose change, the key to my room in the Railway and my new Nokia.

'And sign here.'

'What's going on, Josh?' I asked.

'You heard what Bryn said. It's DS Templeton to you.' He grinned.

Formalities completed, Templeton ushered me past the closed doors of two Victorian police cells towards a third that was open. He pulled the door behind me, locking it. A small hatch high in the door slid open and I heard Templeton say, 'Don't sweat it, Twm. I'll send someone along with some tea and a sandwich.' The hatch slid shut and I heard Templeton walk away.

* * *

Maybe an hour later the cell door was unlocked and opened and in walked the uniformed desk sergeant. There was no sign of tea or sandwiches.

'Okay, Bradley, you're free to go,' he said.

'I'm sorry?'

'Your lawyer's here. You're being released.'

I followed the sergeant back to the counter where to my surprise a smartly-dressed woman in her mid-forties, who I'd never set eyes on before, greeted me like an old friend.

'If we could speed this along, please, Sergeant? I have another client to see in the city in forty minutes' time.' Her voice was educated, her manner confident and assertive.

I waited until all my possessions had been returned to me and we were safely outside the station before I spoke up.

'I'm sorry, I don't know you,' I said.

'My name's Jessica Taylor.'

'I didn't know I had a solicitor,' I replied.

'Tell me, I'm a bit of a stranger around here. Is there somewhere we could get a cup of tea? Have a quiet chat?'

* * *

Grumpy's was usually quiet at this time of the day so we headed there. Breakfast, elevenses and lunch were Grumpy's cash cows but everybody in Porthcoed knew that teatime belonged to Ernie.

At the counter Jessica Taylor ordered and paid for two cups of tea and we sat by the window.

'So you must be new at Woodward & Thomas, then?' I asked her.

'I'm sorry, who?'

'They're the firm the *Gazette* uses. Solicitors. I figured maybe Helen Snow sent you?'

'No, that's not it at all, I'm afraid.'

'Well, in that case, do you mind me asking who you are? And how did you know I was being held?'

'Let's not go into all that now, Mr Bradley, shall we? Suffice it to say that I need to have a conversation with you that we couldn't possibly have in that police station.'

Grumpy arrived with our teas, and at Jessica's request returned a minute or two later with a refilled sugar dispenser. I watched as my slim and expensively-dressed new friend slopped four teaspoons of sugar into her cup and began to stir.

'I understand you were in Italy a few months ago,' she continued. My mind was buzzing. 'Verona, I believe? Can be glorious there in October, so I've heard.'

'Listen, will you just tell me who the hell you are and what's going on here?'

'If you must persist in knowing who I am then let's just say that I am a friend of Mara McKenzie.'

I thought for a moment and then smiled. The woman who dropped Mara off at the station. 'Mara's no more a national newspaper reporter than I am, is she?'

Jessica Taylor may or may not have been taken aback by my response. It was hard to tell. She had a commendable poker face.

'Oh, Mara is a reporter,' she replied after giving it some thought. 'A very good one as a matter of fact. And she does currently work for a London-based broadsheet. But she also works for me.'

'And who do you work for?'

'Let's just say I'm a civil servant, representing some people who are very concerned about the new stadium project. They're awfully keen that it should not be allowed to fail. And so to that end we've been keeping a quiet eye on anyone and anything that might pose a threat to its successful completion.'

'You mean journalists like Humph Blake. And me. And a loose cannon like Eddie Lennox.'

'The timing of Mr Lennox's release from prison did set the cat among the pigeons, I can tell you. Stretched us a little. Out of interest, Mr Bradley, may I ask exactly when, and why, you began to suspect that Mara was not entirely what she told you she was?'

'To be fair to Mara it took me a while,' I said. 'She has a very … persuasive personality. But it was the little things that, added all together, started to give her away.'

'Such as?'

'I noticed that the flow of information between us was a little one-sided. I put this down to journalistic rivalry at first, but eventually I realised there was something more to it than just that. So I reflected back over our relationship and that's when a number of red lights started flashing.'

'Indulge me.'

'Well, firstly, Mara came to us. To Humph. And then to me. Her offer to join forces and go fifty-fifty on a story with a paper like the *Gazette* didn't smell right. That's not how national newspapers work in my experience. She came on just a bit too strong.

'Then when Humph was arrested and I quit my job at the *Gazette*, Mara suddenly lost all interest in Porthcoed and this red-hot stadium story we had uncovered and went back to London. I was confused for a while. Maybe I was drinking a little more than was good for me, but it occurred to me that Humph and I had both suddenly become less of a threat.

And then all that changed again the moment I got a workable lead from Humph in prison. Back she came, eager to pick up on the story again.

'It was in Italy, though, when Ivan Harris started boasting proudly about some "interested parties" back home who were his insurance policy on the stadium – that's when I really turned paranoid. Tell me, are you actually aware of the kind of man you are facilitating?'

'Beggars can't be choosers, I'm afraid,' came her reply. 'The world in which I work is rarely perfect, more's the pity. But then I suppose if it was I'd be out of a job, wouldn't I?'

'You haven't said why you wanted to speak to me.'

'I've been eager to meet you, Mr Bradley, to see for myself the man who Mara has fallen for.'

'She told you that?'

'She didn't have to. I've known Mara a long time, ever since her parents were killed when she was just eight years old.'

'In a car crash,' I said, as the truth hit home. The thin pale scar.

'In all that time Mara has shown little or no interest in forming any close relationship with a man, or with a woman for that matter. She's had boyfriends, yes, but always fleeting. Transactional, if you like. It was one of the things about her that made me think she could do a job for me. But then she came across you.'

She fixed her eyes on mine. 'Mr Bradley, I need to ask you for your help.'

'I'm listening.'

'I need to know *exactly* what you have learned about Eddie Lennox.'

'Then why don't you ask Mara?'

'Your recent … disagreement … with Mara rather puts her on the blind side at the moment. And, anyway, she's got her plate full keeping tabs on Lennox himself.'

'What do you mean?'

'Mara is going to be pretty much in Lennox's company until after the inaugural match at the stadium tomorrow. Ostensibly she's doing a newspaper feature on his return to the scene of a crime that he insists he never committed.'

'Do you have any idea just how much danger she's in?'

'That is exactly what I am trying to ascertain.'

'Eddie Lennox is a dangerous man. He paid the *Gazette*'s picture editor to divert funds from the paper into Humph Blake's wife's account. He was setting him up.'

'Yes, but why?'

'Well, if you believe what Lennox told Smudge Tucker, and I'm not sure I do, for the purposes of revenge. He told Smudge that Humph could have stopped him being sent down for the murder of Delilah Sullivan. My theory is that Lennox killed Humph Blake's wife, though I can't prove that yet. But if I'm right, and if Lennox suspects Mara is not being entirely straight with him, then Mara's life is in grave danger.'

'Yes. If your theory is correct I can see that now.'

At this point I noticed that Jessica's complexion had visibly paled. 'Okay, so what exactly are you going to do about it?'

'There isn't much I can do at the moment, Mr Bradley.'

'You could alert the police for one thing.'

'It's not quite as simple as that, I'm afraid.'

'Why not?'

'There are certain limits on the extent to which the local constabulary can help us in this matter.'

'What do you mean?'

'The force can hardly be seen to be paying overly close attention to a man very publicly involved in trying to overturn an historic conviction at its own hands, can it? Besides, they already have their hands full with the match tomorrow.'

'Well, what about your lot, then? Surely you've got more people than just Mara working down here this weekend?'

'Mara will be perfectly safe until she enters the stadium. It's then that our problems potentially begin. In a crowd of 25,000 people it's going to be awfully hard to stay close to her. Which is why I was hoping that you might agree to step in.'

Chapter 76

Jessica Taylor said she would contact Mara, explain the situation and tell her to expect me. I was the logical and least suspicious choice to ride shotgun for Mara, she said. Lennox knew I was working with Mara and had already met me. I'd neglected to mention to Jessica that with Smudge Tucker back out on the street again, courtesy of Bryn Thomas, Lennox would likely now know that I was onto him. I just didn't want Mara left alone with Lennox.

Jessica then rang me early on the Saturday morning and said I was to meet Mara and Lennox in a city-centre pub around ninety minutes before kick-off. I told her I had some business to take care of in the city first but would get there at least an hour before the game.

The pub was packed to the rafters, and I had to squeeze my way through the door. I found Mara and Lennox standing at the bar. To cut straight through any lingering atmosphere between us I greeted Mara warmly, kissing her on the cheek. Her eyes gave nothing away. I turned to Lennox, whose handshake was cold and clammy.

'Nice to see you again, Tom,' said Lennox, straight-faced. 'Glad you could make it. What's your poison?' And then turning to the bar, 'Can I get some more drinks, here, pal?'

I took my pint from Lennox and thanked him. 'How are you feeling, Eddie? It must feel a bit strange knowing that you're about to set foot in a place that has had such a profound effect on your life?'

'I've thought about that,' answered Eddie. 'And don't get me wrong, son, I may shed a tear or two. But I'm in a much calmer place these days. Forgive and forget, you know? I'm here today to put all that behind me and move on.'

With the arrival of another round of drinks the small talk began to flow a little more easily, and even Mara seemed to relax in my company. With twenty minutes to go before kick-off, she reached into her bag. 'Okay, boys. Ticket time. Today we're going to be on the press benches.'

At that point Lennox smiled and leaned across so that we could hear him clearly. 'I hope youse don't mind Mara, love, but I decided I want to be in the heart of the crowd today, and not stuck with the hacks. Present company excepted, by the way.' He grinned and produced three tickets of his own from his inside jacket pocket, handing us one each. 'Ta-dah! Three seats in the West Stand. Up in the Gods. Hell of a view. My treat.' I looked at Mara and she looked back at me. Lennox smiled and finished off his vodka. 'Who's for another wee belt before we go?'

* * *

It had been more than two years now since a rugby international had been played in the city and in and around the stadium there was a hum of excitement as familiar old habits were being revisited amid the promise of something thrilling and new. As we walked onto the embankment the river flowing past the new stadium rippled in the breezy June afternoon sunshine. Just three entrances were being used for the stadium's first ever match. According to Lennox, ours was Gate 7 at the Central Station end of the ground.

Embedded in a lively and vocal procession of revellers, mostly wearing home colours but dotted here and there with the occasional small cluster of the opposition's yellow and green, we were swept down the embankment. On the road bridge at the bottom of the stadium Mara took Eddie to one side to pose him, thoughtfully, against the backdrop of the city's new landmark. As she fired off a few shots from an expensive-looking compact digital camera, I watched a couple of touts hawking for tickets, some of which I'd read were expected to change hands for three times their face value. Photos done, we took our places in a stationary crowd stretching right back from the entrance gate. As we waited we were watched over by a line of men and women in a mix of orange, red and green fluorescent jackets. According to the *Western Morning Record*'s match-day special edition, around a thousand stewards would be on duty at the game, many of them construction workers based at the stadium.

We waited, motionless, amid the crowd which was becoming a little more restless as the clock ticked ever closer to kick-off. Soon a tannoy announcement revealed that kick-off had been delayed by twenty minutes. The word quickly spread that the new stadium's much-vaunted electronic turnstiles had failed. The *Record* had detailed how each state-of-the-art machine had been designed to admit fans at an orderly rate of more than 650 an hour. Just teething problems, the governing body's publicity machine would no doubt say in the aftermath of the game. Come October it would be all right on the night.

Before long the crowd in front of us started to move and, inch by inch, we approached the turnstiles. Just then a sudden, unexpected surge of bodies swept me away from Lennox and Mara, and I noticed Lennox begin to push through the queue towards a different turnstile, guiding Mara in front of him. I watched, helplessly, as they filed through the approach barriers, gave their tickets to a steward and made their way into the stadium. Twenty yards behind them, surrounded by bodies, there was nothing I could do but bide my time and patiently shuffle my way through the funnel neck towards another turnstile. Through the crowd I caught a brief glimpse of Mara on the other side of the fence, her head turned back, looking for me, but then she was gone.

It took another five minutes for me to reach the turnstile and enter the stadium. I glanced down at my ticket and began to negotiate the succession of numbers printed onto it: there was a gate number, a stair, a level, an aisle, a block, a row and finally a seat number. The stair came next. I headed towards the correct opening and was swept steadily up the switchback concrete stairway. There was no sign of Lennox or Mara in the stairwell, and no way for me to travel faster than the crowd around me. At Level Six the stairwell opened onto a wide concourse that looked like it would circle around the entire upper level of the stadium, with toilets positioned along the inner ring and bars on the outer. I scanned the backs and faces of hundreds of people on the move around me, but to no avail. I checked my ticket once more and set off towards the corresponding block number.

A dozen or so steps up from the concourse I found myself inside the bowl of the stadium, where the claustrophobic crush of the past half hour gave way at last to a vast and open space in front of me. The scale of the stadium was breathtaking. Unfinished, and yet already majestic, its four stands swooped around a lush green playing area. Multi-tiered and studded for the most part with rows of green or red seating, three of the four stands were filling rapidly with fans. At each corner of the playing area immense steel framework structures rose from the stadium floor, like giant red Meccano tent poles, to shore up existing parts of the roof. The roof itself, I noticed, was more complete than I had imagined, with the West and East Stands almost completely covered over.

Another steward squinted at my ticket and pointed me down a short flight of steps towards my row number. Below me the stand dropped away steeply and my stomach churned. Overriding the irrational fear of falling I descended gingerly, carefully finding a foothold on each narrow step. It wasn't until I had reached the correct row number that I took a breath and began to calm down. I checked around me again for Lennox and Mara but, prompted by a large man behind me, I was forced to shuffle along my row, squeezing sideways and apologetically past a line of men and women who had risen to their feet to let me by.

With my back to the void I double-checked my ticket against the number on the one vacant seat in front of me and then politely challenged the people sitting immediately to my left and right. All our ticket details tallied and it was then that I realised that Lennox had deliberately meant to shake me off. He and Mara were always going to be seated in another part of the stadium. Resisting the urge to panic I scoured the stand around me, slowly and carefully but without success. Below me on the green, green grass of the nation's new home of rugby, the regimental band struck up a hymn and was joined by a male voice choir.

I sat in my seat and tried to clear my thoughts. I took out my mobile phone and dialled Mara's, but the call wouldn't go through. Either the stands were blocking my signal or the sheer weight of demand had jammed the system. Around me the stadium burst into a roar as the home team was led out onto the pitch by a regimental Goat Major. I felt completely helpless. The first ever match to be played at the new stadium was about to begin and I was the only person inside who didn't care. I had to find Mara.

As the visiting team's anthem was played I stood up, made my apologies and began to shuffle back towards the end of the row, where I turned away from the pitch and jogged up the steps towards the exit. From the platform next to the exit I started methodically scanning the crowd. To my left a sea of humanity stretched almost all the way to the North Stand.

To my right the rows of occupied seats stopped abruptly somewhere between the ten and twenty-two metre lines marked out neatly in white on the playing area below. From there, all the way around the South Stand to the East Stand opposite, the few blocks of seating that had been installed were either empty or dotted here and there with men and women in hard hats and fluorescent jackets. That end of the stadium was mostly bare concrete and still belonged to the construction workers.

The band now struck up the home team's national anthem. As the singing began I was approached by the steward. 'Is everything all right, sir?'

'I'm … just looking for my friend,' I shouted back distractedly. 'We came in together but seem to have got separated.'

'Well, I'm sorry, sir, but you can't stand here. The game is about to kick off and we have to keep these aisles clear for safety reasons.'

Safety reasons. I hurried down the steps from the stand to the concourse, which was emptying now, with just a few stragglers and late arrivals hurrying towards their seats. North or south? I chose north and ran clockwise around the concourse until I came to the steps leading back up to the next block. With the game underway I worked my way to each block in turn, scanning the crowd until I was inevitably moved on by a steward. If I didn't see Mara, she may at least see me.

Back on the concourse I heard another roar and ran up the steps into the next block in time to hear the stadium announcer namecheck the home team's penalty scorer. For what must have been half an hour or so I worked my way around the stand in this way but I knew in my heart that I was looking for two needles in a haystack.

I had begun to lose faith when Eddie Lennox's words were replayed in my head. *Up in the Gods.* That was it. I knew now how to narrow down my search.

Chapter 77

I ran towards the southern end of the stand until my way was blocked by a barrier and a group of stewards. One of them, wearing the orange jacket of a supervisor, stepped forward.

'I'm afraid it's hard hats only beyond this point, sir,' he said. 'Can I help you to find your seat?'

Breathlessly I explained that I was searching urgently for someone I had become separated from on my way into the stadium.

'It's a young girl,' I lied. 'She's only eight. I need to find her.'

'Perhaps you can give me your name, and her name, and a brief description of what the young lady is wearing?'

Too much fuss, too much time. I turned tail and ran up the nearest set of steps back into the stadium bowl. There was an empty seat right next to the platform at the entrance to the block so I sat myself down to avoid the inevitable attentions of the steward on duty there, then swivelled on my seat and began to scour the top of the stand behind me.

There were perhaps thirty rows of seats between me and the top row of the stand, which was separated from the outermost edge of the stadium roof above it by a gap of what looked to be around fifteen to twenty feet. The gap, open to the elements, was blocked off by thick horizontal safety barriers which meant that anyone standing in the very top row of the stand was silhouetted against the grey-white sky behind them.

I scanned all along the top row, looking for two figures, one short and one tall, but I saw nothing to give me hope. Suddenly the roar of the crowd began to build, the entire stand around me leapt to its feet and the roar burst into a crescendo – the home team had scored a try. On my feet now I was perhaps the only person in the entire stadium looking directly away from the pitch. It was then that in a sparsely-populated row of seats right at the top of the stand I caught a glimpse of one other. A tall, thin figure. Lennox. To my amazement he began to clamber up the safety barriers behind him. It seemed he'd waited for a distraction on the pitch to climb from the top row of seats up onto the roof of the West Stand. What was he doing? I ran from my seat in the direction of what I had seen, pushing past anyone I met on the way.

As the cheering subsided again, I pounded breathlessly up the row of narrow steps towards the top row of the stand, occasionally checking up ahead. There was another roar, a successful conversion no doubt, and I saw a smaller figure – Mara – also pull herself, with difficulty, up onto the roof. I stopped in shock and looked around me to see if anyone else, spectator or steward, had seen what I had seen. But if anyone had seen them amid all the hubbub of the home score, there was no sign of anyone doing anything about it.

I reached the top step, my chest heaving and my head swimming at the thought of the steep drop of the stand behind me, and pushed my way southwards to where the crowd began to thin out, to where I had seen Lennox and Mara. Just as I got there the referee blew the whistle for half-time and the entire crowd rose once more to its feet. Taking my chance I stood on the top of my seat and reached up for the first horizontal metal barrier.

'Oi!' I heard a shout to my left. 'Get down from there. You!'

I ignored the shout and dispelled any thoughts of the reality of what I was about to do by thinking of the danger to Mara. By the time I had scrambled my way onto the roof I was breathless, but too furious to be scared. I got slowly to my feet in the surprisingly cool, breezy early evening air and saw the roof rise on a gentle slope towards the front of the stand, where a tubular framework of white steel ran the length of the stand, guarding the 100-foot drop down onto the playing area.

Midway across the roof Lennox and Mara were entwined, with Mara trying to pull herself from his clasping hands.

'You leave her be,' I screamed.

They both turned to face me. I'd got it wrong. Eddie was trying to escape from Mara.

'Twm!' screamed Mara. 'He's going to jump.'

'Just you stay there, Tom,' shouted Lennox. 'I'm gonna do this and neither of youse are gonna stop me.' He suddenly broke free of Mara, pushing her onto her back, and stepped purposefully towards the inside edge of the roof.

I started to run, enraged now. He turned and saw me coming and picked up his speed. In desperation I hurled myself, arms stretched, at his legs, bringing him down just ten feet from the steel framework guarding the roof edge. But I wasn't the only one with manic energy coursing through me. Lying on his side Lennox began to kick at me with his one free leg. I ducked my head but he caught me with a stunning blow on my temple. This gave him the chance to free himself from my grasp and pull himself further towards the edge of the roof.

'Why are you doing this?' I shouted through the pain.

He stopped and turned his head towards me. 'I'm not going back inside, Twm. Thirty years is enough bird for anyone.'

'Then why kill Bren?'

'Humph Blake and Ivan Harris ruined my life. When I got out of prison I finally got my chance to ruin theirs. I never killed Angie Sullivan. She was a wonderful wee girl. I wouldn't have harmed a hair on her head.'

'But what good does it do ending your life now?'

'I'm even with Blake. This way I get even with Harris. He won't get his precious tournament now.'

With that Lennox climbed to his feet again and approached the steel framework at the edge of the roof. He was about to swing himself through it and launch himself into the void when a voice behind us shouted, 'All of you – stay exactly where you are!' The steward who had seen me climb onto the roof had followed us up.

Thrown by the unexpected, Lennox hesitated. I seized my chance and ran towards him but he saw me coming and started to move again. Reaching out I grabbed his jacket. He swung his arm round violently to dislodge me, but I ducked and tugged hard. Thankfully I had enough of his jacket to swing him around. We both lost balance and landed on our sides, entangled once again. With another manic burst of energy Lennox lifted me over him and threw me towards the edge of the roof. Ahead of me the open chasm of the stadium bowl came into view. Frantically I reached out with my arms to gain a handhold, any purchase on life. As my legs swung out over the edge, I flung my arm around a white steel rail.

'Eddie. I can't hold myself. Help me.'

Lennox took one look at me and another down into the stadium below, weighing up his choice. If either of us fell now he'd get his way. If I fell, he'd maybe even get away with having killed Bren. But suddenly I knew that he intended for us both to take the drop.

'Eddie!' screamed Mara. 'He's going to fall.'

Lennox leaned forward towards me and started trying to prise my arm from the steel rail, clenching his teeth with the effort. I clung on for my life but the strength in me was beginning to fade. Looking down I saw groundsmen wandering over the pitch below me. Summoning one last surge of fury I swung my free arm towards Lennox's face, connecting with my clenched fist and knocking him back into Mara's grasp. With all her might she pulled him over onto his back and fell on him, pinning him down. She turned to me, helplessly.

'Twm!'

I pulled on the steel rail but the muscles in my arm and shoulder were burning now. I swung my free arm again, trying to gain some extra purchase on the roof but failed to grasp the rail. That was the last of my strength. I took one last look at Mara and surrendered to my fate.

Chapter 78

'Twm, are you okay?' asked Mara.

'I must be,' I replied. 'There isn't a single part of me that doesn't hurt.'

'I'd say by now you've used up at least two of your nine lives.'

'Is it always going to be about cats with you?'

Mara smiled at my half-hearted attempt at humour, but we were both past the point where anything was funny any more. That she, I and Eddie Lennox would all make it down from the stadium roof safely had at one stage seemed most unlikely; in my case nothing less than a minor miracle. I had given up the ghost.

As the last drop of energy had leached from the muscles holding me to the stadium roof, I'd looked up at Mara, so near and yet so far from me. The anger inside me which had powered my ascent to the top of the stadium had burned off by then, leaving nothing more than a feeling of disappointment. At that moment I'd moved beyond fear to acceptance, and the memory of that now was terrifying. Then suddenly I'd lost my hold on the roof... but realised I wasn't falling. I'd seen the steward's grimacing face as he, with Mara pulling on him, had dragged me back to life, and the three of us had rolled over in a heap on the rooftop.

The second half of the match had come and gone now and Mara and I were seated in a windowless, brick-walled room deep in the bowels of the stadium, waiting for a police debrief.

'When we got separated I was worried sick about you,' I said. 'I knew Lennox might try something. But I had no idea what was on his mind.'

'He was never going to harm me,' said Mara. 'That was never his plan. He just wanted me to be there at the end to witness his last defiant gesture. He knew you were onto him.'

'I wasn't completely sure until an hour before kick-off that he'd killed Bren Blake.'

'How did you find out?'

'Remember when you took me to meet Lennox for the first time, at his hotel near the station?'

She nodded.

'Something odd happened when we were talking to him which only came back to me yesterday. When the barman spilled Lennox's drink he apologised to Lennox but called him by another name. He referred to him as Mr Edwards. I didn't think anything of it at the time. Eddie. Edwards. I just thought he'd mixed up Lennox's name.'

'I don't even remember that,' said Mara.

'Before I met up with you in the pub this afternoon I called into the hotel. It was a bit of a long shot, but I hoped that with it being a busy match day the same barman might be on shift. Thankfully he was. I showed him a picture of Eddie Lennox from the story you'd written and asked if he remembered him. He said he did and told me that Lennox had stayed at the hotel once before but had checked in under a different name.'

'Edwards?'

'We checked the hotel register and the date tallied with Bren's murder. Hopefully city-centre CCTV and the forensics from Bren will take care of the rest.'

Just then the door opened and in walked a policewoman. 'How are you both doing?' she asked with genuine concern. She turned to me, examining the bruise on my temple. 'Would you like me to find someone to have a look at that for you?'

'No, I'm fine, thank you.'

'What's happened to Eddie?' asked Mara.

'Mr Lennox has been arrested and is in custody. I'm going

to need to arrange to interview you both so that we can get your witness statements written down but judging by the look of you it's been a long enough day. You'd best get yourselves off home.'

'Who won, by the way?' I asked.

She smiled. 'We did.'

CHAPTER 79

In the days and weeks after the inaugural match I finally managed to make some progress with my insurance company and it wasn't long before my flat had been restored to something that promised to exceed its former glory. I was in Grumpy's, taking a break from adding the last coat of paint to the bedroom walls, when I heard a familiar voice above me.

'Mr Bradley, would you mind if I joined you?'

I looked up from my *Gazette* to see Jessica Taylor. 'It's a free country,' I replied, folding the paper. 'Or is it?'

'I wanted to thank you for your efforts at the match.'

I took a mouthful of coffee.

'I also wanted to apologise to you in person about why you were unable to report the events that occurred on that day in exactly the way they happened.'

As if I didn't already know.

'You might be interested to hear that your brief sojourn on top of the stadium on match day didn't go unnoticed. Apart from the steward, with whom we've had a little word, a couple living in a rental across the river on the embankment saw four people scramble onto the roof. It's surprising that with all the thousands of people there that day no one else seems to have noticed, not even with all the telly cameras. Well, that's to say no one else has come forward so far.'

'What can I tell you? We're a rugby-loving nation.'

'Though if someone did try and come forward with a view to selling such a story ...'

'... whichever newspaper or TV company they chose to sell it to would be subjected to an early-evening visit by you or one of your "interested parties"?'

Jessica Taylor merely smiled.

'So, what if a reporter produced evidence that Ivan Harris had taken a short cut on essential safety work prior to the stadium being built? What would you do then?'

'Let's just say that it is in the interests of the greater good that nothing would be allowed to interfere with the final preparations for the stadium hosting the tournament. In any case, whatever Harris may have suggested, I can assure you that the governing body is completely in the dark about what he's been up to. They're not crooks; they're rugby men. Harris is a rogue operator, who has been working in tandem with foreign criminals. And you can also rest assured that a number of world-class construction experts have been drafted in to ensure the safety of the stadium going forward.'

At this point we were joined at our table by Grumpy, who had seen Jessica Taylor enter and was touting for business.

'Can I get you a cup of tea or anything, love?' he asked, rubbing his grubby hands on an off-white tea towel. 'Bakestone, perhaps?'

'She's not staying,' I said, turning to her.

Jessica Taylor smiled and said, 'Yes, I'd better be on my way.'

As she walked away from the table Grumpy began to grumble at me for scaring off business, so I drained my coffee and followed her to the door. Out on Station Road – a tranquil scene at last now that BT had finally filled in their trenches and tarmacked them over – I saw Jessica Taylor's slim and elegant figure walking away from me. I stood on the pavement and turned my eyes back to the *Gazette* building.

In a jointly-bylined piece that had run in both the *Gazette* and in Mara's paper, confounding all my expectations, we had revealed how our investigation into the second Stadium Murder had turned up evidence leading to Eddie Lennox's sensational arrest at the stadium itself during the inaugural match – though of course no mention was made of anyone being on the roof of the stadium during the game.

We'd also broken the news that Lennox had been subsequently charged with killing Brenda Blake at the same location a year earlier, and that both he and *Gazette* employee Alan 'Smudge' Tucker had been charged with fraudulently removing funds from Bentall Newspaper Group and conspiring to pervert the course of justice.

And finally we'd revealed that Mrs Blake's husband, the former *Gazette* editor Humphrey Blake, had been released from the prison in which he was being held on remand for her murder and fraud.

Our joint splash had been enough to earn a grateful Helen Snow sufficient kudos to allow her to return to London with her career back on track. I had been offered my old reporting job back – scant reward for almost falling 100 feet to my death on live television, I thought – but in truth I was undecided on my next move. I had also been contacted by the editor of the *Western Morning Record* and asked out to dinner with him at my earliest convenience.

On my way back to the flat I stopped in at Aarav's for a few supplies.

'How are you, Twm?' asked Aarav from behind the counter. 'How's the flat coming on?'

'I'm fine thanks, Aarav. Just giving it a last lick of paint. How are you?'

'Off to Delhi next week,' he replied, proudly.

'For your auntie's …?'

'For Auntie Prisha's ninetieth birthday. You remembered.'

'Did I really buy that much whisky from you?'

'You know, I almost went out of business when your flat burned down,' he laughed and carried on loading my shopping into a plastic bag.

I was back at the flat, trying to wire up a new music system, when I heard a doorbell chime. After belatedly realising that it was my doorbell, I walked through the kitchen and opened the door to find Mara.

'Brand new staircase,' she shrugged. 'It doesn't creak.'

'I really miss the old one,' I smiled. 'I didn't even recognise the sound of my own doorbell.'

I ushered her inside and showed her briefly around the renovation.

'It looks great, Twm,' she said. 'It must feel so good to be back home.'

'It's cheaper than living with Merve, that's for sure. It's going to take me an age to clean off my slate with him.'

We sat, at a discreet distance from each other, on my brand new settee.

'Drink?' I offered. 'I've just put a four-pack in the fridge.'

'Not for me, thanks. But you go ahead.'

'No, I'm fine.'

The silence was awkward, so I filled it. 'What brings you back to Porthcoed? No offence, but given all the excitement of the past year I'm almost scared to ask.'

'I wanted to see you,' said Mara. It had been a while since we had seen each other, but time had done nothing to diminish the powerful effect that her physical presence had on me. 'I wanted to talk to you.'

'Mara, I …'

'Twm,' she interrupted. 'Can I speak first?'

I nodded. 'Okay.'

'I've been running this over and over in my mind on the train,' she said. 'I changed my mind twice coming up the staircase. So, I'll just come right out and say it, okay? I want to apologise for misleading you. I wasn't honest with you about who I was or what I was doing. And I'm sorry.'

'You should have told me about your parents. About Jessica Taylor. You should have just told me everything.'

'I wanted to, but I couldn't. And then that night in my room … your room … at the Railway. I …'

'You told me you'd fallen in love with me.'

'Yes, I did. And I had.'

'And I told you I didn't believe you. I was …'

'No, that's okay, Twm. You don't need to explain.'

'But I want to,' I said, 'because the truth is I've fallen in love with you, too. It's just that life was complicated back then and I didn't know how to tell you.'

Once again a silence fell between us, until the realisation hit me like a kick in the teeth. 'Oh, okay,' I said. 'I get it.'

'No, Twm, I don't think you do. I still have strong feelings for you, but …'

'But what?'

'But it's not going to work out.'

'Why not?'

'Because … I'm going away,' said Mara. 'I've been offered a job in the paper's New York bureau. It's just too good an offer to pass up. I'm leaving next week but I wanted to see you before I went.'

There was another brief but emotionally-charged moment of silence between us.

'Keeping an eye on the Yanks, eh?'

Mara smiled. 'Something like that, yeah.'

I leaned across the settee and gathered her into my arms, pulling her against my chest, reacquainting myself with the scent of her hair. Mara lifted her head and kissed me. She looked me straight in the eye, smiled sweetly, then got up and left.

CHAPTER 80

'It's so nice to see you back, lovely,' said Teg, who insisted on coming out from behind the front counter to plant another lipstick heart on my cheek.

'It doesn't mean I'm "back" back,' I replied.

'Of course not,' she lied. 'Coma's up in the newsroom. He's expecting you.' As I turned she pinched my bottom.

I climbed into the familiar old lift and pressed the usual brass button. The doors swung to and the machinery seemed to scratch its head for a moment before clanking into life.

The newsroom was humming like the taproom of a pub.

'Twm!' said Coma, staring over his half-specs. 'How's things? Got the flat back up to scratch?'

'Just about, thanks. How's everything here?'

Albie Evans walked by with a smile on his face. George Mellor wheeled a large brown cardboard box through the newsroom on a sack trolley and stopped briefly to stretch and rub the small of his back, straining the zip on the front of his new boiler suit once again.

'Business as usual,' grinned Coma. 'The jobs cull has been called off, for now anyway, and the atmosphere has warmed up ten-fold since the Ice Queen departed for London. And guess what? We're all getting an "Internet Terminal"!' Coma even used his fingers as inverted commas.

'Is that one of the Twins on the picture desk?' I whispered, nodding over to where Smudge used to sit.

'Nige is our new trainee picture editor,' said Coma.

'And I can remember when he didn't know a thing about cameras,' I said, pulling a chair over to sit next to Coma.

'Have you seen Humph?' he asked.

'Not yet, but I heard he was back home.'

'Been a dreadful time for him. Still, once he gets his feet back under the table here, he'll be right as rain. Best thing for him. And the same goes for you.'

'We'll see,' I told him. 'I haven't made up my mind about that just yet.'

As ever at the appointed time of day, the sound on the newsroom telly was turned up to allow the duty reporter to monitor the local lunchtime news. But when the WTV anchor delivered her top headline a disbelieving hush fell across the newsroom.

'There is shock in the rugby community this lunchtime at the news of the sudden death of construction entrepreneur Ivan Harris, the man behind the redevelopment of the new national stadium.'

The anchor handed quickly across to Mike James-Jenkins, WTV Hairdo, who was 'live for us' outside the national stadium.

'Yes, that's right, Jane,' said Mike, visibly excited at the tale that was his to convey. 'Police in northern Italy have just confirmed to me that Ivan Harris, the 55-year-old Porthcoed-born owner of Harris Construction, was killed this morning in a boating accident on Lake Garda. Witnesses reported seeing the engine of the speedboat in which Mr Harris was travelling erupt into flames just after dawn around half a mile off the lakeside town of Bardolino. Police have revealed that the only other passenger in the boat, a Mrs Caterina Bianchi, was also killed in the explosion. Mrs Bianchi is the wife of the prominent Italian businessman Andrea Bianchi at whose villa Mr Harris was staying as a guest. A spokesman for the Italian police has confirmed that an investigation will take place into the deaths but that early indications suggest nothing more than "a catastrophic mechanical failure with tragic consequences".'

The *Gazette* newsroom was gravely quiet for a second or two and I turned to look at Coma, who had turned to look at me.

'Okay, boys, let's go,' said Coma, snapping back into the moment. 'Aled, see if you can get hold of Harris Construction, Ken Thomas at the Buzzards and the PR department of the governing body. We're going to need reaction, a tribute piece and a backgrounder on Harris, okay? Nige, maybe you can start pulling together a good spread of pictures from the archive and anything you can get off the wire, all right?'

Coma looked at me over his specs. 'Twm?'

'Okay,' I replied, taking off my jacket, 'but I'm strictly freelance for this one.'

Chapter 81

I didn't get back to the flat until late in the evening. At the bottom of the staircase I found my father, pacing around.

'I wasn't sure if this was where you lived,' he said. 'Doesn't look like a burned-out flat to me.'

'The insurance firm finally pulled its finger out. Are you coming up?'

'Yes. Yes, please. Did you hear the news?'

'I was at the *Gazette* when it broke. I just helped them compile a pack of lies about a leading businessman and philanthropist who gave millions to charity and was a much-loved figure in Porthcoed society.'

I turned the key, pushed the door and switched on the kitchen light, leaving my jacket on the back of a chair at the kitchen table.

'I need a drink,' I said. 'Beer?'

'Okay,' said my father closing the door behind him.

'You're in town to see Jacqui Harris, I take it?'

'She's had a hell of a shock.'

'I bet she has. She's just found out her husband was knocking off Caterina Bianchi. How's she bearing up?'

'She's doing okay.'

'Wait till she finds out he murdered his ex-wife too.'

'What did you say?'

'Nothing. I'm just tired, okay? Long day.'

I handed my father his beer. He looked at the label disapprovingly.

'Ivan Harris's death rather clears the way for me,' he said after a pause.

'With Jacqui?'

'With the stadium,' he said, clearly annoyed. 'If anything comes out now about the circumvention of safety procedures they'll hang it around his neck and not mine.'

'It won't come out,' I told him. 'Trust me. Apparently it's not "in the interests of the greater good".'

'What do you mean?'

'Ever hear of a woman named Jessica Taylor?' I asked him.

'Name doesn't ring a bell, I'm afraid. Who is she?'

'It doesn't matter.'

'Well … thanks for the beer,' he said, leaving it unopened on the table.

'Back to the grieving widow?'

'For God's sake, son, show some respect will you? Her husband's just been killed in a tragic accident.'

I heard the kitchen door click shut behind me. 'Some accident,' I said.

Chapter 82

From the top of Deri mountain you can reduce Porthcoed and all its good intentions and dashed dreams into a town small enough to fit between your thumb and forefinger. It was a breezy late September day, and the clouds above us were scudding eastwards across the valley in the direction of the city.

'What got into you?' I asked Humph who was standing beside me admiring the view. 'For a smoker you shot up that last part of the hill like a man possessed.'

'It was all I could think about when I was in prison,' said Humph, who I'd rarely seen outside in the open air. 'I used to walk up here all the time as a boy, but I let all that go when I got into newspapers. Let that be a lesson to you.'

We stood side by side for a few minutes, watching a lone buzzard circle on the breeze below us.

'Thank you, Twm,' said Humph.

'For what?'

'Don't be daft,' he said. 'For doing what you did to get me out of trouble.'

'Worst part was looking after Modlen. Vicious little …'

'I thought it was Coma who took her in?'

I let it go, rubbing my hands together to warm them up. 'Well, you'd have done the same for me. Wouldn't you?'

'Bloody Ivan Harris,' said Humph. 'I got so obsessed with that bloody man I took my eye off the ball and that was that. I stepped into it right up to my neck, didn't I? And it cost Bren her life.'

'It wasn't your fault, Humph. It was the act of a madman. Just what was it between you and Eddie Lennox anyway?'

'Eddie had it in for me, all right,' said Humph, turning to look at the hillside around us. 'And with good reason.'

'What do you mean?'

'I'm saying that if I'd got out of jail after serving thirty years for a murder I didn't commit I'd probably want to hurt the bastard who could have stopped me getting sent down in the first place, too. I've realised that much in the past couple of months inside.'

'You mean that line Smudge Tucker and Eddie Lennox fed me was actually true?'

'I could have got Lennox acquitted,' said Humph, scratching his moustache with his forefinger. 'And I didn't.'

Chapter 83

I can see it just as clearly now as I saw it thirty years ago, Twm. The figure of a man dragging the body of a woman across the dirt. The light was bad, it was night-time, but there was a moon in between the clouds. There was no mistaking that it was a woman. That it was Delilah. That it was the woman I loved more than anyone or anything else in this world. The woman who should have had my child.

First he carried her over his shoulder, but her body slipped and fell to the ground. He rested a moment, looked around him, but where I was I knew he wouldn't see me. He took a handkerchief from his pocket and wiped the sweat from his face. Then after a few minutes he bent down and took her arm and began to drag her. It looked like harder work than carrying her had been.

Of course I wanted to intervene but it was as if I was paralysed. I couldn't move. I was waiting to see what he was going to do. I watched him prop her body up near the edge of the excavation, then after regaining his breath he tipped her over backwards, her long legs over her head, down into the cavity. There was no sound. He peered around him once more. Then he was gone. I was crying then as I'm crying now.

When I was sure I was alone I walked across to where they had been. I leaned over and stared into the void. Just darkness. Nothing but the smell of damp and dirt. I looked down into that hole where she had simply disappeared. And so I walked away. But I stood on something. A shoe. It was Delilah's shoe. I bent over and picked it up and cried more tears over it and then dropped it to the floor.

I didn't know what to do. I was in shock. I went back to my digs and tried to wash the smell of death and disgust off my skin. But then there was a hammering on my door. I opened it and there he stood. He told me to forget what I had seen that evening or else he would fit me up for killing Delilah. He said he'd waited before leaving the stadium site, just to check that the coast was clear. And that's when he'd spotted me picking up Delilah's shoe. And after I'd left he'd gone over and picked it up with a pencil, taking good care not to smudge any of my fingerprints. And he'd kept it. He'd kept it hidden away from her other shoe, the one which had Eddie Lennox's prints all over it, the one that ended up convicting him.

He told me if I so much as breathed a word he would put together a case against me so watertight that a jury would have no choice but to convict me, and that I'd go down for life. He told me that Eddie Lennox had killed Delilah and that Ivan Harris had seen him dump her body and that I had seen nothing because I hadn't been there. He said Harris's witness statement would be enough to send Lennox down. That and the other shoe. I had no choice, Twm. It was either a thug like Eddie Lennox or it was me.

Chapter 84

'You're talking about Bryn Thomas,' I said. 'It was Thomas who killed Delilah?'

'She was a beautiful woman. She was young, and innocent, and wild. Bryn Thomas fell for her just like Ivan Harris, Eddie Lennox and I did.'

'But why would Bryn Thomas kill her?'

'Because she spurned his advances, I expect. She didn't want anything to do with him. Delilah knew, like Annie Léchet did, that Bryn was a bad 'un; that he was in the pay of the protection mob that came round each week demanding money from Annie.'

'Did you see him kill her?'

'No, thank God. I was spared that.'

'But why would Bryn Thomas want to set up Eddie Lennox? And where does Ivan Harris come into it?'

Humph bent over to pick up a small rock. It was smooth and he stood upright again, rubbing his thumb over it repeatedly.

'I suppose Bryn set up Lennox purely because it was Lennox who'd been out clubbing with Delilah that evening. They'd have been seen together. Maybe Bryn himself had seen them rowing or something. He must have known he could put together a convincing case. Lennox was an angry lout and a drunk. It can't have been all that hard. And when Lennox got out of jail thirty years later Bryn must have made sure he knew what I had done.'

'And Harris?'

'Ivan Harris was a greedy little shit,' said Humph. 'He was on the make even then and eager to buddy up to someone like Bryn Thomas. I think Ivan saw a lifetime of doors opening for him with a bent copper on his side, especially one who owed him a favour. I know for a fact Harris thought he could own me, too, but I never let him. I never let him blackmail me even though he tried. After Lennox's trial I knew, because of the two of them, that I had to clear out of the city. But I drew a line. I was always going to stand my ground back in Porthcoed.'

'There's still one thing you haven't explained to me.'

'What's that?'

'How come you were at the stadium site on the night that Delilah was killed?'

'Simple. I followed her there. I never got over loving her, and yet I had to watch while she moved on from me. I had to stand back and watch while Ivan Harris moved in on her, married her, beat her up according to Annie.

'When they separated, and I heard about Delilah being seen around town with this violent drunken footballer, I was no less worried about her. I followed the both of them to the Morocco Club that night. And I saw her leave. But just as I had decided to go up to her and make sure she was all right, I saw Bryn Thomas moving in. I followed them both back into town and down towards the stadium. Then suddenly there was a shouting match between them and a struggle. Bryn took hold of Delilah and dragged her into the stadium site, and that's where I lost them. Just for a few moments. By the time I managed to find a way inside he was carrying her body. He must have just snapped. It still kills me to this day that if I'd managed to get into that site quicker I might have been able to save her.'

Humph walked off on his own, and I let him go with his thoughts. After ten minutes or so, he worked his way back round to me and started back down the hill.

I stood alone on the summit for a moment more, taking in the view, before I set off after him. 'Coma reckons it'll do you the world of good to get back to work.'

'I'm not going back,' Humph replied. 'There's nothing left there for me now.'

'Well how about Bryn Thomas, for starters? Isn't it high time that justice was served on that man? Let's get back to work, Humph. Let's find a way of bringing him down. You can't let him beat you. There's still time to make amends.'

'He's won, Twm,' said Humph. 'There's no fight left in me any more. That's a job for a younger man. Have you decided what you're going to do, yet?'

'I've been offered a job on the *Record*,' I said, tucking my hands into my coat pockets. 'Chief reporter.'

'That would be a good move for you,' said Humph. 'A couple of years there and then off to London. Or TV maybe. Fancy that?'

'Me as a Hairdo? I can't exactly see that, can you? No, it's newspapers for me or it's nothing.'

'Newspapers have had their day, Twm. You know that. They'll never be able to survive in an era when you can get your news live on a TV or computer screen, 24/7. They've had their time and so have I.'

'We'll see,' I said. 'If there's one thing I've learned in the past year or so it's that there's still a future for old-fashioned, painstaking newspaper journalism; for measured thought as opposed to instant gratification.

'When you took me over the road to Grumpy's that morning and told me about Bren, and the missing cash, my life began to unravel around me. Everything I thought I knew started to look like a lie. I lost my perspective. I lost my job, my home. I almost lost my life. It was only when I got a grip and started working the problem, when I started doing what you taught me to do, Humph, that I found a way through the bullshit and the lies.

'Now, you can say newspapermen like you and I are a dying breed. You can even tell me that corrupt folk like Ivan Harris and his "interested parties" are going to win more than they lose. But you can't persuade me that newspapers, even a small-town newspaper like the *Gazette*, haven't got a unique role to play in keeping these people honest. And there's no way I'm going to give up on that.'

Humph looked at me and nodded and we walked on.

Epilogue

The atmosphere in the stadium just before the first game of the tournament was everything the city fathers could have hoped for and more. The colourful opening ceremony had been an unabashed celebration of the nation's culture with the eyes of the world looking on. And now, to the accompaniment of a regimental band and massed male voice choirs, the nation was doing what it was known for doing best: warming up for a big rugby match with a crowd of 70,000 fans in full voice:

'Sheeeeeee stood there laughing,
(Ha ha ha ha ha)
I felt the knife in my hand and she laughed no more.
My, my, my Delilah.
Why, why, why Delilah?
So, before they come to break down the door,
Forgive me Delilah, I just couldn't take any more.
Forgive me Delilah, I just couldn't take any mooooore.'

As the song ended I felt a tap on my shoulder.

'You sure you're okay?' asked the young man beside me. 'It looked for a minute or two like we'd lost you again.'

'I'm sorry,' I replied. 'I was just ... mulling over a story I've been working on.'

'I knew I recognised you,' came his reply. 'You're the journalist who put Eddie Lennox back behind bars for the stadium murder. My name's Wynne Jones. *Western Morning Record*. News reporter. Pleased to meet you.'

'Twm Bradley, *Porthcoed Gazette*,' I said and took his outstretched hand. 'Editor.'

We absorbed the spectacle around us for a moment or two more before Wynne turned back to face me again. 'Bizarre when you think about it, though, isn't it?'

'What's that?'

'Five or six times a year we gather in our thousands on this patch of ground to watch a game of rugby, and how do we get ourselves in the mood for kick-off? By partaking in something akin to a mass ritual sacrifice.'

'I'm sorry?'

'It's been the same for the past thirty-odd years. The band starts playing, the choir kicks in, and before we know it we're all arm in arm, religiously singing along. But even after all this time we never seem to stop and think that this song we're singing is about a woman who's stabbed to death by a jealous lover. Poor old Delilah. Do you suppose the guy who kills her gets what's coming to him in the end?'

'He will,' I said, thinking out loud. 'He will.'

Rhodri Wyn Owen has worked in journalism, PR and online production for the BBC, and as a journalist for the *Western Mail* and the *Wales On Sunday* newspapers. He also works as a freelance editor for a number of Wales-based publishers.

He is the author of three popular pocketbook titles published by Graffeg: *Castles of Wales*, *Coast Wales* and *Mountain Wales*, and co-wrote *The Green Room*, a 30-minute sitcom broadcast by BBC Radio Wales in 2005. *Delilah* is his first novel.

Rhodri is married with two grown-up sons and lives in the Vale of Glamorgan.